CAPITAL GIRLS

CAPITAL GIRLS

ella monroe

ST. MARTIN'S GRIFFIN ☘ NEW YORK

CAPITAL GIRLS. Copyright © 2012 by Marilyn Rauber and Amy Reingold. All rights reserved. Printed in the United States of America. For information, address St. Martin's Press, 175 Fifth Avenue, New York, N.Y. 10010.

www.stmartins.com

Design by Anna Gorovoy

ISBN 978-0-312-62303-6 (trade paperback)
ISBN 978-1-250-01426-9 (e-book)

First Edition: August 2012

10 9 8 7 6 5 4 3 2 1

for celia, phoebe, ben, and olivia,

our favorite capital kids

CAPITAL GIRLS

ONE

There was something about cemeteries. Something eerily calming. As she always did, Jackie felt the urge to hold her breath as she pulled into Oak Hill Cemetery. A futile attempt to silence the whirlwind in her mind.

"Quick, hold your breath! Quick!" Taylor said, nudging me. She took a deep breath, closing her eyes and pursing her lips—Dior Addict Scarlet Siren. Even at twelve, she had a signature color. And I was stuck wearing clear gloss until I was thirteen. I was jealous as hell.

She opened her eyes and shook my arm. "Hold your breath until we pass a white house!"

I did. We all did, holding our breath until our cheeks burned and we felt light-headed. Afterward I asked her why.

"Because you have to!" Laura Beth answered, as if I'd been asking her.

"People always hold their breath when they pass a cemetery. It's to keep from breathing in the spirits. If you breathe them in, they could possess your soul."

"I just thought it was to be nice," Lettie said, blushing the way only she could. "Since dead people don't breathe, you have to hold your breath for them."

Taylor laughed. "I just wanted to see if you'd do it!"

Jackie shifted the bouquet of gardenias and calla lilies in the passenger seat next to her and tried not to gag at the overwhelming perfume. She preferred subtle scents, like Coco Mademoiselle. Her flowers of choice would have been long-stemmed roses, freshly cut, in a white box with a red bow. The kind Cary Grant would have given to Katharine Hepburn.

But this wasn't about her. It was about Taylor, who collected perfume and La Perla lingerie the same way she collected guys. And Taylor's favorite flowers were gardenias.

It took a week to get permission to cut these blooms, but it was worth it. They were from the White House garden where Taylor always stole a single gardenia on her way out. She'd put it behind her ear or twirl it through her long fingers, showing it off for the rest of the day, like everyone would know, just by glancing at her, where she'd gotten it—would know she could get behind the most guarded gates in D.C. And that was so Taylor, to want the most unattainable flowers even if no one knew just how exclusive they were. She would've loved these.

Jackie bought the purple callas separately, just for color, because putting plain white flowers on Taylor's grave wasn't right.

When she parked the car and turned off the ignition, she felt fine. But one second later, it was like she was going to pass out if she didn't get fresh air *right now.* She swung the door open, and fled the cool air-conditioning into the sauna of D.C.'s summer humidity. The sun beat down on her and she shifted her Chanel sunglasses to avoid the glare, leaning against the car until she had her breath back. *Anxiety attacks,* her doctor told her yesterday. They were happening more and more. This one was quick though, and aside from the inescapable heat, she felt fine again. Or as fine as she could, considering where she was.

The heels of her strappy sandals sank a few inches into the ground, and she wished for a moment that she were at Laura Beth's, lying flat on her back on one of the pool floats, letting her long blond hair trail in the water while she worked on her tan. That's how she and Laura Beth—and Taylor—had spent most of their summers since elementary school. But instead of her hot pink bikini and a day at the pool with nothing on her mind, Jackie chose a navy blue sundress and a trip to the cemetery. To see Taylor.

Because even if she'd gone to Laura Beth's, *just like I did yesterday and the day before and the day before that,* she wouldn't have been able to have nothing on her mind. If only.

She recognized Taylor's headstone instantly by the little yellow daisies at the base. Someone had left a fresh bouquet every week since Taylor's death, but Jackie didn't know who. She'd asked Taylor's twin brother, Daniel, if they were from him. His response? *"Taylor thought daisies were practically weeds."*

The marble headstone itself was nondescript. No color. No details that said *Taylor!* It was just . . . ordinary.

Jackie frowned as she stepped closer. *Taylor doesn't belong here.* It was a familiar thought that always came with a tightening in her chest and a shortness of breath. Her eyes burned a little as

3

she leaned over and placed the bouquet in front of the headstone, wishing she'd brought candles or a picture or something to go with it.

Straightening her back and lifting her chin, Jackie composed herself, fingering the silver charm bracelet on her wrist until her breathing evened out. She focused on the reason she was here. The thing she could only talk to Taylor about.

Eric.

She couldn't stop thinking about him. The flirty grin he'd given her when they first met the other day at the White House. His perfect, but not too perfect, white teeth. The way his brown hair curled at the back of his neck. She could practically feel the faint stubble on his cheek. Their kiss . . .

Oh my God, the kiss!

The way his lips had come down on hers, forcefully, like he needed her kiss to survive. The touch of his tongue against her own—the way he had sucked on her bottom lip, reluctantly pulling away, like he didn't want to stop.

Jackie brought a hand up to her lips, almost feeling the way he'd lingered. Just remembering it made her hot. It wasn't just the sun. Glancing around to make sure she was alone, she knelt down, leaning forward as if she could still whisper in Taylor's ear and tell her all her secrets.

"Tay, you wouldn't believe it," she breathed, a conspiratorial smile coming to her lips. "I've been dying to tell you. I met a guy. Eric Moran. He's a lawyer—a top aide to a *senator*! And he's into me.

"You wouldn't have believed Laura Beth when I told her. She was so jealous! And Lettie was mortified, of course. Her eyes almost popped out of her head."

And that's why Taylor was the one person she had to tell about Eric. None of her other friends would want to hear the *details*. Taylor would. Tay would love it. Taylor would understand.

Jackie bit her lip to keep from letting her smile get away from her. "Oh, Tay, you'd love him. I was outside the Oval Office, waiting for my mom to come out of a meeting with Aunt Deborah and Senator Hampton Griffin. You know, he's that sketchy Republican from Texas—who's of course an *old family friend* of Laura Beth's."

She stuck out her tongue and shuddered at the thought of the senator's gaudy pinky ring with its oversized diamond. "Anyway, Eric was waiting outside Aunt Deborah's door. I thought he was some cute new intern, so I offered to take him on a tour of the West Wing. I know, lame, right? But the entire time, he was flirting like crazy, saying stuff like, *No wonder Deborah Price's first term has been charmed if she has an angel on her side.*" Jackie giggled. "Okay, so I *know* that's a line. And on another guy it would have been totally cheesy and lame, but he smiled when he said it, like he knew it was ridiculous, but he had to say it anyway.

"And when we got to my mom's office, we went inside, and within thirty seconds half our clothes were off.

"He's older and so hot. Swoon-worthy. And he was so hot for *me*. It was like he'd die if he couldn't have me." She'd never felt like that before. Of course, she'd seen guys fall all over Taylor like that. But no guy had ever wanted Jackie like that. Not even her boyfriend.

At the thought of Andrew, Jackie sighed. "But I couldn't exactly tell Lettie and Laura Beth the details—or that no one's ever kissed me like that before. I started to, but they both freaked out. Lettie did one of those gasps she always does, and Laura

Beth just asked, 'What about Andrew?' And you know the whole time she was thinking we might break up and she could have him. And she can have him. I'm so sick of Andrew. He's always so careful and predictable—always worrying about his public image. Nothing like Eric."

She leaned in closer, lowering her voice again to a whisper. "And who knows how far we would've gone, but we heard Senator Griffin and Mom coming down the hall." Okay, so that was only partly true. She couldn't *really* be sure she would have let him take things much further. But Taylor would have done it in a heartbeat.

She remembered the surprised look on her mom's face when she and Eric came out of her office together. No wonder Taylor was always taking risks. Even just thinking about it made Jackie's heart race a little faster—made her feel a little more alive.

She leaned back and fingered her charm bracelet again. "Oh, Tay, I wish you were here. I need your advice. I mean, Eric's not even a Democrat! If Andrew and I broke up it'd be all over the tabloids. Can't you see the headlines: 'Top Democrat's Daughter Dating Republican'."

Jackie giggled. "Okay, well actually it might be more like, 'Underaged Daughter of Presidential Aide Mauled by Republican Sex Maniac' because you know how the tabloids exaggerate everything. And my birthday isn't for another eight days. Eight days! I can't possibly go eight days without seeing Eric. What am I going to do?"

What am I going to do? She was so used to asking Taylor that question. So used to throwing herself on Taylor's king-size water bed, burying her face in the satin pillows and waiting for a slice of no-bullshit advice to cut through what everyone else wanted her to do.

Only now it was a more loaded question. Because even though she was here asking what she should do about Eric, there was a much deeper sense of restlessness in the back of her mind. One she had been swallowing down with each lump in her throat and pushing back into a tiny corner of her heart for the last six months.

Jackie got to her feet and brushed the top of the headstone, almost like saying good-bye. Taylor had always had her own gravitational force. She was infuriating, but impossible not to like. Just when you wanted to strangle her for flirting with your boyfriend, or being high in front of your parents, or skipping school then demanding you give her your class notes, she'd redeem herself. Like the time she accidentally-on-purpose dumped her Coke and tray of marinara pasta on Christie Haggart's new white Dior pants to get back at her for spreading a rumor about Jackie. Or when she snuck into Dan Hayman's house and stole his journal and photocopied the especially *sensitive* entries and passed them out to people at school after the girls found out he'd only asked Laura Beth to prom because his friends bet he couldn't score with a sophomore. She didn't think twice about cheating on guys yet she was absolutely loyal to her three best friends. They could totally count on her when they really needed her. And as lame as it might sound, she gave great advice.

She never took her own advice, of course. *"Hey, do as I say, not as I do,"* she would say with a shrug and a laugh. And God, her laugh. It was infectious. When Taylor laughed, everyone laughed.

And right when Jackie felt completely lost, as if coming here had only made her feel more alone rather than help her figure things out, a light breeze played over her shoulders and ruffled the bouquet of flowers. No. She knew what she had to do. She'd take a page out of Taylor's playbook and not worry about Andrew or her mom or even political allegiances. Eric was hot. He wanted her.

And maybe it was time she went after what *she* wanted for a change. Consequences be damned.

TWO

Lettie Velasquez knew this summer would be different.

Jackie and Laura Beth had been complaining about how awful their last month of summer would be, stuck in D.C. Usually in the summer *anyone* who actually lived in the most powerful city in the world would pack up and leave, heading for a quaint cottage in Martha's Vineyard or a villa in the south of France—really, anywhere but here—to get reacquainted with their families after Congress finally quit meeting at the beginning of August.

Anyone except Lettie, of course.

It wasn't as if she preferred washing dishes over basking under the Tuscan sun. And it wasn't that the girls excluded her. They always invited her to go with them on their family vacations, even though they knew she'd have to say no.

But this summer was different for most of the pampered

rising seniors at Washington Excelsior Preparatory School for Girls. (School motto: "Simple in my virtue. Steadfast in my duty.") No prolonged Paris shopping trips, no lying on the beach in St. Tropez, no partying in clubs in Ibiza. Not for them.

They were sentenced to spend most of their vacation on mindless college tours with over-caffeinated student guides who all walked backward and spoke variations of the same script. Where parents asked dumb questions like, "Who cleans the dorms?" or "Are the chefs here restaurant-grade?"

But Lettie couldn't help feel excited—even a little giddy—at the prospect. College was going to be her ticket out of an embassy dishwashing job. Her chance to actually do something that mattered. So, unlike Jackie and Laura Beth, who dreaded the upcoming month, Lettie had been counting down the days.

Sure, she saw the absurdity of it all if she looked at it from Laura Beth's and Jackie's perspectives. When they weren't on the road in their shiny new Priuses (the Democrats) or Made-in-the-USA BMW convertibles (the Republicans), they were stuck at home, busy mailing off slick letters of recommendation from the connected friends of their connected parents. For them it wasn't so much a matter of which college would want them but which prestigious institution they'd deign to accept.

They just. Didn't. Get it.

Most days, Lettie could look the other way. Just not worry about it. Lettie lived in *reality,* and she knew it. *Reality* included living in a cramped two-bedroom apartment on Sixteenth Street in Mount Pleasant with her parents and her two sisters, Maribel and Christa. They were squished even tighter before her older brother, Paz, was packed off to the Paraguayan army.

In *reality,* her largely Latino neighborhood was slowly being gentrified by lawyers, lobbyists, and other Democratic loyalists who swarmed into town after President Deborah Price's inauguration. They fell in love with the 1920s Art Deco apartments with their twelve-foot ceilings and marble lobbies and the close proximity to the Capitol. They turned a blind eye to the drug dealers on the street corners and the crumbling schools because they didn't venture out on foot at night and they paid $30,000 a year to send their kids to private school.

Unlike her friends, *realistic* Lettie didn't spend much time worrying about guys or dating. She was too busy studying to keep up her grades, working part-time, and babysitting her little sisters. Anyway, her parents didn't approve of dating and Lettie didn't care enough to rebel.

But in *reality*, she knew she was still better off than if she were home in Paraguay, where the crime rate was one of the worst in the world. Where women and girls vanished from the streets, leaving only a trail of rumors that they'd been smuggled off to Brazil or Argentina. Where her education would never have been what it could be here. It didn't mean she didn't miss Paraguay sometimes—that was where she'd been born, and in some corner of her heart and mind, it would always be home. But dwelling on what she didn't have, whether that was bits and pieces of her old life or the connections and free time her friends had here, could make a person crazy. It was better instead to focus on the opportunities now within reach. That's what she reminded herself every time Laura Beth tried to force a new designer hand-me-down on her or when Jackie tried to find her a boyfriend.

Although Laura Beth's mother, Libby Ballou, had sent her driver to pick up Lettie from work, rather than just letting her take the bus, even the buttery soft leather seat couldn't make her relax. The irony wasn't lost on her—the daughter of the Paraguayan Ambassador's chauffeur getting picked up by Mrs. Ballou's driver to go to a tea party. She felt extra irritable after working all morning in the stifling embassy kitchen. As the chauffeur pulled into the circular driveway, part of her wanted to storm inside and ask Laura Beth if she needed to get an understudy for her role as the token Latina in case her work schedule didn't fit her mother's social calendar. She would never say that, though. She knew Laura Beth didn't mean it the way it came off. Because she knew Laura Beth wanted what was best for her, which included networking with important people. People who might help Lettie build a different future.

She just needed to suck it up and keep working hard. Washing dishes at the embassy didn't have to be her life forever.

When the cab dropped her off at Laura Beth's house, Jackie couldn't help but smile at Lettie standing at the front door as if she didn't want to go inside. She knew exactly how she felt. Libby Ballou had invited—no, ordered—the girls to come over for "Sunday afternoon tea" to welcome a father and daughter who'd just moved to D.C. from California. The new girl, Whitney, would be joining their senior class in the fall.

Lettie stood, twirling the silver charm bracelet around her wrist. Her dark hair was piled into a messy bun on top of her head and she was still wearing her work uniform—shapeless black pants with an old-lady waist and bad pleats, and a white collared shirt that looked like she'd spilled something on the sleeve. Coffee? Gravy? Poor Lettie. Jackie knew she hated her job.

Jackie lifted her sunglasses as she got closer.

"Want to make a bet on how many drinks Libby's had so far this morning?" she whispered to Lettie, who whirled around in surprise.

"I thought you were already inside," Lettie gasped.

Jackie shrugged. "I went to see Taylor. Drop off some flowers." As soon as she said it, she wished she hadn't. Lettie paled and looked away, her big brown eyes a little watery. Jackie felt a prickle of resentment. Taylor was *her* best friend.

But she took a deep breath and pushed those feelings down and locked them away. Lettie cared about Taylor as much as she did. They were all going through this together. Jackie steadied herself and threw her arm around Lettie's shoulder, ignoring the brown stain. "Come on, how many drinks you think Libby's had?"

It was rarely too early for Miss Libby to start drinking. Of course to be fair, she wasn't the only Excelsior Prep parent who drank too much. But the Ballous' open bar was notorious. And the girls were happy to take advantage.

"Too bad she doesn't smoke weed too," Taylor used to say. *"It'd be one-stop shopping."*

Lettie smiled and looked at her watch. "Less than an hour before tea time and neither of us are inside yet? Oh, she's at least on number two."

"You're too nice; I'd have her downing number four and wasted." Jackie laughed. "Let's find Laura Beth and make sure she isn't contemplating suicide."

The Ballous' maid came to the door and ushered them through the house and into the rear garden, where a table was already set up.

Laura Beth sat slouched under a large custom-print umbrella that matched the vase of creamy roses on the linen tablecloth. When she saw Jackie and Lettie, she immediately perked up, folding her hands in her lap and adopting the mannerisms of Scarlett O'Hara. She had gorgeous dark auburn curly hair that Jackie had always been envious of when they were younger (her own hair wouldn't hold curls no matter what she did), but sometimes Laura Beth tried too hard to look like the perfect image of her very Southern mother.

Jackie flopped down on the chair next to Laura Beth and poured a peach daiquiri from an icy pitcher on the table, taking a long sip.

"Where have y'all been?" Laura Beth asked as Lettie sat down on the other side of her. "I thought you'd never show and you'd leave me here to deal with Mama and these crazy California hippies all by myself."

Jackie fought to keep from rolling her eyes.

Lettie smiled. "Don't worry, Laura Beth. When have we ever left you to deal with your mama alone?"

Laura Beth looked over at Lettie as if she was seeing her for the first time. "Lettie, you look wiped out."

Lettie nodded. "Work."

"What you need is a cool shower and some fresh clothes to make you feel gorgeous," Laura Beth said, using her soothing voice—just like her mother's. "I've already laid everything out for you upstairs."

Lettie blushed and smiled, which Jackie knew was her way

of saying thank you. To be polite, Jackie looked away and reached into her Louis Vuitton handbag to check her iPhone. Not just polite, she wanted to see if she had any texts or missed calls. But nothing. Not from Eric, or Andrew either.

Laura Beth motioned to Jackie's phone. "Have you told Andrew yet?" she whispered. "About that other guy?"

"Of course not!" Jackie hissed. "Why would I tell Andrew?"

"You kissed another guy," Lettie said softly. "Andrew's your boyfriend. Telling him *is* probably the right thing to do."

"Taylor cheated on guys all the time, and you never gave her a hard time."

"Taylor made mistakes," Lettie said quietly, her face flushing.

"But it's Andrew!" Laura Beth squealed over whatever Lettie had intended to say next. "Besides, let's not talk about Taylor. It just makes it worse. I mean, I know that's just awful to say, but it's true."

Jackie swallowed her reply when she saw Laura Beth's mother appear at the French doors. In true Libby Ballou fashion, she was ready to entertain in a red linen Escada pantsuit—her pet designer ever since the Republican Senate Leader's wife started wearing the brand. She wore her perfectly dyed ash-blond hair in a chin-length bob and accented her look with a jeweled flag pin custom-made by local jeweler Ann Hand, a glass of bourbon and branch, and a lacy linen handkerchief that she waved at the girls.

"Hey, girls!" she greeted them in her Charleston drawl, the bourbon sloshing in the glass. "Y'all having a wonderful day today? It's almost time for our little garden party." She frowned at Laura Beth as she drew closer. "Laura Beth, your hair's gone all frizzy in the sun, darlin'. I've told you to keep out of the heat."

Jackie wrinkled her nose. "It did frizz a little." Normally she would have tried to soften Miss Libby's critique of Laura Beth's appearance, but the whole Taylor thing grated on her nerves.

"Laura Beth, take Lettie upstairs so she can change into the dress you picked out for her," she said, draining the last of the bourbon. "Lettie darlin', you're such a pretty girl when you're presented right."

"Thankfully, you've still got time to take a shower, Lettie," Laura Beth added.

Lettie didn't say anything. She just offered Miss Libby what Jackie knew was a fake smile and headed for the house. Before Laura Beth followed, she leaned over and whispered, "We'll talk about Andrew later."

Jackie nodded, but couldn't help thinking: *As if it's any of her business*.

Laura Beth had always had a crush on Andrew Price—even before his mother was elected president. And even though they joked about it, Jackie knew Laura Beth well enough to know she was still drawing hearts and writing First Lady Laura Beth Price on her books, just like she did back in sixth grade.

Jackie didn't need to mention that Laura Beth's daydreams conveniently skipped over the fact that Andrew's Democratic parents and his own political aspirations wouldn't allow him to marry a Republican—unless it was a way to get more votes. And the Ballous weren't just any Republican family. Laura Beth's dead father practically invented dirty campaign tricks.

Okay, so maybe Jackie hadn't exactly been speaking the truth when she told Taylor that Laura Beth could have Andrew. She wasn't really sure she was ready to give him up quite yet.

As much as he drove her crazy lately, Jackie and Andrew

had known each other their whole lives. Their mothers were college roommates and political soul mates, and she'd grown up with him and his younger brother, Scott. Andrew was tall and cute in that lanky Robert Pattinson way. He had these amazing bright sexy green eyes and sandy brown hair that always looked like he'd just climbed out of bed.

And he could be so sweet. Like when he bought her the Tiffany earrings her dad had promised to get her. Andrew had wrapped them and tried to pass them off as a gift from her dad. But she knew better. Her dad never remembered her birthday on time, at least not since he and her mom split. And certainly not in time to buy her a gift. He usually just handed her an envelope with a hastily scribbled check inside.

That's the kind of guy Andrew was. The guy who knew exactly what you wanted, would shell out a couple hundred for it, and then let someone else take the credit. Sweet. Genuine. Caring.

Boring.

Okay, that sounded bad—she knew it did, because Andrew *did* have so many great boyfriend qualities, but he was just too predictable. And even though she cared about him, *loved him,* they didn't have any romance—any *passion*—anymore. It was like they were barely a couple. And no matter what she did to try to get that back, he just seemed so disinterested.

"Jackie, darlin', are you listenin'?" Miss Libby asked, sounding more and more like Blanche DuBois with every word. She paused to make sure she had Jackie's full attention. "Her name's Whitney Remick. She's a rising senior like y'all and she loves to surf and sail. I bet she's just darlin'."

Jackie was listening but she remained skeptical about the

new family. Who just let their parents pick them up and move them their senior year of high school?

As if answering her question, Libby continued. "I heard they're abandoning the West Coast so that William Remick, he's a Berkeley economist, can head a new liberal think tank that hopes to curry favor with the Price Administration. His wife, Tracey Mills—she still goes by her maiden name—is an African American gossip columnist who writes tidbits for *Entertainment Weekly* in Los Angeles. She even has a regular gig on that TV show *Hollywood Secrets,* and she's stayin' behind in L.A. She's goin' to spend her time commuting back and forth between Washington and L.A. because of her filming schedule. Can you just believe that?"

Not really. If her mother was staying in L.A., why wouldn't Whitney have wanted to stay there, too?

"Did y'all ever watch that *Hollywood Secrets* show?" Miss Libby asked.

Jackie shook her head. Taylor always said people who needed gossip to live vicariously through celebrities weren't living their own lives. *"After all, people should be gossiping about us!"* And after the tryst with Eric, Jackie tended to agree.

Miss Libby kept talking, and Jackie smiled, nodded, and shook her head at all the appropriate moments. It was easy to take her cues from the expression on her face.

Jackie would have asked why the hell Miss Libby wanted to have tea with the enemy—a Democrat *and* a gossip columnist's husband, it couldn't get worse than that. But she already knew. Libby Ballou was a mover and shaker who knew how to maneuver political battlefields. She made sure to court all "the liberals," as she referred to them with distaste—and that included this new California family. She told the girls, and maybe even herself, that dealing with the enemy was a charitable act. What she meant was it was a way to get a foot in every door.

Laura Beth emerged from the house with Lettie trailing behind her. Lettie looked beautiful, her dark hair loose and wavy, and the dress hugging her curves. Laura Beth had tried to smooth down her hair, but it still looked stubbornly frizzy. There was really only so much overpriced salon products could do.

"Wouldn't it be nice if this Whitney could take Taylor's place in y'all's little circle?" her mother said to the girls, as if the idea had suddenly occurred to her.

Lettie's mouth fell open.

Jackie's heart pounded in her chest and blood thundered in her ears. As if some random surfer chick from California could move in and immediately replace Taylor. Taylor, who they'd known forever. Taylor, who'd pushed Angie Meehan into a pool after she purposely bought and wore the same silk Prada dress as Jackie at the Excelsior Junior Banquet. And then, of course, she assured Jackie it looked bad on Angie anyway.

No one will ever replace Taylor.

And in her newfound spirit of channeling Taylor, Jackie imagined herself grabbing Miss Libby's glass of bourbon and dousing her with it before storming out. Only the glass was already empty, and Laura Beth beat her to saying something.

"Mama, you can't suddenly become best friends with someone you just met."

"Well, Laura Beth, I'm just saying, if it gets you what you want." She stood up to pour herself another drink. "You girls are going to have to instruct Whitney on the ways of Washington. Not being raised here, she won't understand how this town works."

Jackie knew exactly what she was up to. Trying to get them in good with Whitney would assure Miss Libby easy access to gossip and a heads-up when anything hit too close to home.

"Y'all need to show the poor girl around, where to shop, where to get her nails and hair done, and of course wherever y'all go to have fun."

The doorbell rang before Laura Beth could shoot back a retort.

A few seconds later the Ballous' maid led William and Whitney Remick into the courtyard, and Jackie smiled. Miss Libby might also have a more devious motive for befriending Whitney and her *lonely* father.

In her earlier description of Mr. Remick, she had failed to mention he was a George Clooney lookalike.

Laura Beth's mom clearly hoped to show him around D.C. because then she'd be able to flirt with him. She wasn't the kind of woman to take it any further than that. None of her affairs had ever been with married men—at least not that Jackie knew about. But she loved, above all, attention.

Whitney followed only a step behind. She was willowy and beautiful with flawless caramel skin, and her untamed brown hair flew wildly around her head. The bitch was also braless. And it showed.

Jealousy burned in Jackie's chest. Clearly, Whitney'd mastered the whole Californian art of total casual. The "effortless" look, the one that probably included daily runs on the beach followed by yoga, a massage, and an Adderall washed down with a wheatgrass concoction to suppress her appetite and keep that "natural" glow.

As Whitney walked across the patio, her short, washed-denim Joe's Jeans skirt swished around her thighs, and a diamond-studded hoop in her belly button twinkled through her white peasant blouse. Two toe rings on her manicured feet glinted in the sun.

"I think I hate her already," Laura Beth whispered before lifting her cocktail to her lips.

Lettie leaned closer and whispered, "How can she dress like that in front of her father?"

Jackie smirked. "All that *shopping* advice your mom wants us to give her will just be wasted. Obviously she only wears half the amount of required clothing."

Laura Beth almost spit her drink out across the table. Thankfully those Southern manners taught her well and she swallowed it down, coughing. Lettie patted her back.

Jackie smiled, glad she could lighten the mood a little, but really she felt butterflies in her stomach. Whitney walked with the kind of confidence that Jackie used to have. Jackie knew she was still Washington's It Girl. Everyone wanted a piece of her, the most popular girl in the school, the daughter of the woman behind the president, the girlfriend of the president's son. But she seemed to have lost her self-assurance since losing Taylor.

She'd continued to play her roles and fake her way through the last six months, but it hadn't gotten any easier. If anything, she felt less inclined to stick to her lines. She wanted to break down the walls around her, climb into someone else's shoes—or even their skin. With a perfect new girl in town, *who didn't wear a bra,* she wondered what this would mean for her. Would she be replaceable to her friends if she decided not to be Andrew's girlfriend? If she decided not to be the perfect daughter? If she couldn't be Washington's It Girl anymore?

Laura Beth turned her head, her face hidden by a curtain of hair. "Butterfly belly-button ring? Gaudy."

"She probably has a matching tramp stamp," Jackie breathed.

Lettie smiled for a second and then shook her head. And that was Lettie for you. She was probably thinking to herself right at this moment, *We should give her a chance.*

"Welcome! Welcome to our home," Miss Libby said, her eyes only on William Remick as she signaled to the maid to bring out the refreshments.

"Thank you. I can't tell you how thoughtful it was for you to invite us," Mr. Remick said, giving everyone a broad smile.

"Of course! We want you to feel at home in Washington."

Whitney stood next to her father and smirked. "We really don't know too many people on the *East Coast*." And from the way she said it, she obviously didn't want to. Like *she* was looking down on *them*.

"Whitney, darlin', you sit opposite me, between Lettie and Jackie, so I can see your pretty face," Miss Libby ordered. "William, you sit right by me. My girls are probably feeling a bit shy, Whitney, so let me introduce them."

"Mama, that's—" Laura Beth started to protest but quickly shut up when her mother delivered The Look.

"This is my daughter, Laura Beth. She's the spittin' image of her mama in every way except her red hair, which is natural, you know," she said, pausing only to instruct the maid, who'd appeared with a large silver tray laden with refreshments. "She got it from her father, Preston, God rest his soul. She's growing into such a gracious Southern young lady, he'd be so proud. And with the loveliest singing voice! Perhaps she'll sing for us later—"

"Mama!" Laura Beth, horrified, tried to cut in again.

"Oh, don't be so modest, darlin'." She was on a roll as she poured everyone tea from an antique silver tea service. "Whitney, it's so fortunate that you're doing your senior year at Excelsior. The best colleges just *adore* our graduates. What are your college plans, dear? Laura Beth plans to attend my alma mater, Sewanee, where I graduated magna cum laude, of course."

Laura Beth looked at Jackie and then at Lettie. She still hadn't worked up the courage to tell her mother she had no intention of going to Sewanee—something that practically everyone else on the planet knew. Not that Jackie could blame her. Laura Beth's mother listened about as well as a brick wall when it wasn't something she wanted to hear.

"Swanee, like the song?" Whitney asked.

Her dad reached over, like he was going to explain, but before he could open his mouth—

"Oh, my Lord!" Libby Ballou said. "I just assumed everyone knew about Sewanee: The University of The South! All the best families send their children there." She added, only half-jokingly: "It's been upholding the same wonderful traditions since before the War of Northern Aggression."

Mr. Remick laughed, but it sounded tight. Definitely forced. "I'm sure," he said.

Jackie smirked. *This is actually way more interesting than I expected it to be.*

"Oh, and Miss Jackie Whitman here needs no introduction, what with her pictures all over the papers. She and Andrew make such a lovely couple. And I'm so proud of them both for taking that chastity vow. And Andrew even wears the promise ring to prove it." She leaned into Mr. Remick and whispered just loud enough for the whole table to hear her. "You know, them bein' Democrats 'n all."

Laura Beth slid down even farther in her chair. And even though Jackie's heart plummeted to her stomach, she refused to let her embarrassment show. Instead she kept her back straight and feigned the look of polite boredom she'd learned over the years. She determinedly did not glance over at Whitney, who was trying to cover her laugh with a fake cough, or Mr. Remick, who was shooting his daughter a look and shifting in his chair like he wanted to get up and run.

"A chastity vow?" Whitney asked.

"Apparently those are banned in California," Jackie whispered to Laura Beth.

Apparently not softly enough. Whitney's head swiveled in their direction and lifted her chin. "It'd be a little too late for that anyway."

Still in conversation—however one-sided it was—about Excelsior, the two adults either hadn't heard the exchange, or pretended they hadn't. "And of course, this is *Laetitia Velasquez*," Miss Libby said, trying to say Lettie's name with the appropriate Spanish accent. Jackie cringed inwardly on Lettie's behalf, though Lettie didn't let anything on her face betray how she must have been feeling. She just sat there demurely, like she didn't mind being treated like an object. *I don't know how she does it.*

Lettie had more strength and more grace than anyone Jackie knew.

Miss Libby kept talking. "Lettie, tell Whitney how you came

to go to Excelsior Prep." She waved her handkerchief in Lettie's direction. "Lettie is just such a wonderful example of how anyone in this country can achieve their dreams."

Lettie dropped her eyes, staring intently at her teacup.

Jackie opened her mouth to say something. But what? What could she say that wouldn't just embarrass Lettie further?

"Lettie's a little shy," Miss Libby said, dropping her voice to another loud whisper. "Her parents work at the Paraguayan embassy." And then she looked at Lettie. "Tell them, darlin'."

Lettie put on a brave smile and looked at Mr. Remick and then Whitney. "I won a scholarship."

"Isn't she a clever thing!" Laura Beth's mother said, leaning toward Mr. Remick. "What an opportunity! And our girls have taken her under their wing! Doesn't it just make you so proud to be an American?"

Nobody seemed to know how to respond, and without Miss Libby's chatter, silence surrounded them, weighing down on their shoulders. Jackie watched Mr. Remick shift in his seat and lean back a little, as if trying to distance himself from Miss Libby, and Jackie felt comforted that at least she wasn't the only one who was finding it hard to breathe.

"What's with the bracelets?" Whitney asked.

Jackie groaned inwardly. She desperately wanted to keep the bracelets to herself, but she held out her arm so Whitney could see. "We got friendship bracelets in seventh grade. We add a charm every year." She tried to sound casual.

But in true Miss Libby fashion, she disclosed more than Jackie would have liked. "Laura Beth designed the charm. Isn't it just darling?"

Laura Beth had designed the charm, but Taylor had been

the one to come up with the monogram and officially name the group.

Whitney looked closer. Each charm had four hearts joined at the points to form a four-leaf clover. She turned it over and saw a date and an intricate monogram that looked like a back-to-front C intertwined with a G. "What's that?"

Jackie didn't answer. She didn't want to tell her about why Taylor made them each take a shot of tequila—her first shot of alcohol ever—that summer night they stayed up until the sun rose and decided nothing would ever come between them. Not politics. Not money. Not men.

"Oh, that monogram stands for Capital Girls," Miss Libby announced. Jackie pulled her hand away and leaned back in her chair, wishing she could find something about Whitney to pick apart. Other than the skanky braless attire and trampy belly-button ring, of course. "The girls and their friend Taylor Cane, God rest her poor soul, started this club. They called it the Capital Girls Club and no one else was allowed to join. They made one of those sweet little-girl pacts, that they would always wear them as long as they remained friends. I had my jeweler make them up especially for their seventh-grade graduation."

Whitney looked unimpressed.

"I thought they should be eighteen carat gold, of course. But Jackie thought that would be too gaudy for every day and persuaded me to do sterling silver," she added.

They'd fought over that—Taylor and Laura Beth—over whether the bracelets should be silver or gold. Laura Beth had a lot of gold jewelry and gold looked better with her skin tone. But Taylor insisted silver would be better. They wanted the bracelet to be a symbol, not a billboard. Taylor also insisted Jackie be the one to make the decision.

"It's all so sad," Miss Libby said. "The four girls were inseparable."

"Yeah, sorry about your friend," Whitney said, never taking her eyes off Jackie's, as if she was challenging her. "Drunk driving is such a problem."

"She wasn't drunk!" Jackie hissed, pressing her palms against the table. "She wasn't drunk," she repeated, and sat back again, her eyes fixed on Whitney's.

"Alcohol had nothing to do with the crash," Lettie added.

Whitney glanced at her father, who gave her an almost imperceptible shake of his head. "So," he said, clearing his throat and attempting to change the subject. "Are you girls applying to colleges in—"

"There was so much inaccurate press coverage at the time," Miss Libby said, her voice rising in outrage. Poor Mr. Remick. He'd never get a word in. "What with the president's son being in the car too. Some of it was just plain vicious, claiming she and Andrew must have been drunk when Taylor ran into that tree. Those vultures didn't even wait for her to be buried before they wrote all those hurtful lies."

"Mama, please," Laura Beth said quietly. "Let's not talk about it anymore."

"You're right, honey. I'm sorry. I didn't mean to upset you wonderful girls and I certainly don't want to make our guests uncomfortable." She picked up a tiny gold bell by her plate and rang for the maid. "How about a drink, William? Bourbon? Scotch? I think I'll have a teeny-tiny bourbon. Whitney? Girls? Iced tea? Soda?"

"It's a little early in the day for me, I'm afraid. But you go ahead, Libby," Mr. Remick said with a pleasant smile. "I'll stick with tea."

"I do so love an afternoon tea party, William, don't you?"

Miss Libby liked to think of herself as the Pamela Churchill Harriman of the Republican Party. Except, while Mrs. Harriman could discuss foreign policy, the sex life of the British royal family, and pheasant hunting, Miss Libby relied on her cleavage, her Southern charm, and her well-stocked bar to attract men.

Jackie watched as William Remick tried to keep his composure from cracking as he choked out his next words: "To tell you the truth, Libby, I think this is my first tea party ever. Thank you so much for inviting us."

Good thing his wife wasn't here. Jackie could just see the gossip column: *Colorful Republican socialite and political dynamo Libby Ballou doesn't mince words when it comes to affirmative action, her daughter's Latina friends, and rewriting the Civil War.*

"Well, I just think it's important for us transplants to stick together, don't you? Washington is such a beautiful city, but it can be so daunting at first and of course we want to teach our girls the same culture and manners we learned growing up. And good friends are always important. Being a widow's not easy, especially when one's husband was such a prominent Republican and so beloved by his party. And his country, for that matter."

She gave a dramatic sigh.

Jackie had to stifle a guffaw at the idea of Libby Ballou, notorious man-chaser, playing the role of lonely widow lady.

"My mom said you were engaged," Whitney said with a yawn.

Jackie looked over at Laura Beth, who literally drooped in

her seat, looking sick. Who knew how the gossip columnist discovered her cougar hook-up with Laura Beth's voice coach? The four of them had spent hours in Laura Beth's bedroom scheming over ways to break them up. The "engagement" only lasted six weeks.

Poor Laura Beth. She quit singing that winter and besides dance, she'd barely left her room.

"Oh, that was just a silly little rumor. You know those over-imaginative gossips," Miss Libby said dismissively. Then she feigned a gasp. "Oh my goodness, William, I didn't mean to be rude. I mean . . ."

"I've never been a huge fan of the tabloids either," Mr. Remick said with a wave of his hand, but Jackie noticed he was clenching his jaw.

Miss Libby turned to the girls. "Why don't you take Whitney for a walk around Georgetown while I make sure William knows where to get decent help and the best places to dine? Show her Dumbarton Oaks and the canal and I bet she'd love all those little boutiques along M Street."

Despite being home to the extremely rich and the very powerful, Georgetown was an eclectic mix of student bars and posh restaurants, exclusive boutiques and bargain fashion outlets, pricey antique stores and goth shops. With a fake ID and a trust-account credit card, the possibilities were endless.

The girls scrambled gratefully to their feet.

Escape.

No sooner had they shut the front door behind them Laura Beth collapsed against the wall and flung an arm over her face. "Oh, I do so love a tea party, especially when there's bourbon!"

"Oh, William, I didn't mean to call your wife a low-life

gossip-mongering bitch. I do hope you didn't take offense," Jackie joined in. "And little inferior Lettie, honey, aren't you just so grateful you've been saved by superior white people like us?"

"Oh Jackie, I'm so proud of you! Even if you are a Democrat," Lettie laughed. "Laura Beth, how many bourbons had she had already?"

"Seriously," Jackie laughed.

Laura Beth blushed so Jackie offered her a quick hug. It wasn't her fault her mother was such a drama queen.

"So, Whitney, do you want to come with us?" Lettie asked.

Jackie looked over to see the new girl intently studying one of her bright blue fingernails. "You guys *do* owe me some fun after that torture."

Lame. We don't owe her. "I don't know if we owe you anything but it's definitely time to get out of here and do something fun," Jackie replied.

"You guys smoke weed?" Whitney shrugged. "I got some great Cali medicinal grade."

Medicinal grade? Who is this girl? The best Taylor ever got was hydro.

"Oh! Let's show her Roosevelt Island. There are lots of great spots where no one can see you," Laura Beth suggested. "And the breeze is great for getting rid of the smell."

When Whitney got home, she logged into her computer and opened her mother's e-mail.

How did it go? Did you get to meet any of their parents? Make sure you send me all the details. Don't forget to take pictures of everything too.

And that was it.

Whitney sighed. The Virgin Queen Bee, a Southern Belle Wannabe, and their Token Charity Case—even if they did get high—were poor substitutes for all of her friends and the celebrities back home.

Her mom had practically forced her on the plane to D.C. "I need to focus on some things here for a while," she'd said. Career ranked higher than Parent. Like always.

She just wanted to get out of this sweltering hellhole and go back to L.A. The heat here was life-sucking, and it showed everywhere in the city. Aside from this tea-party-whatever-it-was, Whitney'd only been outside once. It was when they'd first gotten here. She'd barely waited for all her boxes to be moved inside before she took the keys to the car that her dad had shipped ahead of time, and drove off—from Foggy Bottom to Georgetown's narrow streets to downtown. Just looking. For something. She didn't know what.

She found nothing she recognized from California—things here just had a different vibe. It was all so put together and organized and stressed looking: from the redbrick buildings with the neat, white pillars to the girls in conservative skirts. It drove Whitney to the brink of insanity—she just wanted to go in and mess it all up; give it some life.

Finally, she'd turned onto H Street. As a sprawling white structure came into view, she felt as close to excited as she was going to get here. She'd never seen the White House. And it was supposed to be majestic or something, right? But as she got closer, she saw, beyond the sweaty crowd of tourists standing in front of the black gates, the White House wavering like a mirage. And it was just a house. Men in ties and women in suit jackets were striding past it, trying to strip away all their extra layers without breaking ear-to-cell-phone contact.

That's all this city was. Hot. And stressed. And boring.

And it still was. She had nothing much to tell her mom about today either. It was hardly news that they'd gotten high. No one cared about that anymore, and she hadn't gotten any pictures to prove it. But she'd still relay everything that happened. Finding a big story was the only thing that might make her mom happy enough to bring Whitney back to California.

THREE

Everything about the Oval Office—from the elaborately carved Resolute Desk to the massive presidential seal woven into the pale blue carpet—exuded *power*. It was designed to intimidate. And most people facing down the president of the United States would be overawed, or at least nervous.

Andrew Price simply felt annoyed and exhausted. But this wasn't just the president to him—this was his mother.

For the third time, he pinched the bridge of his nose, hoping to relieve some of the tension in his headache.

"This is supposed to be a press conference on immigration reform, Mom," he said, shaking his head, and falling back onto the couch in front of the fireplace. "Why does it sound more like a celebrity photo op for Jackie and me?"

His mother raised an eyebrow from where she stood behind her desk, a single strand of her auburn hair falling into her face.

When standing, she was almost as tall as Andrew, and she knew how to look intimidating. She'd known how to do it even before she was president, back when she was just his mom. "The immigration bill is important. We want the press to be happy, so we have to give them something to make them happy. Come on, Andrew, you know how this works."

Andrew knew too well. No gossip column was complete without a celebrity sighting of Andrew and Jackie—or "Ankie," as the press had ridiculously dubbed them: "Ankie" enjoying a candlelight meal at the latest Fourteenth Street hot spot, or dancing at a State Dinner, or walking the Price family labradoodle, Leftie, on the White House lawn. It was all so planned and choreographed.

"Besides, you know how much the press loves Ankie," his mother teased, smiling now.

Andrew couldn't manage to return it. He knew he could tell his mom that he and Jackie had been fighting. And she'd listen to him. She'd take him seriously. But she'd also be devastated.

The press, on the other hand, would be thrilled. That would be a juicy tabloid piece for them: "Trouble for the It Couple?" "Ankie on the Outs?" He wanted to ask why his parents couldn't pose as the happy First Couple themselves. But he already knew the answer. His father helped when it came to campaigning, but they were only a *couple* when it suited their needs and they appeared in public together just often enough to keep the press from asking questions. So he and Jackie got stuck with posing as the happy White House couple to quash any rumors of a rift.

"You're turning me into the new Chelsea Clinton." Andrew hated that he sounded almost whiny. He wanted to talk to her like an adult—not a three-year-old. He forced his voice to sound more even-toned. "She just stood around and did nothing. Like a prop."

"Don't be ridiculous," his mom said, moving toward him and dropping a hand on Andrew's shoulder. "She was nowhere near as popular or well-respected." She squeezed. "I promise."

And that was why, as always, Andrew didn't really have the heart to fight her on this. She wasn't trying to make Andrew a prop—she was trying to create a solid foundation for Andrew's own political future. Which was the other reason he always went along with the photo ops. He did have aspirations, and he'd do whatever it took to turn them into a reality. Of course, as the bulbs were flashing, he'd be wondering if it was enough that he was the son of the president. Shouldn't he be doing more—be more involved? But if Ankie kept him popular, and it helped keep his mother in office *and* happy, he'd do it.

It was harder sometimes than others. Hardest now, when he and Jackie were fighting. Lately he wondered if his brother, Scott, had the right idea. Maybe getting exiled from the family and sent to Wilderness Survival Camp, or wherever he was this summer, was the smarter choice.

Whatever he planned to say next died away when Jackie breezed into the room, a Secret Service agent holding the door for her. For a moment, all the things he wanted to say to his mother, even the headache, it all just slipped away.

And all he could see was Jackie.

Bare tanned legs, the way her black skirt hugged her ass, the way she smiled when her blue eyes met his.

God, she was beautiful.

But then his chest tightened, and it felt like something inside him hollowed out, as it did whenever he looked at her lately. He didn't deserve her anymore.

"Sorry I'm late, Aunt Deborah," Jackie said, brushing her hair over her shoulder. "There's picketing outside. It's a madhouse." She didn't need to mention *who* was picketing, since it was the same group who had been calling for Deborah Price's impeachment for months now—the Patriotic American People's Party. The PAPPies had sprung up a month or so before Taylor's accident and had been gaining popularity ever since. Jackie smiled at Andrew again, hoping he'd come over and give her a kiss. Instead he just offered her a weak grin. The door opened again and the president's press secretary, Brian Gillespie, walked in.

"Madam President," he said.

"Now that everyone's here," Aunt Deborah said, giving Andrew, then Jackie, a last smile before she slipped back into president mode, "why don't you tell them exactly what you want them to do?"

Brian nodded, unbuttoned the jacket of his three-piece navy suit, and pulled out a notebook. Jackie fought to keep from rolling her eyes when he started talking. *Of course, Madam President. Anything you want, Madam President.* She never could stand the guy. His former boss, a New York senator, had loaned him to Aunt Deborah during the presidential campaign, but after she won, he ended up staying on rather than heading back to Capitol Hill.

"We'd like the two of you to stand behind President Price,

just to her left," Brian said. "We don't want you blocked from the cameras. And make sure you're holding hands."

"Should I be wearing a pink shirt?" Andrew joked, looking down at the Brooks Brothers button-up. "The press might question my manhood."

"Only real men can wear pink," Jackie said. "The press knows that." They probably also knew it had been a birthday present from her. She grinned, hoping Andrew would look at her, and know that she was remembering the night she'd given it to him. But he kept his gaze straight ahead, like she wasn't even there. Her smile faded.

"Listen," the president said. "This bill is important. You need to look supportive while I'm talking." She stretched her arms. Her sleek outfit, a beige linen pantsuit, was a nod to Hillary Clinton, who helped shatter Washington's glass ceiling—though the cut was more stylish than Clinton's mannish suits and a ruffled shirt softened the overall look. A fist-size pin of pink and aqua rhinestones was another nod to another feminist mentor, former Secretary of State Madeleine Albright.

"I'll be staying on point about the immigration bill," she said as Brian handed her a sheet of talking points. "We want the bill to be the sole focus of the press conference. So don't answer any questions, even if they're directed to you."

Jackie nodded. She and Andrew knew the drill. Even before they were a couple, each was accustomed to playing a public role in Aunt Deborah's never-ending popularity campaign: two doting children representing American Democratic family values. It was only for the first couple of months after Taylor's death that the White House kept them under wraps. Andrew because he'd been in the crash and Jackie because she was an emotional wreck. But now that six months had passed and the acceptable grieving period was over, the White House was happy to use them for optics again.

"You'll both be wonderful, of course," Aunt Deborah added, offering Jackie a smile.

"Ready?" Andrew asked.

Jackie looked over to see his hand outstretched to her. For a second, a flicker of annoyance went through her. Why did she always have to go to him? Why couldn't he come to her? But she went anyway, and when she touched his skin, her irritation melted away. Her hand fit inside his like a missing piece of a puzzle, and she automatically relaxed.

But Brian, on his mission to be important, wasn't finished. "Oh, Jackie, we should have had you bring along that friend of yours, Lettie. She would have been perfect."

He looked at the president, who nodded and pressed the intercom button on her phone. "Carolyn?"

Jackie's stomach did a flip. Lettie probably would have loved to play a role in pushing the immigration bill, but not propped up on stage as the token Latina. Especially not after yesterday's afternoon tea with Miss Libby. Allowing two parents to use Lettie's ethnicity twice in two days was too much.

"Aunt Deborah, you know how shy Lettie is." Jackie turned to Brian. "She'd be fidgety in the background. It wouldn't look good on camera." *And I don't want you using my friends.*

Andrew squeezed her hand, and she squeezed back. At least they could offer a united front on the topic of Lettie.

Brian's brow furrowed and jaw clenched—the picture of irritation. "But she's perfect—a family friend, a hardworking, brilliant young woman who's here on a temporary visa because under the current law she doesn't qualify for permanent residency. It's a great example of how this issue affects everyone, even the president."

The Oval Office door opened, and Jackie's mother entered, wearing an Armani black skirt and suit jacket, with her long blond hair pulled back into a tight bun at the base of her neck. "Don't worry, I have the Secret Service investigating that crank caller." She was talking before she was even through the door, as usual.

"What crank caller?" Jackie asked.

Her mother looked over and gave her a reassuring smile. "We got a crank call this morning from someone threatening the First Family. They specifically mentioned you and Andrew. It's probably just another attention-seeker, honey. It's nothing to worry about."

"Of course not. The White House gets dozens of threats every week," Aunt Deborah said with a dismissive wave. "Actually, Carolyn, that's not why I buzzed you."

Jackie's mom was back in chief-of-staff mode instantly. "Is everything okay?"

Carolyn Shaw was one of the most powerful women in the world. The "woman behind the president," she commanded attention whenever she walked into a room. And she was a single mother, who'd raised a daughter all by herself after she and Jackie's dad split.

A lot of kids admired and looked up to their parents—when they were *kids*. But Jackie still admired her mom and aspired to follow in her footsteps—as a smart, intelligent, independent woman of the world, her mother was still her idol.

"I understand you want to protect Lettie," Aunt Deborah was saying. At the mention of Lettie's name, Jackie made eye contact with her mother, ready to all but plead to leave Lettie out of this, but she didn't need to. She caught her mother's calm posture and easy smile, and knew it wouldn't come to that. Her mother had obviously anticipated what weasely Brian might say and had a plan. Her mother always had a plan. Aunt Deborah continued. "But Brian does have a point: I want the press to understand I have a personal stake in this immigration bill—we all should."

"You're absolutely right. It does affect everyone. I've had the staff round up about a dozen foreign students with temporary visas to stand in the background with Jackie and Andrew. And, as human interest pieces after the press conference, they'll be able to give their own personal stories of coming to America," Jackie's mother said. "We should really start making our way to the East Room in about five minutes."

"Good—we can do a meet and greet with them before the press conference," Brian added.

"Do you need Jackie and me for that too?" Andrew asked. Half-heartedly in Jackie's opinion. If he didn't want to do it, why didn't he just tell them?

"No," Jackie's mom said, before Jackie could get any more frustrated with him. "You just need to present a united front for the cameras. Just make sure you and Jackie don't get cornered by any reporters. Remember, we have to keep the focus on the immigration bill. It's critical for the re-election campaign."

Aunt Deborah flashed them a charming smile. "Just think, Andrew, if this bill passes you will have helped make history."

Andrew looked like he was about to say something, but the door opened, and he shut his mouth. Silenced. The president's secretary, Agnes Ford, slipped quietly into the room and handed a folded slip of paper to Jackie's mother. Carolyn Shaw read it with a raised eyebrow, then passed it to the president.

Aunt Deborah gave the slip of paper a similar look. "Fine. Send him in," she said.

Agnes nodded, and smiled at Jackie as she made her way back out of the room.

The door opened again seconds later, and Jackie dropped Andrew's hand as her heart leaped into her throat.

Eric!

Impeccably dressed in a dark suit, crisp white shirt, and a blue tie that accentuated his piercing blue eyes, he strode into the room like he was claiming the office for his own. He moved straight to the president. "Madam President," he said, shaking her hand. "I have a note from Senator Griffin. He wanted to make sure you got it before the press conference."

When he turned, the corner of his lips went up, forming a flirty smile and revealing the dimple in his cheek. "Ms. Shaw," he said, then nodded to Brian.

He turned to Jackie next and her pulse pounded in her ears. It felt like all the air had suddenly been sucked out of the room and her mouth instantly went dry. "Miss Whitman," Eric said, taking her hand lightly in his. "As always, it's a pleasure."

He let her hand go, and she felt dizzy, as if she might start swaying.

And then he turned to Andrew, and her temperature seemed to bottom out. "You must be Andrew." He offered his hand. "I'm Eric Moran, Senator Griffin's AA."

Jackie could have sworn time stopped dead until Andrew
reached out and shook Eric's hand. She could tell by the way he
squinted his eyes that he didn't like Eric's confidence.

"Tell Senator Griffin I'll take it under advisement," the president said as she finished reading the note, folded it, and stuffed
it in her pocket. Eric nodded and took that as his cue to leave. But
he caught Jackie's gaze before he did.

As soon as the door shut behind him, Aunt Deborah groaned.
"The *senator* is terrified we're going to let in too many *illegals*."

Carolyn Shaw nodded. "Just remember not to use that dirty
word 'amnesty.' Stress how many new taxpayers we'll be gaining rather than giving a free pass to illegals."

While she waited for President Price's press conference to start,
Lettie pulled out her scrapbook and pasted in the most recent
editorial on the proposed immigration reform onto a blank
page.

The scrapbook was Lettie's secret. No one knew about it.
Well, she'd told Taylor a few months before the accident. But
no one knew *now*. It had actually started as a kind of Burn Book,
a place where she vented her feelings about how much she hated
so many of the girls at their school and their money and condescending apathy. It was also where she poured out her heart
and soul, admitting how much Laura Beth's advice about her
clothes and appearance made her feel like crap or how much she
wished she could be popular and comfortable in the public eye
like Taylor and Jackie.

But it was so much more than that now.

She still kept newspaper clippings of her and her friends

every time the press snapped a picture of them. And sometimes she did still vent about things that bothered her.

But the focus of the scrapbook had changed. A couple of years ago, she'd started collecting articles about political issues and topics she felt passionately about. She kept track of the arguments on both sides, trying to understand what exactly her position was and why she felt that way. It was an exercise in civic discourse, really. She was determined to be more informed and better prepared to handle the world she wanted to change.

Then Taylor died. When it first happened, Lettie didn't pick up her scrapbook for several months. World policy, political debates—none of it seemed important anymore when life was so short.

She'd almost forgotten about the scrapbook too, kicking it to the back of her closet. Then she'd read about the immigration bill President Price was pushing. This affected *her family*. If the bill passed, she, her parents, and her three siblings could become permanent citizens of the United States. They would never have to go back to Paraguay, where things were getting worse. Bad enough that Paz was in the thick of it, Lettie didn't want Christa and Maribel to ever see home the way it was now. Not until things changed.

Lettie flipped the scrapbook open to the page that had the clippings from Taylor's car wreck and read the obituary for the hundredth time:

TAYLOR CANE, 17
Potomac, MD
     Passed away suddenly. Beloved daughter of Jennifer and Aaron Cane, loved twin sister of Daniel, and baby sister to

Samuel, cherished granddaughter of Elizabeth and Barry Duncan and Cheryl and David Cane. Will be greatly missed by family and friends. Taylor's beauty and adventurous spirit touched us all.

A celebration to honor her life will be held Monday at the Washington Excelsior Preparatory School. Donations in lieu of flowers should be sent in her memory to Martha's Table.

People at school had laughed about Taylor's "adventurous spirit" and claimed it was code for wild, promiscuous party girl, but that was only because they didn't know Taylor the way Lettie did. Sure, she *was* wild and promiscuous, but only because she felt stifled by D.C. What Taylor really wanted was the kind of adventure that would stop the world in its tracks. She seemed even more restless just before she'd died.

"You know how it is, L. Everyone acting like back-stabbing hypocrites, worrying about how much money they have, who's the most powerful, who has the latest designer handbags, and hoping their husbands don't find out they're cheating too. I can't wait to get away from it."

She thought fleetingly of Sam, Taylor's older brother. She'd had a small crush on him before Taylor died. He'd always ask her about school and about her family and even about Paraguay whenever she saw him. At first Lettie thought it was because he liked her, but then she realized he was just being nice to her.

After all, Taylor had told them Sam was gay.

Jackie's hand was starting to feel sweaty. But she and Andrew stood still, their hands locked together, surrounded by the foreign students. Aunt Deborah stood in front of them, a large American flag hung behind her, her hands resting on the podium bearing the presidential seal. She looked completely collected as she called on the reporter from the *L.A. Times*. Protocol dictated all the major daily newspapers and TV networks each got a chance to ask a question at every presidential news conference.

"Madam President, isn't your bill just an excuse for amnesty?"

"No, not at all. If you remember, Ronald Reagan successfully implemented similar immigration reform. My bill, just like his, will create hundreds of thousands—possibly millions—of new taxpayers. They're already here illegally so it won't cost Americans any jobs, but it *will* provide untold billions of dollars to financially strapped states and it will help us pay off the federal debt. It's a win-win."

She pointed to a reporter Jackie didn't know. Pasty-skinned, overweight, and looking a little too eager—probably a radio reporter.

"Thank you, Madam President. As you know, the Patriotic American People's Party"—Jackie tightened her grip on Andrew's hand to keep from wincing—"claim to have almost eighty thousand signatures on a petition demanding your impeachment, alleging you overstepped your constitutional powers by—"

"When there is a serious accusation leveled against me, I will be the first person to answer it," Aunt Deborah said, the muscles in her neck tense. The PAPPies had been going after her for months now, but so far they had nothing concrete.

"Last question," Brian Gillespie said, stepping to the microphone.

She reluctantly pointed to the Fox News reporter.

"We haven't had the opportunity until now to ask Andrew about the tragic car accident that killed his friend, Taylor Cane. I'd like to ask him a two-part question. How are you feeling, and do you have any regrets that you weren't the one driving that night?"

Jackie could feel the tension grip Andrew as his body went rigid. Every eye in the room changed focus. The silence was suffocating.

"This news conference is about immigration policy," Aunt Deborah said tartly. "My son is coping as well as can be expected. He has not commented publicly about this tragedy and will not do so now. The death of his and Jackie's dear friend, Taylor, is not something we wish to see exploited for political purposes.

"Thank you all for coming," she added, then she turned her back and walked out of the White House East Room.

Someone touched Jackie's shoulder and herded her and Andrew out of the room as well. Members of the press shouted questions after them, but she couldn't hear any specifics. Not that she would have wanted to.

"Damn it!" Aunt Deborah swore, then lowered her voice as Brian Gillespie came up beside her. "Andrew and Taylor's accident is going to be the lead on every network broadcast tonight instead of the immigration bill."

The person behind Jackie squeezed her shoulder. A familiar squeeze. Her mother.

"Is there any way to spin this, Carolyn?" Aunt Deborah strode past Andrew and Jackie, pausing only to raise an eyebrow at them—a subtle "Doing all right?" look she gave them whenever the press crossed a line. As always, Jackie nodded, even though she was having trouble catching her breath. Andrew stared straight ahead, his mouth tightened and his grip on Jackie's hand slackened, but said nothing. Obviously it had bothered him—why not say so? Or put up a good front and move on? She took her hand out of his; she wasn't going to stand here and be part of his passive aggression.

"Better leave it alone," her mother said, giving Jackie's shoulder another squeeze before turning to follow her boss. "Stick to immigration. I have a few of the teenagers lined up to tell their immigration stories to the media. I'll take them down to the press room right away."

"Let's go upstairs," Andrew finally said.

Jackie thought about telling him no, but he was already walking away, and it felt childish to simply stand there and not follow him.

Five minutes later, she sat blankly on a traditional upholstered sofa in the living room of the second-floor family quarters. Andrew paced in front of her, ranting, saying everything he should've expressed to their mothers—the two people who could actually do something about this.

"Asshole reporters. Why can't those douchebags leave it alone?"

"Because Taylor's dead," Jackie whispered.

"What's that supposed to mean?"

"Nothing, just that she's dead. My best friend is *dead*," Jackie shot back. Part of her still couldn't believe it. There were still mornings when she woke up and reached for her phone to dial Taylor's number. She still had moments when something goodbadinterestingfunnyexcitingridiculous happened, and her first thought was she'd have to tell Taylor. She'd never quite caught

47

her breath, and now it was getting worse. It was like her throat was getting smaller.

"What, and it's my fault Taylor's dead? Is that what you mean?"

Jackie stood up. She needed air. The window, maybe. "No, of course not! I mean it's not surprising that they're still asking about the accident. Someone's always going to bring it up. Even Libby Ballou was talking about it yesterday."

Andrew scowled. "Fuck her too."

"Fuck you." Jackie shook her head. "I don't know what your problem is."

Forget the window. She turned and moved for the door, only to stop with her hand on the doorknob. She didn't want to leave things like that with him. She wanted him to stop her. To promise her everything would be all right. To say something that would make the tightness in her throat vanish, and make things right between them again.

She looked back over her shoulder.

He sat on the edge of the couch, his head down, his hands in his hair.

And she instantly felt guilty.

Jackie sighed and leaned her back against the door. "Let's not fight again."

Andrew looked up, twisting the plain silver band—his stupid promise ring—that he wore on his wedding-ring finger.

He had been one of her best friends since she was little. Even if their relationship was all but over, she didn't want to hurt him. She couldn't imagine a life where they weren't friends. "Let's talk about something else. Did I tell you we're all going to do the Princeton college tour tomorrow?"

He dropped his hands in his lap. "That should be fun."

Jackie shrugged. "Well, it should have been. But the new girl, Whitney, is coming. I'm *not* her biggest fan."

"The gossip columnist's daughter?" He stared at her in disbelief. "Why would you want to hang out with her?"

"I don't," Jackie said, moving back toward the couch. "But I have a sneaking suspicion that Carolyn Shaw, Libby Ballou, and Deborah Price have determined the best way to get in good with a gossip columnist is by making us BFFs with her daughter."

Andrew slapped his face in mock surprise. "They would never do that!"

Jackie smirked. "Whatever. We got stoned with her after Libby's tea party."

Andrew leaned back. "God, that's what I needed yesterday, something to help me relax."

Jackie thought she might know a better way to help him relax. Only every time she'd suggested *that* lately, rather than smile or show *some* kind of reaction, Andrew just ran a hand through his hair and made excuses. *Exhausted. Rough day.* It was enough to almost make her feel unattractive.

"You up for a movie?" she asked instead.

"Yeah, sure." He slid over on the couch and she sat down next to him while he reached over to grab the remote. "What do you want to watch?"

Nothing romantic. "Whatever. Your choice."

He put his arm around the back of the couch and started flipping channels, and a deep wave of *dissatisfaction* rolled through Jackie's heart.

She wanted excitement right now, and Andrew wasn't delivering. There were no surprises. No passion. When she was a little girl, she and her mother watched *The Philadelphia Story,* and the moment she saw Cary Grant and Katharine Hepburn in that scene at the pool's edge (the one where she's wearing that elegant white poolside gown), she knew she wanted a man like that, a man willing to challenge her, stand up for her, excite, surprise, and inspire her.

Once upon a time, she thought Andrew might be that guy.

He had a lot of great qualities. He was a rising college sophomore, a straight-A international studies major at Georgetown University (okay, it wasn't an Ivy or anything, but he wanted to stay in D.C.), a member of the varsity basketball team (so he rarely ever played, but he *was* on the team), and the star of the debate team (just like his mom).

"Oh, how about this one?" Andrew said, settling on an action movie with The Rock.

"Sure." She leaned back trying to get comfortable when her iPhone vibrated. She reached into her purse to glance at it.

A message from Eric: *You looked so hot today. When can I see you?*

She tucked the phone back in her purse without answering. But while Andrew watched the movie and she curled herself under his arm and tried to snuggle into him, she couldn't seem to shake the one thought stuck in her mind.

Andrew wasn't The One. He just wasn't the kind of guy who'd fight for her. He wasn't the kind of guy who would show up at a wedding to prevent her from marrying someone else.

She caught a cab home a few hours later, and as she looked out at the city, backlit by a warm, orange sunset, the niggling thought fled her mind, along with every other worry she'd accumulated lately. No, she didn't know what she'd do about Andrew, or how she'd feel if the reporters from today rehashed Taylor's accident *again* on the nightly news, or even how she was going to get through senior year seeing Whitney every day. But despite all that uncertainty, there was one thing that Jackie was absolutely sure of: the D.C. landscape. It had looked the same since Jackie was a little girl, and somehow, that reassured her. Jackie knew it was strange to be sure of something like nineteenth-century brick sidewalks and lovingly restored row houses. But it'd always been comforting to her to think that no matter where *she* was in two, five, ten years, D.C. would be here.

As she sometimes did when she was driving through the city, Jackie tried to imagine what it would be like if she were seeing this for the first time. The women in silk dresses disappearing into the historic wood-paneled restaurants; the glass storefronts of the new boutiques lining M Street; the White House lit up and glowing. What did it all look like to people who'd never seen it before? What would they think of it all?

Jackie rested her head back against her seat and smiled to herself. She knew exactly what they'd think, because it was the same thing Jackie thought: this was the greatest city in the world.

FOUR

Laura Beth let out a sigh. It didn't matter, though. Not one of her friends looked over at her. Whitney was drinking from her "water" bottle (vodka) and texting. Jackie was watching a new Russell Brand video on her iPod, and surprise, surprise, Lettie was reading Malcolm Gladwell's latest. After leafing through the latest issue of *Teen Vogue*—twice—Laura Beth was just plain bored.

Six days to Jackie's eighteenth birthday (and Laura Beth still couldn't decide what to get her), it was a muggy summer day. They were on their way to New York, taking the Acela Express, the luxury train popular with politicians, celebrities, socialites, and K Street lawyers heading to Manhattan for business and pleasure.

"Oh, look at this," Lettie said, passing her book over to Jackie, who paused her video to read.

"What's it say?" Laura Beth asked.

Lettie turned to her, blushing a little, before she shrugged. "He's talking about rational drug design versus mass screening and how the pharmaceutical industry has gone too far in the rational direction."

"Lettie, how can you read that leftist crap? Don't you know they're tryin' to brainwash you?" Laura Beth said.

Jackie rolled her eyes and Lettie bit her lip, pulling the book up to cover her face.

Laura Beth sighed again, this time loud enough for Whitney to look over at her. She usually loved taking the high-speed Acela. Yes, it was twice the price of the Northeast Regional, but it got you to New York in less than three hours without adult supervision and she usually saw a celebrity or two. As per usual, her mom's driver had dropped them all at Union Station a little before nine. And like it always did, the sight of D.C.'s gorgeous 1907 Beaux-Arts train terminal with its high arched ceilings and marble floors took her breath away. Before Taylor died, they would often take the train to Manhattan. She and the girls would get on, and Taylor would say something like, *"We're off to New York, dahlings,"* in a ridiculous posh accent that sent them all into giggles. They'd scope out guys and celebrities, and talk and laugh, and something about it made Laura Beth feel . . . not *safe* exactly, but secure. Confident that they would always be this way—that nothing would ever tear them apart.

But today, everything felt stale. They were each sitting around, doing their own thing. Somehow without Taylor, it felt like they weren't a group anymore. Like the glue that held them together had somehow vanished with her.

Laura Beth was determined to get that back. All this melancholy moping was just startin' to drive her *crazy*. It was bad enough that Mama controlled her future—she'd even quit singin' because of her. She didn't want Taylor's death to control her social life. The four of them used to laugh until they cried and their sides burned, and there was always something to gossip about. Not anymore, it seemed. But Laura Beth had a plan. She wanted to *be* the glue. She wanted to slide into the shoes Taylor had left behind. She just wasn't quite sure *how* to go about doing that.

"Are they glaring at us or just perving?" Jackie whispered, pulling Laura Beth out of her thoughts.

She looked over to see two middle-aged businessmen in dark suits settled into another four-person banquette. They were both glancing at the girls. Repeatedly.

Whitney put her phone in her pocket. "How much do you want to bet I could get them to buy me a drink?"

"I dare you," Laura Beth said.

Whitney pulled down her lime-green silk cami so it hugged her boobs (she was still totally going without a bra). Then she stood up and arched her back. She squeezed past Jackie and gave her butt an exaggerated wiggle as she crossed the aisle.

"Wow, how many times you think she's done this before?" Jackie laughed.

"Maybe she specializes in old guys," Laura Beth added.

"Much older," Lettie echoed.

The girls tried to smother their giggles as Whitney leaned toward the gray-haired guy in the aisle seat.

Whitney said something to the men—Laura Beth couldn't hear what it was. But the men obviously asked to her to join them, because seconds later she was performing stripper-like moves to maneuver over to the window seat.

"Oh my God," Jackie said, staring and moving forward in her seat. Like she didn't know whether she should get up and stop Whitney or just get a better look. Laura Beth, personally, wanted to see what'd happen.

With an ultra-sexy drop into the seat, Whitney began chatting up the mesmerized stiffs. The men couldn't take their eyes off her legs as she kept crossing and uncrossing them, like she was trying to find a comfortable position.

One of the men got up and disappeared for a few minutes, returning with three drinks on a cardboard tray. The minute a glass was in her hand, she jumped up from her seat and raised her voice. "What kind of men are you?"

Her voice was raised a couple of octaves and her lips quivered as if she were about to cry. "You are disgusting!" she said, abruptly switching to a Southern accent. "No wonder my mama didn't want me to go all by myself on the train."

The bewildered men looked around furtively and sank as low as they could into their seats. Whitney even pushed one of them as she stepped into the aisle. "Do you gentlemen know how old I am? I am barely seventeen and here y'all are trying to get me drunk and comin' on to me. And it's only eleven o'clock in the mornin'!"

Laura Beth buried her face in Jackie's shoulder to smother her laughs.

One of the guys finally found his voice. He turned, addressing no one in particular: "This girl is insane! She came over here—I don't know what she's talking about!"

Whitney turned on her heel and marched back to her seat,

muttering, "Dirty old men!" She sat down just as one of the conductors made his way to the businessmen to find out what was going on. Whitney raised her glass in a mock salute and drained it.

"That was pure genius," Laura Beth said with a laugh. And she meant it. If Whitney hadn't been here, Jackie would still be watching her iPod, Lettie would be reading, and *she* would still be waiting for something to happen.

Even if Laura Beth didn't *like* Whitney all that much, having her around for entertainment could be fun.

"I gotta admit," Whitney said with a smile, "traveling by train is way less boring than I thought it'd be."

Laura Beth watched Jackie finally relax back into her seat. "The Acela is my favorite way to travel," Jackie said. "Except for Air Force One, of course."

Whitney opened her mouth to respond, but Laura Beth didn't want to hear more about Jackie's trips on Air Force One—at least not until Laura Beth got to take one herself. "Whitney, that was hilarious! We need to keep this fun goin'. What else have you got in mind for us?"

Whitney looked at Laura Beth with raised eyebrows. "Well, wait'll you hear how I'm collecting on my bet."

"But we didn't actually bet anything," Lettie said, brow furrowed, like she was concerned Whitney was going to make *her* go over there next.

Whitney shrugged. "You didn't stop me; so I say the bet stands." She smiled, slow and devilish. "Tonight, we're crashing a college party, and I'm showing you East Coasters how us California girls live it up."

Jackie's hand went white-knuckled on the armrest. But Laura

Beth couldn't help but smile. It was nice having someone around who wasn't all mopey about Taylor. And Whitney had courage and spunk, different from Taylor's, but still fun. Laura Beth could take a cue from Whitney and have more fun this year. "Let me get a sip of that," she said, reaching for Whitney's "water" bottle. She ignored Jackie's frown. Just like she ignored the gawd-awful burn as the alcohol rolled down her throat.

After all, maybe it was time for Washington to have a new It Girl. A Republican.

Libby Ballou's hired chauffeur stood waiting for them on West 34th Street outside Penn Station. Jackie tucked her iPhone back into her purse and breathed in the New York air. Despite the faint smell of rotting trash, greasy bus fumes, and last night's rancid hot dogs, the air always made Jackie feel invigorated. Here the bad smells and rude crowds were expected and even exciting. Those smells meant shopping on Madison Avenue and Fifth Avenue and in Soho.

Unfortunately, they weren't staying. They were headed to Princeton for their last college tour of the summer.

"We need to stop by Magnolia Bakery in Greenwich Village first, please," Laura Beth instructed as they got into the limo.

That was the reason they'd taken the detour to Manhattan. It wasn't like they couldn't get cupcakes in D.C. The cupcake craze provided a lot of options, and Georgetown Cupcake was certainly nothing to scoff at. But nothing compared to Magnolia. That sweet, sugary vanilla smell could lead a person five blocks to the bakery's doorstep. Even the *Sex and the City* girls went there to talk about men and get their dessert fix. They had the best, and most famous, cupcakes in the world. And cupcakes at Magnolia was a Capital Girls tradition.

"Capital Girls take Manhattan!" Taylor said, throwing her arms up in the air as she twirled around, her Betsey Johnson skirt flaring just enough to reveal her black lace thong decorated with cherries. When she paused, she blew me a kiss and I grabbed her right arm and linked it through mine.

She was right. The four of us in New York City on the freshman class trip, our first trip to the Big Apple without one of our mothers hovering over us. We could do anything. "We have two hours before the show. Where should we go?" I asked.

"Well, we just haveta go to Newman Jewelers. Mama says they have the most beautiful Pickard china, like the White House has, and Vera Wang place settings," Laura Beth said, as she linked her arm through my free one.

Taylor gave a snort. "Unless you're planning on putting together your wedding trousseau, Laura Beth, I refuse to waste a second of my free time in New York City shopping for something your mother would buy. Lettie?" She beckoned. "Isn't this your first time in New York? What do you want to do?"

Lettie shrugged and linked her arm through Taylor's so the four of us stood in a line. "We're supposed to get lunch?"

Taylor smiled, the scarlet of her lips emphasizing the devilish plan forming in her mind. "I know exactly where we'll go."

Jackie bit her lip and looked out the window, remembering the red velvet cupcake she and Taylor had gotten the last time they were there. She turned and looked at Laura Beth and Lettie. "What kind are you getting?"

"Chocolate for me!" Lettie said, clapping her hands.

"I'm having banana pudding," said Laura Beth. "Red velvet for you?"

Jackie thought for a second. She always got red velvet. It was her favorite. But for some reason, she had the urge to try something new. "I think I'm going to get the devil's food cupcake this time. I've always wanted to try that."

Jackie caught Whitney rolling her eyes. "What?" she challenged.

"Oh nothing, just that here we are in one of the world's most exciting cities, and all we're doing is going on a fucking cupcake tour?"

"You were more than welcome to stay home," Jackie said.

"Devil's food cake was Taylor's favorite," Lettie said to no one in particular.

"So this is the Taylor Memorial Cupcake Tour? That's pathetic."

Jackie refused to get into an argument with Whitney about Taylor. It was obvious the girl would never have understood what it was like to have a *best* friend. And besides, she was dangerously close to crying and she'd be damned if she ever shed a tear in front of Whitney.

"Come on, you think your friend would want you all constantly thinking about the fact that she's not here? She sounded cooler than that." Whitney took another sip from her water bottle.

"Whitney's right, Taylor wouldn't want us all moping," Laura Beth agreed.

The fact that Jackie held her composure and didn't lose it

right there simply had to be one of her greatest accomplishments ever.

Lettie bit her lip but nodded. "You should try a cupcake. They're really good."

"I'll stick with vodka," Whitney said.

"Anybody need their bottles topped off?" Laura Beth asked, reaching for the bar. "I don't think I've ever had straight vodka this early in the morning. We should've mixed it with orange juice, the way we usually do."

Whitney shrugged. "Who needs the extra calories?"

Laura Beth topped off Whitney's water bottle and then took a swig of vodka herself. "You sound a little like Taylor," she giggled.

Jackie rolled her eyes. Great, Laura Beth was getting hammered already. By tonight she'd be throwing herself at every guy she met. And Whitney. *Ugh!* Jackie couldn't help hating her.

It was ridiculous she was even with them. Only Jackie and Lettie had any real plans to apply to Princeton. Laura Beth had the grades and connections to get in, of course, but Libby Ballou would die before letting her baby go to a northern Ivy. As far as Libby was concerned, Laura Beth was only applying to one school: Sewanee. What she didn't know was that Laura Beth was applying to Juilliard, provided she worked up the nerve to defy her mom.

Lettie's family couldn't afford to send her on the trip, but Mrs. Ballou's way of helping "those less fortunate" meant she didn't mind splurging on train tickets and the driver for the girls. After all, Laura Beth might meet and marry a nice Princeton boy so long as he was a Republican.

But what was Whitney's excuse? Why did she even want to *be* here?

The limo stopped outside the Bleecker Street bakery and Laura Beth shoved a $50 bill into the driver's hand so he could run in and pick up their order.

"Y'all get yourself something too," she yelled after him.

Jackie couldn't help laughing. She half expected Laura Beth to call the driver *darlin'*. "The farther north we go the more Southern you sound," Jackie teased her, mimicking her perfectly. "Y'all talk so cute, darlin'."

"You're just jealous now, Jackie Whitman." Laura Beth laughed even as she flushed. "Oh, there's Marc Jacobs across the street. Do you think we have time to run in?"

Lettie shook her head and made eye contact with Jackie, who knew exactly what Lettie was thinking. *How much more MJ could they possibly want?* "Let's plan a New York weekend later in the summer. Then we can come back and do all the shopping your Southern lady heart desires."

The driver returned carrying a white package.

Heaven in a box.

Jackie bit into her cupcake and savored the deep, rich chocolate. It was so aptly named—anything that tasted this good had to be a sin.

"Lettie, you *have* to try a bite," she said, passing it over. Lettie nibbled a small piece.

And then her eyes widened. "Oh my God."

Jackie laughed. "I know, right?" And before she could stop herself, she said what Taylor would have, because it was Taylor's standard of measurement when anything was simply divine. "This has got to be better than sex."

Laura Beth started coughing and Lettie turned away from her.

"Nothing's better than sex." Whitney laughed. "Trust me."

"So, Whitney, where are you applyin' to college?" Laura Beth asked, obviously hoping to avoid more Taylor comments.

She shrugged, eyes fixed dazedly on the redbrick buildings they passed. "Somewhere on the West Coast," she said, like she hadn't even thought of it.

But she had to have, didn't she?

Jackie met Lettie's eyes briefly, then Laura Beth's. They both looked as disbelieving as Jackie felt. "You don't have any specific schools picked out?"

"Whatever," Whitney said, turning to meet Jackie's eye line, testing her gaze. "I'll just apply to all of them." She smirked, then slung back the last of her water bottle. "I'll go to the one closest to the beach."

God, was she joking? And how was she not falling over wasted by now?

Laura Beth, voice high and scandalized, asked, "But if you don't know which schools you're applying to, that would mean you haven't started on your applications?"

Whitney laughed. "Shit no. Those things aren't due for ages, right?"

Annoyance bubbled up in Jackie's chest as she *again* wondered what the hell Whitney was doing here. Almost as if Whitney read her mind, she threw a scornful look at Jackie and made a big show of relaxing back into her seat.

"Well I for one don't want the extra stress during senior year," Jackie said. "I'm going to have my applications finished before school starts." Which wasn't exactly true. A few schools didn't release their applications until September. But for some reason, the less Whitney did, the more Jackie wanted to look accomplished.

"Oh please, like you need to be worried about them, either," Whitney said. "Jackie, you could get in anywhere because your mom is BFF with the president. And—"

"That's crap! I have to work as hard as anyone," Jackie snapped, even though she was well aware that her mother's relationship with Aunt Deborah and her own celebrity status gave her a huge advantage. But that didn't mean she could just slack off. She had straight A's and would graduate in the top five of their class, and she'd spent hours and thousands of dollars at that stupid SAT class every Wednesday night last spring.

Whitney just raised an eyebrow. "As I was saying. Lettie's lucky too. I bet you've got colleges begging to have you." She laughed. "They'll probably just eat up your essay. Don't admissions officers get wet dreams about the little immigrant girl whose poor family came to America for better lives? Just play up all the sad shit. You'll be fine."

Lettie frowned. "You don't know what you're talking about."

The last of Jackie's patience fled—Lettie worked harder than anyone she knew. "Seriously, Whitney, lay off. You don't know a thing about Lettie—or any of us."

"Whatever," Whitney said, and went back to staring out the window, like none of this had bothered her. It just made Jackie angrier. How could she just judge them all like that?

"Last year my cousin, Sue Lynn, she made up her entire essay," Laura Beth said. She talked fast and high-pitched, the way she always did when she was trying to change the subject. "She claimed she found out that her mama used to be some sort of high-priced call girl! It was hysterical! She got in to Yale, early action!"

"Oh my God!" Whitney yelped. "Wouldn't it be hilarious if it was true, and she came to visit her daughter on parents' weekend and ran into a customer?"

"I know someone whose mom died of cancer his senior year and he wrote about that and got accepted at Berkeley," Lettie said.

"See?" Whitney said. "Just play up the drama. I think that's what I'll do—come up with some dramatic way to kill off my mom. My life would be way more fun without her, anyway."

Laura Beth laughed, a nervous tinge in her voice, and Lettie just stared, wide-eyed. Jackie might have been offended too—only she'd watched a few clips of *Hollywood Secrets* just to check out Tracey Mills. Just from the way the woman acted on that show—obviously the apple hadn't fallen far from the tree.

"Enough college talk. I'm only here for one reason," Whitney said. "College boys. Which is why we're finding a party before we leave."

"We could stop at one of the college bars on the way home," Laura Beth suggested, looking at Jackie.

"Hell yeah," Whitney said with a smile. "Or a frat party. They're always pretty tight."

"You in?" Laura Beth asked Jackie.

She shrugged. Part of her would rather just get away from Whitney as quickly as she could and go home. But it wasn't like much was waiting for her there. She didn't have any new messages from Eric, and Andrew was . . . Andrew. Besides, she hadn't been able to spend much time *having fun* with Laura Beth and

Lettie in the past few months. And if she said no, she was sure Whitney was going to throw that stupid bet in her face.

"I'm in. But we have to make sure no one knows who I am."

Whitney smiled and lifted her water bottle for Laura Beth to top off.

People knowing who you are will be the least of your problems.

FIVE

From the moment Lettie stepped on campus, she just *knew*.

She was meant to go to Princeton. It was as if everything she'd done in her life had all just been a detour. Her brother's gang history and taking care of her younger sisters and sweating during her long work hours. None of it mattered anymore. In a year she would trade washing dishes at the embassy and Laura Beth's hand-me-downs and her parents' strict rules for the fresh smell of recent rainfall on gothic brick buildings in one of the oldest universities in the country.

Will Yao, their tour guide, originally from Taiwan, smiled at Lettie and pointed out Nassau Hall. "It's the oldest building on campus, built in 1777."

"That was the seat of the Congress of the Confederation for a few months in 1783, right?" Lettie asked, even though she'd read about it.

Will nodded with a smile. "From June to November. I'm actually hoping the weather will be nice next year on graduation day. This year we were able to have the ceremonies on the front lawn of Nassau Hall, which everyone here calls Old Nassau."

Lettie could picture it.

"The AWCS meets on the front lawn sometimes too."

"The AWCS?" Lettie asked.

"Oh yeah, the American Whig-Cliosophic Society. It's one of the coolest clubs on campus," Will said. "It's the nation's oldest debating, literary, and political society. We oversee the International Relations Council, Model Congress, the Debate Panel, Mock Trial, and Model UN." His face flushed. "At least *I* think it's one of the coolest clubs on campus."

"No, it sounds great!" Lettie said, and turned to look at Jackie, who nodded.

"We're coming up to McCormick Hall. One of my favorite professors teaches a class right now. We could pop in if you want?"

Lettie clapped her hands and started to say *"YES!"* before she realized it was actually Jackie's call. She looked over just in time to catch Jackie smiling at her.

"We'd love to see a Princeton class."

They both ignored Whitney's groan from behind them.

Much to Whitney's everlasting *and vocal* disappointment, they were getting a private tour. Jackie had wanted her identity kept under wraps and her mother had negotiated the tour with the admissions office before they came. Not that it mattered. The dean of academics was there to meet them when their limo pulled onto campus. She looked like a stereotypical Ivy League academician with her gray hair pulled into a straggly bun and her smudged reading glasses propped on top of her head. The only thing missing was a tweed jacket and a pipe.

For once, though, the special treatment didn't get under Lettie's skin. The dean was all eyes on Jackie at first, but when Jackie introduced Lettie and sang her praises, she was clearly just as interested in her.

"And this is my best friend, Lettie," Jackie had said. "I'm in awe of her. She works almost full time in the Paraguayan embassy, is helping raise her little sisters, and still has time to help me with my homework. She's going to be our valedictorian."

"Nothing's for sure yet," Lettie had said, her cheeks turning crimson.

But Jackie had just laughed and said, "You've been ranked number one since seventh grade. It's sure."

She could have hugged Jackie. She would have, had that been appropriate in front of the dean *and* had Whitney not been there. She was really trying to think the best of Whitney and give her a chance, but Whitney seemed determined to make it hard. So Lettie was putting Whitney and the prospect of being real friends with her on the back burner for today. She had too many other things to worry about on this trip.

Lettie was grateful for her friends, despite their differences. It didn't matter that they could spend their summers at luxury resorts all over the world while she had to stay home and work. It didn't matter that they never thought twice about buying clothes they didn't really need—and wore some of those outfits only once—eating at the best restaurants, or insisting on front-row concert seats. It didn't even really matter that Laura Beth wanted to treat Lettie to a haircut at Aveda in order to make her look more like Laura Beth and less like *her*. Both Laura Beth and Jackie—and of course Taylor—cared about her. Just in their own way.

It was a fluke, really, that Lettie became friends with them.

It was the night Angie Meehan mistook her for a waitress at the seventh-grade dance. Or at least she pretended to. Lettie had glanced down at her plain black dress and then at the nearby drinks table and floundered over what to do.

Then Jackie Whitman, the most popular girl in school, had stepped in and saved her.

Jackie grabbed a glass and poured Angie a Diet Coke, then pretended to stumble, splashing the front of Angie's dress. "Oops, sorry! I am such a klutz!" Lettie found out later that the dress had cost more than five hundred dollars.

At the time, Jackie linked her arm through Lettie's and led her away. "Ignore her. Angie Meehan's awful. I'm Jackie. You're Lettie, right?"

A few minutes later, Jackie introduced her to Laura Beth, Taylor and her twin, Daniel, and Andrew. And suddenly, they were all friends.

Jackie needed a drink, bad.

They were almost done with the Princeton thing and now all she wanted to do was get out of there and forget today. Eric still hadn't freakin' texted her. She was starting to get a complex.

And of course, Whitney seemed bent on embarrassing her. When they finished their tour and said good-bye to Will, the dean came out one more time to talk to them. She mentioned something about the Princeton experience, and Whitney had the nerve to say, "I'm just interested in the guys."

Thankfully, Lettie changed the subject. "Actually, I heard that you can sign up to be an *extra* in a lecture class, and you can audit the whole semester. Is that available for all classes or just lower level ones?"

Only to have Whitney ruin it again. "Hey, isn't this the spot where they filmed that scene in *Gossip Girl*?" She pulled out her phone to take a picture. She forced her cell into Jackie's hand and posed for the shot.

Beyond embarrassed, Jackie quickly clicked the shutter and tossed the phone back to her. Even worse than Whitney's clueless behavior was the fact that Laura Beth kept giggling at everything Whitney did.

The dean gave Whitney a withering look before she turned to Jackie and Lettie and continued to rattle off the standard speech: twenty-nine academic departments, eighteen foreign languages, no teaching assistants, a sixteen-billion-dollar endowment, almost three dozen Nobel prize–winning faculty members and alumni.

"Look at this," Whitney said as she flipped through the thick course guide. "Race and the Pornological! I think I will apply here. How hard could a porno class be?"

Thank God Princeton wasn't Jackie's first-choice school.

Lettie and the dean were still talking.

Jackie flexed and pointed her feet until they finished the conversation, suppressing the urge to go sit down on a nearby bench. It seemed liked they'd walked all five hundred acres of campus.

"Jackie," the dean said, moving toward her. "It was fabulous to meet you. I recommend Café Vivian at Frist for dinner, if you're hungry. Don't hesitate to contact me if you have any questions about your application or the school."

"Of course," Jackie said with a nod, not that she'd likely have any questions. She and her mother talked constantly about everything she had to do in order to get into an Ivy League school— and how important it was. Jackie, unlike Whitney, was completely prepared.

"Oh my Lord," Laura Beth laughed as she and Whitney grabbed mocha frappuccinos at the Taproom Café. "Whitney, you should have come on all our college visits. I haven't had this much fun at any of 'em."

Whitney smiled as she looked out the café window to see Lettie falling all over the dean of academics and the dean falling all over Jackie. It was so ridiculous. It's not like *Jackie* was the president's daughter. . . . Why was the dean drooling all over her, anyway?

But according to her mom, even people in California wanted to read about Jackie Whitman. She was America's freakin' sweetheart. Whatever. If people wanted to spend their time drooling over Jackie's every move and stalking her on blogs, fine. All Whitney had to do was provide the material.

She'd seen on the drive over that Jackie's patience had a limit. She just had to find a way to break her. She'd tried today, because how juicy would that have been? "Jackie Whitman Loses Her Shit in Front of Princeton's Dean." But Jackie had completely ignored everything Whitney did. Even the porno comment.

There was something about her—about all of D.C.—that Whitney just didn't get. There was some way to unravel it all, to snap Jackie's image; she just wasn't seeing it yet.

"Is that our driver?" Laura Beth asked, her eyes on the door. Just like they'd been for the past half hour.

Jackie looked up from her second Long Island Iced Tea to see a guy who looked nothing like their driver. "Stop worrying. You gave him a hundred bucks to go get dinner. We've got plenty of time."

"Did you seriously just give him a hundred dollars?" Lettie squealed.

"I don't want him spying on us and telling Mama," Laura Beth said.

"Yeah, relax, *chica*." Whitney nudged Lettie's shoulder and laughed.

Jackie looked at Lettie and shook her head. She had half a mind to ditch Whitney somewhere and head home. They were supposed to be having fun, unwinding after the tour, partying it up. Instead they were sitting around a table with drinks, hardly talking to each other while Laura Beth watched the door in a crazy bout of paranoia.

Not that this bar was all that great. *Money* magazine ranked Princeton as one of the top fifteen places to live in the United States—not surprising since it was dead center between Manhattan and Philadelphia. But as a college town, it was dull. Standing on Nassau Street, the main hangout, they'd found that this lame bar was pretty much their only option.

They got inside without any problems, thanks to a friend of

Andrew's who was the go-to guy for high-quality, high-priced fake IDs. Taylor had slept with him in exchange for an awesome discount for Lettie. Andrew passed on one for himself. He didn't want to get caught like the Bush twins, who made tabloid headlines for using fake IDs. Just one more example, in Jackie's mind, of Andrew needing to live a little.

The music changed and the Black Eyed Peas came on. "Hell yeah!" Whitney said, jumping out of her seat. She arched her back and stuck her chest out and started swaying her hips. She immediately commanded the attention of every guy in the bar.

All seven of them.

But just when Jackie was about to suggest they leave, four guys who looked like standard white-bread Princeton students walked in.

And they were *hot.*

They saw Whitney instantly, of course, and paused for half a second before moving to the bar—their priority was alcohol over sex, apparently. But the fourth guy, and the cutest, with wavy dark hair and blue eyes that matched his light blue polo, let his eyes sweep the room. When they landed on Jackie, she met his gaze and smiled, before glancing down at her drink in mock shyness. When she glanced back, he was smiling.

At least the night was looking up.

"Oh my Lord," Laura Beth gushed. "Did y'all see that? One of those boys—I bet they go to Princeton—he just smiled at me. He's so cute! Should I go talk to him?"

"No," Jackie said. "Stay here. They'll come to us."

"But what if he thinks I'm not interested? What if—"

Whitney laughed. "Dude, Laura Beth, c'mere. Dance with me. We'll give them something to look at." She grabbed Laura

74

Beth's arm and jerked her out of her seat. Laura Beth stood awkwardly, while Whitney danced around her.

"The blond guy in the black hoodie is so cute," Lettie said with a smile.

Whitney leaned over to grab her Jack and Coke. "So you don't only date Latin guys?"

It took Jackie longer than it should to process that comment. She just couldn't *freakin' believe* the words so she kept replaying them in her mind over again. Either Lettie was going through the same thing, or she was being typical Lettie and trying not to say anything.

"Whitney," Jackie started. "What, do you only date African Americans?"

"Oh my gosh, no! I'm sure Whitney didn't mean it that way," Laura Beth jumped in.

Whitney shrugged, and her lips turned down in a frown. "Whatever. He's hot—I'd do him."

Maybe we should go before Whitney does something stupid.

Laura Beth must have caught the tense expression on her face. "Worried about Andrew? Or Eric?"

"Oooh, who's Eric?" Whitney squealed.

If Laura Beth hadn't slapped Tommy Rockefeller across the face in the first grade after he told Jackie she had hairy arms, Jackie might have killed her. How could she mention Eric in front of Whitney? Had it only taken two fruity umbrella drinks to make her forget that Whitney wasn't one of them?

But she just shrugged and played it off. "Just some guy."

Whitney nodded, though she didn't look entirely convinced. "Screw waiting. I'm gonna talk to them and invite them over." She pulled her cami down a little, all but flashing the whole bar as she started walking toward the guys. Then she paused and looked back. "Aren't you coming, LB?"

Laura Beth nodded and chased after Whitney.

"LB?" Lettie asked as soon as they were out of earshot.

Jackie laughed. They both watched Whitney practically throw herself at the four guys.

"Do you really think she's . . ." Lettie didn't need to finish the thought.

Jackie shrugged. "Maybe that's how she got attention in L.A."

"I don't get that," Lettie said.

And neither did Jackie, but she wasn't about to waste her time trying to analyze Whitney's behavior. She just knew she didn't like it.

"You know, if you want to get out of here, you can always blame it on me," Lettie added.

"No, don't be ridiculous. We can have a drink with them," Jackie said. "Besides, you think the blond guy's hot. Maybe we can hook you up."

Lettie blushed and opened her mouth to say something, but Whitney was back with the four boys in tow, Laura Beth trailing awkwardly behind them. Tall-Dark-and-Blue-Eyed sat down next to Jackie, turning his chair slightly toward her.

"I'm Tom," he said. "And this is Ed, Jason, and Gordon."

Ed and Jason slid into Whitney and Laura Beth's empty chairs, while Gordon grabbed an extra chair and squeezed in next to Lettie.

Up close, Jackie had to admit, Ed was the cutest. He wasn't that tall, but he obviously worked out. And he had an infectious grin. But he was clearly taken with Whitney, who was already on his lap.

"Do you need a drink?" Jason, the blond, asked Lettie.

"I'll have a beer," she said with a smile. "Or 'beast.' I'll have some beast. Isn't that what you Princeton guys call beer?"

Jackie almost dropped her drink. She'd never seen Lettie flirt before, and there she was, her cheeks flushed, a tense smile on her face, as she half leaned toward Jason with a hand tentatively hovering near his upper arm.

She looked so awkward it hurt. Jackie needed to save her and quick.

"Another round sounds perfect to me, what do you think?" she said, turning to Laura Beth, who apparently was having flirting issues of her own.

Laura Beth's complete attention was on Gordon. Standing next to him, she looked like she was trying to channel her mother—hanging all over him, flattering him with an admiring smile, and erupting into ridiculous fake giggles whenever he opened his mouth.

Oh, God. Awkward was bad, but guys could sense desperation a mile away, and Laura Beth was giving it off in waves.

"I'll get your drink," Gordon said, and then he looked at Jackie. "You need another one?"

"Sure, but you don't have to get it." Jackie started to stand up. Then Laura Beth could sit down in her seat.

But Tom grabbed her hand. "Let Gordy get the drinks. He's got an open tab anyway."

Jackie turned to Laura Beth, but Gordon was already halfway to the bar, with Laura Beth right behind him.

"You're the first Princeton boy I've met. Smile!" Whitney laughed right before she took a picture with her cell phone.

Jackie sighed in disgust and then looked over at Tom, who was laughing.

"What?" she asked.

"You aren't from around here, are you?"

"Why do you say that?"

Tom leaned toward her, putting his arm around the back of her chair. His lips moved close to her ear, not quite touching her skin, but close enough that she could feel the heat of his breath caressing her neck.

"Jersey girls. There's something about them," he whispered.

"And you're saying I haven't got that?" Jackie asked, leaning back.

But leaning back was a mistake. This close, she could smell mint and beer on his breath. His blue eyes were only an inch away from hers, and the look he gave her—it was so intense, as if he wanted to know everything about her, down to her very soul. It was the way Eric looked at her.

"I'm saying you're something better."

Tom shifted his gaze to her lips and Jackie knew what was next. He was about to kiss her and she had a split second to decide whether she was going to let him. Part of her wanted to. There was something erotic and sexy about kissing this guy she'd just met in the middle of a college bar. She knew Taylor wouldn't have thought twice about it.

But at the same time, she didn't feel the passion or urgency she felt with Eric. And she at least owed Andrew some sense of loyalty. If she was going to ruin everything she had with him, it should count. She should feel swept up in the romance of it all.

It should be more than just some random guy in a bar with a bad line.

Jackie pulled back. "So you go to Princeton? What year are you?"

"Sophomore," he said, leaning back in his chair.

"Where else did you apply?"

He shrugged, looking a little disappointed that the conversation had turned back to school. "The usuals. Harvard, Yale, Dartmouth, Duke."

Laura Beth drained the last of her beer and set it on the table. Jackie was grilling Tom about why he chose Princeton over Yale. What a waste. He was so hot. With the way his brown hair had a little wave to it, he looked a little like Clark Kent in *Smallville*. And even though Laura Beth had never really seen that show, Clark Kent was cute.

She turned back to Gordon, who wasn't nearly as gorgeous, but was the only one left, since Lettie and Jason were laughing and talking about the decay of American culture or something else equally ridiculous. And Whitney . . . Laura Beth looked over at her. She was still in Ed's lap, and giggling loudly.

"So, what do you want to do?" Laura Beth asked, moving closer to Gordon.

Ugh, what am I sayin'?

"Oh my God!" Whitney screamed, collapsing into laughter as Ed's hand slid underneath the back of her top. "At least I don't come from New Jersey."

"Hey, this isn't anything like New Jersey. This is Princeton." He laughed. "Are your friends from California too?"

"Are you kidding? No one from Cali would get so dressed up to go on a lame college tour. Don't you know who she is?" She lowered her voice to a whisper and pointed at Jackie. "That's Jackie Whitman. Her mom is some big deal at the White House."

Laura Beth saw Whitney gesturing toward Jackie, and could just make out what she was saying. She cringed at the use of Jackie's full name—and the way Ed suddenly looked over at her with more interest. Jackie would be *pissed* if she knew.

"No way," Ed whispered, a look of awe spreading across his face.

Whitney leaned forward and whispered something else into Ed's ear. For a second, Laura Beth thought she might still be talking about Jackie, but Ed's attention shifted from Jackie to Whitney again. He laughed and grabbed the back of her head.

"Oh, you're bad!" he said, before pulling her closer into him.

"You have no idea," Whitney said. Laura Beth looked away.

"I'm going to the bathroom and then we've got to go," Jackie said abruptly, standing up. "I want to get back to Washington before morning," she added over her shoulder as she headed across the room.

Laura Beth looked up at Gordon and hoped he would kiss her, but he stood up. "I'm getting another beer, you want one?"

Ugh. No, she didn't want another beer. She wanted him to sweep her off her feet, tell her he'd never met a girl like her before, that he'd always just been a player, but now that he'd met *her,* Laura Beth Ballou, he knew his life would never be the same.

Or something epically romantic like that.

SIX

Eric's hands slid up Jackie's thighs and over her hips. She arched her back underneath the roughness of his hands, and she glanced up to see a look of possessiveness in his eyes. His face seemed to say he wanted her so badly, he'd die without her. Her breath caught in her throat and a rush of heat went through her.

Two delicate Baccarat crystal champagne glasses stood half empty next to them on the nightstand. Red rose petals were strewn all over the floor and hundreds of tiny scented tea candles shimmered on every surface. Eric had spent hours creating the perfect romantic scene, handpicking even the love songs playing softly in the background.

There couldn't possibly be a more perfect moment for me to lose it.

He kissed his way up her body until his arms supported his weight and he hovered above her. "Are you sure?" he asked in between kisses.

81

"*Yes,*" she whispered.

And then her phone rang.

Only half awake and wishing she could have finished her dream, Jackie fumbled around in a tangle of satin sheets, reaching across the nightstand to silence her iPhone. The ugly red numbers of her clock glared at her.

6:17

Her hand hovered over the phone, which continued to ring as she looked at the clock. It was exactly the same time of day six months ago that she'd gotten the call from Andrew, the one that changed all their lives. She knew from the ringtone that it was her mother calling now—not Andrew. But the similarities— being awoken from a dead sleep and a *good dream,* disoriented and feeling around for the phone in the heavy darkness of her room, wondering why the hell anyone would be calling her right now— they were still hard to ignore.

"Jackie . . ." Andrew sobbed. "It's Taylor . . ."

Even before he'd choked out the words between sobs, I knew what had happened. I knew it, but every inch of me refused to believe it. My heart was racing but I could feel myself freeze up and I felt hot and cold all at the same time. I was gulping in air but it was like my lungs were refusing to take any in. I was crying but there were no tears.

"She's dead."

Once he got the words out the first time, it was like a floodgate had opened and he couldn't stop repeating them—over and over.

She's dead. She's dead. She's dead.

Stop. Stop. Stop!

Andrew fell silent.

It took me a moment to realize why. I'd just screamed that out loud.

Please, God. Not again. Jackie answered her phone. "Mom?! What is it?"

"Jackie." Her mother's tone was just this side of mad. "What have you done? Why didn't you give me a heads-up?"

What the—

"At least if you'd told me first I might have been able to spin it—"

Jackie desperately racked her brain to think of what could possibly have happened to have her mother so upset. Maybe it was just that she was still sleep-logged, but she honestly couldn't think of a single thing. Could her mom have possibly found out about Eric? What was there really to find out? She still hadn't seen him since the press conference.

Her mother raised her voice. "But now it's *everywhere*. How could you be so irresponsible?"

"Mom, calm down. What are you talking about? What's wrong?"

"Oh, nothing!" she sputtered. "After all, what's a photo plastered all over the newspapers and the Internet, not to mention the morning news, showing *my daughter* drunk and making out with some random boy she met at a bar in Princeton?"

"Me? Making out? What are you talking about?"

Jackie didn't understand anything her mother was saying. The only way there would be photos of her making out with one of those Princeton guys would be if someone took a picture of *Whitney* and then Photoshopped in Jackie's face. She and Tom had spent most of the night talking college choices.

But how could someone have doctored a picture if no one there knew who she really was?

Her mother was still ranting. "You should have more common sense or consideration for Deborah or for me. Do you have any idea what this could do . . ."

It had been two days since they'd been in Princeton. Two days since Whitney brought the four boys over to their table and started acting like a slut.

"Jackie! I want an explanation!"

Jackie's stomach lurched.

"I have no idea what's going on. I didn't hook up with anyone. I—"

"Jackie. Just tell me exactly where you were and what you did. I want the no-bullshit bottom line."

"Can you stop interrogating me for a second and listen?" Jackie said, her voice breaking.

She heard her mother take a deep breath, exhaling into the phone. When she spoke next, she'd shifted from full, stressed-out chief-of-staff mode back into a seemingly rational person. "It's you and me, Jackie. Just you and me. And we agreed a long time ago that we would be honest with each other. That's what I need right now. The truth."

Jackie took a deep breath herself. The truth actually wasn't so bad. "We went to a bar, and four Princeton guys came in. We all sat around a table. I talked to this guy named Tom. Whitney made out with one guy and Lettie and Laura Beth flirted with the other two. I didn't see anyone take any pictures. Maybe someone recognized me? Or—"

"Of course someone did. Pictures of you and Andrew are in every supermarket tabloid every week of the year. You can't just go to a bar without thinking like that. It's reckless. Because of who you are and because you're underaged." There was a definite shift again as her "mother" tone came back. "What were you doing in a bar, anyways? How did you even get in?"

"I'm sorry. I'm so, so sorry."

Her mom sighed. "Sorry doesn't always cut it. You're almost an adult, and you're an intelligent young woman. You have to think things through before you jump in."

"You're right," Jackie agreed.

"The president's already called me, demanding an explanation. We can't afford this distraction—especially not now, when all our energy is focused on trying to get this immigration bill through."

Jackie opened her mouth, trying to think of the right thing to say. "I did not hook up with anyone. I swear."

"It doesn't matter, Jackie," her mother said, suddenly sounding tired. "Perception is all that matters."

"We'll fix it. I'll issue a statement, and—"

"*The Washington Post* and the Associated Press have already left messages on my voice mail and your new friend's *mother* wasted no time getting the pictures up on her new political gossip blog that sprung up overnight."

Jackie sat up straighter. "Whitney is not my friend! *You* are the one who made me hang out with her!"

"Don't raise your voice with me. I've been so busy doing damage control, I haven't even had time to find out who actually broke the story."

"But—"

"No. Stop. No excuses. You are not some average teenager. You can't just go around barhopping, waving around a fake ID, and throwing yourself at random guys. You've just embarrassed yourself, your family, and your president. You've just given those so-called 'family values' Republicans ammunition to use against Deborah. Not to mention you can probably kiss Princeton good-bye."

Maybe I didn't want to go there anyway.

But she didn't say that. Her mom was overreacting. This wasn't a big deal, and she *hadn't* done anything wrong. She *never* did anything wrong. But that didn't matter. Because despite how fiercely she wanted to defend herself, she knew that as soon as she started talking, her voice would crack and she'd end up crying.

"What should I do?"

"You can start by coming here and apologizing to President Price. She has a little time this morning before she leaves for Boston. Be at my office by eleven. I'll let the Secret Service know you're coming."

The phone clicked, and Jackie groaned.

And what her mother didn't have to say was that she was grounded. It didn't matter that her eighteenth birthday was in four days.

Slumped in her chair, her hand still on the phone, Carolyn Shaw wanted to just melt into the background.

In moments like these, when she felt all the order and structure she'd worked so hard to establish and maintain was crumbling around her, she felt the sting of loneliness. On the rarest of moments—and this was one of them—she almost regretted divorcing Harry, Jackie's father. Despite the fact that he was completely unreliable, especially when it came to doing *his* share in raising *their* child, in his own way he loved Jackie. And since Princeton was *his* alma mater, he should have been chaperoning them on the college tour.

Oh, who was she kidding? Had Harry been there, he probably would have been buying them the drinks.

She ran a hand through her hair and thought—not for the first time—she should have married Deborah's husband, Bob. She'd dated him for a year before dumping him for cheating on her, and he'd eventually moved on to Deborah. He'd turned into a serial womanizer, but at least he was a good father to Andrew and Scott—and even a supportive husband to Deborah when she needed him.

The phone rang and jolted her back into reality. "Carolyn Shaw," she answered, standing up. "Oh, Brian. Yes. Tell them we have no comment at this time. You can tell them the president is busy running a country, not gossiping about teenage love lives."

Whitney's voice mail picked up *for the third time*. She couldn't believe Whitney wouldn't answer her phone. Not that Jackie really thought she'd be dumb enough to leak a photo to her mom. It would be too obvious. It would be social suicide.

Her phone rang.

God, who was calling now? "What!" she snapped, not caring who was on the other end.

It was Laura Beth. "Oh my Lord, Jackie, you better turn on the TV."

Jackie's anger deflated. It was strangely comforting to think Laura Beth had called her as soon as she'd seen. "I know. My mom just called. Apparently this is worse than some country declaring war."

"I didn't even see you kiss him!"

"Because I didn't, Laura Beth!"

Silence on the other end.

"Did you see anyone taking our picture?" Jackie asked. She picked up the remote and punched in the local NBC channel just in time to catch the seven o'clock headlines on *The Today Show.* "Oh my God."

She and Tom were the lead story. The camera zoomed in on a photo of the two of them, their heads together. It was that moment when Tom had been just about to lean in and kiss her. That moment *before* she pulled away. Who had freaking taken that picture?

"Crap, Laura Beth, are you watching this?"

"At least y'all aren't actually kissing in the picture," Laura Beth said.

"You can see my drink in my hand, and it's obviously alcohol. And have you seen the freaking headline? 'Ankie's Hanky Panky'? This is a nightmare."

"Yeah . . . they *are* makin' you look pretty bad."

Jackie turned off the TV and chucked the remote. "God! Isn't there any real news?"

"At least you look cute in that DVF dress."

"Cute? I look like I'm about to suck face with Tom! Who cares about the dress!" Jackie paused to take a deep breath and thought of her therapist and all the breathing exercises and relaxation techniques he'd taught her. "What I really need to figure out is who took that picture. You don't think it was Whitney, do you?"

"No. She was way too into Ed. They were both too busy feeling each other up to be holding a camera."

So had one of the other guys recognized her?

"What the hell am I going to say to Andrew? What am I going to say to Aunt Deborah?" Jackie's voice cracked.

"What are you goin' to wear? You need to make the right impression. Sugar sweet and repentant."

"Laura Beth! Forget the clothes. What am I going to say?"

"Well, we better get our story straight. Do you think there are any other photos still out there?"

"I hope not, but how would I know?" She stopped to think. "Our story." She repeated what she'd told her mother. "I'll say we think it must have been one of the guys who recognized me."

"Yeah, make it sound like it was no big deal. You can blame some of it on Whitney for bringing the guys over. But mostly blame the media for distorting the facts. And also sound really, really sorry at the same time."

"Good idea. Call Lettie and fill her in, and I'll keep calling Whitney and tell her to go along with whatever we say. We all have to have the same story." Jackie sighed. She felt exhausted already, and the drama had barely even started.

Something in her chest squeezed and she felt short of breath. *God, what am I going to tell Andrew?*

Whitney sat on a stool in front of the marble-topped island, slouched protectively over her coffee—unsweetened, black, and as strong as motor oil—just the way she liked it. Nothing woke her up or relaxed her the way coffee did. So what if she loved It's a Grind coffee the best and had to have it shipped? Some comforts were worth it, no matter the cost or inconvenience. Good coffee in the morning was one of them.

Only this morning, it wasn't quite working. Her phone was buzzing consistently at five-minute intervals, and even though she wasn't looking at the screen, she knew it read *Jackie*. All the gourmet coffee in the world couldn't take away her desire to just crawl back in bed and sleep the day away.

Scratch that. Sleep this D.C. nightmare away.

Maybe if she slept long enough, she'd wake up back in Cali.

Her dad came into the kitchen, the phone to his ear, huffing as he dropped his copy of *The New York Times* next to her. "It's absurd," he said into the phone. "All this talk about whether illegals should be allowed to stay. They're already here. Who cares? The problem isn't a bunch of people who don't vote, it's that no one in this country can focus on anything other than their political affiliation long enough to actually come up with a solution."

He paused to listen into the phone.

"This isn't something to laugh over *or* make Libertarian jokes about. This country is spiraling out of control," he added, and Whitney rolled her eyes. Her father was always so serious about everything. Like any one drama would lead to the end of the world.

He paused again. "Yes, well, of course we're lost without you," he added, and Whitney realized he was talking to her mother. She sat up straight and reached toward the phone so he'd give it to her when he was done.

He nodded and held up a finger. "Right, and we'll see you

next weekend at least . . . oh, well, we'll figure it out. Okay, talk soon."

And then he hung up and put the phone down. "She had to run to a meeting." This early, on West Coast time? Whitney doubted it.

Her father gestured to the newspaper. "Your mother would be back in the cotton fields or deported to Africa if these PAP-Pies had their way."

"What are pappies?" Whitney asked. They sounded gross.

Her father gave her a sidelong glance. "The new political party?"

"Right," Whitney said even though she had no idea what he was talking about.

Once upon a time, she would have asked more about it. But she'd stopped making that mistake. Every minuscule question—even yes or no ones—turned into a three-hour lecture. Once she asked him a question about the Civil War and her whole night was shot. She was stuck on the couch listening to him re-enact the whole battle and list the histories of *every* soldier.

Her father flipped the newspaper open and didn't say anything more. They hadn't had an easy conversation in years. Not since Mara. She quickly pushed those sad memories back into the dark recesses of her mind.

Taking another sip of coffee, she smiled at her dad as he said good-bye and slipped out of the kitchen. She grabbed the phone and dialed her mother.

No way could she talk to her mom about gossip in front of her dad. He hadn't liked it in L.A. when she'd fed her mother tidbits about her Hollywood friends and their movie-star parents. And she'd heard her parents arguing about it again, just before she and her dad moved here. Apparently in Washington, politics and political gossip were serious business. He was worried he'd be frozen out and not taken seriously in his new job. As if that would happen. He was always too damn *serious* about everything.

Her mom answered on the second ring. "Guess how many hits my new blog had this morning?" she gushed.

Whitney opened her mouth to guess.

"Two hundred thousand!" her mother said, a hint of a squeal to her voice.

Whitney shut her mouth and just let her mother talk, wishing she were in L.A. too.

"And that was only an hour after the story broke. I'm betting I'll have at least a million hits by the end of the week. All thanks to you." Whitney could hear the excitement in her mom's voice. "My new boss at the *Washington Tattler* will be thrilled—a D.C. scoop before I've even started the job!"

Whitney couldn't help but smile. No one could rival her mother when she was like this—happy. No one was more fun or more exciting. The last time she'd been this excited was when Whitney'd gotten her the scoop on the Selena Gomez/Miley Cyrus feud and her mother had spent the day with her. They'd gone to Raya to get massages and facials and then went shopping on Rodeo Drive, where her mother pretended they were sisters and flirted with a group of men in their thirties. Best day ever.

"When you come out here next weekend, we'll have to go shopping to celebrate. I can show you some of the cool George-town stores," she suggested. "Jackie and Laura Beth said I should go to Urban Chic." Not that she cared much for their taste in clothes. Laura Beth always looked a little too formal, too dressed up, and Jackie was so put together it was boring. But still, she couldn't deny they knew shopping.

"Jackie!" Her mother really did squeal this time. "The public acts like she and Andrew are royalty. Just imagine the reaction when you dig up some *real* dirt for me!"

Whitney frowned. It was going to be a lot harder to earn her allowance here in D.C. than it had been in Cali. There, no one was trying to hide it. Half the time some of her friends even *paid her* to tip off her mom because they wanted the publicity. Then she made bank and had money rolling in from both directions. But these uptight political types were different. And Jackie and the *Crapital* Girls were freaking prudes. She was going to have to practically throw Jackie in front of the camera in a compromising position if she wanted to make her look like anything other than Little Miss Perfect.

No. It wasn't even that. She'd *understood* California. Shit, she was going to have to figure out D.C., wasn't she? Like really figure it out.

The picture the other night was luck. It would have been better had she managed to get one of Jackie actually cheating on Andrew. But she could only do so much. Noticing how Jackie and Tom's eyes met when he came in the door, then whispering in his ear that Jackie was into him when she went up to the bar was one thing. That was easy and deniable. Blatantly doing something to jeopardize Jackie's reputation—doing something Jackie could trace back to *her*—that was different. She had to be careful.

Whitney took another sip of coffee. She'd figure this out. She always did. And in the meantime?

"So next weekend?" Whitney prompted. "Or we could go to Ginger in Bethesda."

"Of course, wherever you want to go," her mother mumbled. Then, like she was just tuning in again, "Oh, but I won't be there next weekend. I have too many loose ends to tie up here."

"Oh, well . . . maybe—"

"What are you doing today? Anything with Jackie? You need to see her and her friends and be comforting."

Whitney did have a ton of missed calls—all Jackie. And a few texts from LB. *Princeton was fun!* and *Come over today.* But no way did she want to be interrogated by Jackie.

"And make sure you get in good with their parents," her mother added. "They have to think you're really their daughters' new best friend."

"But—"

"We can go shopping any time the weekend after next when I fly out."

Yeah, but we won't.

Whitney hated it when her mother did this, always promising face time then finding some excuse not to do it.

"Remember your cover story. You were on the phone with me last night and I got an important call. You think it might have been a source. You think someone in the bar recognized Jackie from the tabloids and took the picture. The source must have spent a while trying to figure out who to sell it to and somehow he got my name. Tell them that's how it happens in Hollywood all the time."

Whitney rolled her eyes as her mom continued to recite the same cover-up routine they'd used only a hundred and one times.

It's amazing you don't put a fucking wiretap on me.

"Maybe I could fly to L.A. this weekend," Whitney said.

"Oh, I can't believe I forgot. The *Post* says the Price family is attending some Kennedy Center thing this weekend. Jackie and Andrew will have to be there, showing a united front. Try to wrangle an invite. I'd love to be a fly on the wall."

Whitney slumped over the kitchen counter, wishing she hadn't drunk so much damn coffee. Then she could go back to sleep. "Okay."

"And don't forget the story. We'll see each other soon, okay?" She hung up without waiting for an answer.

This was shaping up to be the worst year of her life.

SEVEN

Jackie had a problem. She couldn't find a single thing in her closet to wear to the White House. Sure, she'd bitched out Laura Beth for bringing up clothes when they were on the phone, but she *did* need to think about it. Her mother would want her to dress for Aunt Deborah and the media—high neckline, knee-length at least, drab colors, something that said apologetic and repentant. In order words, something that didn't say *whore*.

But what you wore to apologize to the president and what you wore to apologize to your *boyfriend* were entirely different outfits.

Not like I can wear that slinky vintage Azzedine Alaïa, can I?

No. She couldn't. Tight, form-fitting, or anything that showed too much skin was out.

Jackie leaned over to check her iPhone. She felt a little

light-headed as she pressed the center button to see if there were any calls.

There weren't.

Disappointment and relief swirled in her chest, settling in her stomach. She felt like she might puke.

Why the hell hasn't Andrew called?

What had she expected? A furious phone call? Or a demanding text message? Something. It didn't really matter what. She almost wanted him to be downstairs right now, banging on her door, threatening to kick it down, demanding an explanation.

But instead, nothing.

Maybe he was sulking? Maybe he hadn't heard?

Yeah, right. Like Aunt Deborah wouldn't have told him. I bet he was the first person she called.

Scratch that. Second person. She'd certainly called Jackie's mother first.

Maybe he just didn't care?

Unable to stand it anymore, she speed-dialed Andrew's cell.

Only to have it go straight to voice mail.

So his phone was off. Did that mean his battery had died? Or that he'd turned it off?

She chewed on her bottom lip.

The last two days he'd been on the road again with her mother and Aunt Deborah on one of those quick red-eye trips to the West Coast that pretended to be official White House business but was really an early campaign swing billed to taxpayers.

She nodded. He always forgot his charger on those trips. He must still be sleeping.

Jackie turned back to her closet, packed with dozens of dresses (though it was nothing compared to Laura Beth's "dressing room"), squared her shoulders, lifted her chin, and thought of what Taylor would say to her right now.

"You're Jackie Fucking Whitman, Washington, D.C.'s It Girl. You're not going to let a little rumor get to you, are you?"

No. She wasn't going to let some trumped-up piece of gossip that wasn't even true make her feel bad. She was the one who dictated the fashion trends for Excelsior girls. And everyone else who mattered. At their first ever White House State Dinner last year, Laura Beth had chosen an attention-grabbing neon-green Marc Jacobs ballgown with enough ruffles to cover three brides. But it was Jackie who stole the scene in a simple midnight-blue David Meister draped gown that gently hugged her curves.

She slipped on a black mesh Stella McCartney thong and bra. *That's for Andrew.* Then she picked out the most conservative shift she could find, a navy-blue knit from Tory Burch, and matching London Sole ballet flats. She tied her hair into a high ponytail and dabbed some cream on a zit on her chin.

No makeup, no jewelry. Virginal and repentant.

If only it weren't so true.

"Oh, come on. What's the big deal? We love each other," I breathed, sucking on his bottom lip.

He managed to speak, mid-groan. "We should wait."

I pressed closer to him, feeling just how much he didn't want to wait, and then I kissed him again, deeper this time, tasting the beer we'd swiped from his dad's "secret" stash. "For what? Till when?"

"Till we're ready."

"I am ready," I whispered, raking my fingers down his back, just enough to promise more to come. "It's not like anyone would catch us. No one ever comes in here." An advantage of living in the White House was privacy. It was the perfect opportunity for sex. Even though the promise ring was a bigger road-block than the Secret Service.

But just like I always did, I pushed too far, and suddenly, he was moving away from me and crawling out of bed and pulling his jeans back on.

"Let's go down to the tennis courts. I haven't kicked your ass lately."

"You haven't kicked my ass in tennis since we were ten," I said, even though I just wanted to scream "Why won't you have SEX with me?" instead.

In the cab on the way to the White House, Jackie kept thinking about their last *almost* moment in Andrew's bedroom.

What nineteen-year-old guy still wanted to be a virgin?

There *had* to be more to it than just the ring on his finger.

The way he looks at me and touches me. He wants me.

She knew that he did. But ever since Taylor died, every time they made out, he'd pull back, looking worried and guilty, and suggest something lame like tennis.

And it wasn't like people weren't supposed to have sex in the White House.

The Kennedys had even used his room while the presidential suite was being renovated. And everyone knew what a sex maniac JFK had been. Too bad Andrew didn't have that sex drive. She just wanted to push him against the wall or throw him down on his bed and have her way with him. Was that really so much for a girl to want—something *romantic* and *passionate* with her *boyfriend*?

Jackie quit daydreaming about sex—*God, if only the press could read my mind, then they'd really think I was a slut! Either that or they'd feel sorry for me and blame Andrew.* She tried to think about what she was going to say to Aunt Deborah. The truth, obviously, that she and Tom had just been talking. She wanted to blame the whole thing on Whitney, but that would just look like a cop-out.

She glanced out the window as the taxi drove through her Foggy Bottom neighborhood. All of Washington had been built on a swamp, but Foggy Bottom was so low-lying, fog often got trapped there, which resulted in the embarrassing name. Not that there was any fog today. Just sun and humidity.

The car turned down 21st and drove past George Washington University's Marvin Center, where a group of people milled outside, for some kind of conference, most likely, since school wasn't in session. Some of Jackie's classmates wanted to stay local and go to GW, but Jackie didn't get it. Not that GW wasn't a good school. It was *fine*.

But Jackie had a different philosophy. Everyone needed to live outside the beltway some time to see how the real world lived. Besides, why would any sane person *want* to live anywhere near their parents during college?

With almost ten minutes to spare, the cab pulled up to the White House official visitors' entrance. A group of protesters wearing I'M A PROUD PAPPIE t-shirts and waving IMPEACH PRICE signs milled around outside the black wrought-iron fence.

She knew one of the agents manning the guard box, though he still had to check her ID—she'd brought the legal one this time—and send her through the Magnetometer.

"Hey, Jackie. You're on the list," he said cheerfully, handing her a visitor's pass.

"Thanks, Rob."

The West Wing entrance was right by the White House press office and TV reporters were milling around, getting ready to do stand-ups for the news cut-ins. She ducked her head and stared at the ground as she walked past them.

Damn, I should have worn a hat and sunglasses—or maybe a freaking parka.

"Hey! It's Jackie! Jackie Whitman!" one of the reporters yelled.

Suddenly there was a crush of reporters and camera crews closing in on her, microphones thrust in her face.

"Hey, Jackie, are you in the doghouse?"

"Are you going to see the president?"

"What are you going to tell her?"

"Jackie, look over here!"

"Have you and Andrew broken up?"

"What's Andrew think of you fooling around?"

They were pressing in, smothering her. She couldn't even move a step forward. Her throat started to tighten in a now-familiar way. *Oh, God, not here.* But the more worried she got about having an anxiety attack in front of the press, the more imminent it seemed. She tried not to look up, and when she finally had to, several flashes went off and immediately blinded her.

It wasn't like she hadn't been surrounded by reporters before, but it had always been when she was with Andrew or his parents or her mother in a tightly controlled setting and the press was held back by the Secret Service.

Or there were the few times when Taylor had been there, and she'd taken charge by announcing something ridiculous. Like the time when they were sophomores, when she'd spent the night at Taylor's and they'd snuck out to meet up with Andrew and Quentin Loftin, one of his friends from St. Thomas Episcopal. That was before the White House realized that reporters were fascinated with Carolyn Shaw's teenage daughter and Deborah Price's teenage son.

And the press hadn't given them that ridiculous nickname yet.

The reporters had caught Jackie and Taylor—high from a couple of beers and smoking weed—just as they were sneaking out of Quentin's house. It was the first time the press had caught Jackie doing something *wrong*. She almost panicked and dialed her mother, but Taylor thankfully kept a level head.

"I have a statement!" Taylor yelled above their voices.

Immediately they fell silent, all of their eyes directly on her, as she smoothed her white-blond hair and pursed her red lips for the cameras. She pushed them gently, and they stepped back, eagerly waiting for whatever she would say.

"I just think it's important that you know . . ." she began.

Her fingers curled around mine and she squeezed. Three times. A signal.

"I seem to have misplaced my thong."

And before the last word was out of her mouth, we were running, Taylor half-pulling, half-dragging me with her, as we left the dumbfounded and shell-shocked press behind.

"Is this the first time you cheated on Andrew?" the reporters were shouting at her now.

"Who was he?"

"What are you going to tell the president?"

This time the Secret Service was nowhere to be found, and Taylor was long gone. Which was, of course, *worse*. Not only was Jackie trapped in a mob of reporters, but never again would Taylor distract them by pretending she was about to flash them or announcing she wanted to sleep with a senator in his forties or that she only believed in wearing *boots you leave on*.

All the bodies around her and the sun beating down—the heat suddenly felt stifling, the humidity too thick. Jackie tried to take a deep breath and compose herself, but she couldn't. Her vision started to blur and she swayed on her feet.

"Hey, guys, back off."

The voice behind her was familiar. The crowd of reporters seemed to part. Air rushed in and she could breathe again. She whirled around, looking for Andrew, ready to hurl herself into his arms. Who cared what the reporters did then?

Only she couldn't throw herself into Andrew's arms.

Because it wasn't Andrew coming to her rescue.

It was Eric, who gave her a quick, dimpled smile and motioned for her to get behind him. She did as she was told as he focused the mob's attention onto himself.

"Haven't you guys got anything more important to report on?" he teased the pack of eager scribes. "There's been a development on the immigration bill, if you're interested."

Jackie was instantly forgotten as they surrounded him. She moved to the doorway, pausing only to glance at Eric for a few precious moments.

"As you know, Senator Griffin is chairman of the Senate Judiciary Committee, which has chief oversight of immigration issues. In the spirit of bipartisanship, the senator reached out to President Price this week, but she has chosen to ignore his overtures. He sent me here today to make it clear to the White House that any attempt to pass this foolhardy and anti-American immigration legislation will be met with resounding defeat."

"Hey, Eric, what about the rumors Senator Griffin's going to defect to the PAPPies . . ." one reporter yelled.

That was enough.

She signaled the Marine guard to open the door and disappeared inside. Jackie couldn't believe her luck. Eric seemed so in charge. He knew exactly how to handle those creeps.

She pulled out her phone and texted him.

You totally saved me. I need to thank you in person.

"So you're the one bringing the daisies."

Lettie jumped in surprise. Her heart seemed to leap into her throat, her face grew hot, and her mouth went dry as Daniel Cane walked toward her. Standing in front of Taylor's gravestone with the small bunch of daisies in her hand, she felt like she'd been caught doing something wrong.

She looked down at the flowers, embarrassed and uneasy about what she should say. The truth was, it was Jackie who'd befriended her and Laura Beth who enjoyed dressing her up and giving her makeovers, but she and Taylor had a different kind of friendship—a stronger kind. They didn't have secrets from each other. Lettie had told Taylor *everything*.

"I always wondered who was leaving these," Daniel said with a shrug as he came to stand beside her. "I've seen them here a lot."

Lettie nodded, still unsure of what to say. She glanced over at Daniel to see what kind of flowers he'd brought, but he was empty-handed.

He smiled, as if he knew what she was thinking. "I just brought myself."

Daniel was Taylor's twin, but apart from their pale blond hair and blue eyes, they looked nothing alike. He was taller than Lettie, which wasn't saying that much since she was the shortest of all her friends, and he looked strong. Not that she was surprised—Daniel went to a boarding school in L.A., where he was a champion skateboarder. He didn't dress like one, though. At least not like the kids Lettie saw on TV, all grunged out with messy hair. Daniel looked put together in his jeans and black tee.

"Tay would only care that I was here," Daniel added. "She hated being alone, you know."

Lettie nodded. Taylor had confessed that in the summer before their sophomore year when she was begging Lettie to come to Palm Beach with her to visit Taylor's grandparents. Jackie was visiting her dad at his summer home in the Hamptons. The Prices were out in Martha's Vineyard, and Laura Beth was in London with her mother. Daniel was already back at school, and their older brother Sam had just started his first week of college on the West Coast.

"I just hate being alone. It's the whole twin thing. I wasn't even alone in the womb," Taylor pleaded. *"Please, please come with me. I promise you'll have the time of your life."*

And she did. Whenever people talked about the *best time of their lives,* Lettie thought of that week in Palm Beach. They'd done the usual stuff—laid out on the beach, gone shopping downtown, flirted with guys—but they'd also done some charity work with Taylor's grandmother, gone into the pockets of the county where people didn't speak English and didn't have health care. And they'd stayed up every night until the sun was coming up, talking about politics, boys, philosophy, and just life.

"This is too sad," Daniel said. "Let's talk about something else. Are you still planning on going back to Paraguay after college?"

Embarrassed, Lettie ran a hand through her hair and nodded. "I want to go to Princeton and then Harvard Law, and then go back home."

"I think it's cool that you want to change things there."

"It's not just that I want to," Lettie said. "I feel like I *have* to. I mean, Paraguay is my country. No matter how long I live over here, it will always be my home. It would be irresponsible of me if I didn't try to help others who weren't fortunate enough to come here and learn."

Daniel smiled and Lettie, flustered, dropped her gaze back to the daisies. "*Our* country could use more people like you," he said quietly.

"What about you?" Lettie asked, her voice barely above a whisper. "What do you want to do after college?"

Daniel let out a long sigh. "I'm not exactly sure. I'm thinking CIA or special ops or something. Maybe the FBI . . . as a last resort. Not that my dad will ever go for it—he really wants me to join his software company. Groom me to take over 'the empire,' as he calls it."

He looked so annoyed, Lettie didn't know what to say. Taylor never had anything nice to say about her parents either. Everyone knew how scary her mother was and her dad didn't have a much better reputation. He had a lot of old family money and a habit of strengthening his investments through bribery.

Daniel turned to look at her, and something in his face caught her off guard. She sucked in a breath and held it. "I can't stop going over the car accident, Lettie." Suddenly, instead of seeing a cute athletic guy with a devastating smile, she saw a guy who'd lost his sister—his twin—and subsequently his whole world. "And the more I think about it, the less it makes sense."

It didn't make sense to Lettie either—how could Taylor just be *gone*? But then she caught Daniel's gaze—direct and intense—and realized that wasn't what he meant. He dropped his voice to a whisper and leaned in closer. "Taylor's death wasn't an accident like they're saying. There are things that don't add up."

EIGHT

Jackie paused right before she reached her mother's office and redid her ponytail. She was going for clean and put together, not I-just-got-mobbed-by-the-press and certainly not I-just-rolled-out-of-bed. And there was no *way* she was going to tell her mom about her latest run-in with the White House vultures. Despite her mom's "Tell me everything first, then I can be prepared" attitude, Jackie knew better.

Had she actually noticed someone taking her picture—or had she really hooked up with Tom in a public bar (really, how stupid did they think she was?)—she would have told her mother. And Carolyn Shaw, *the* woman behind the president of the United States, would have been just as pissed off as she was this morning. In fact, she probably would have been even more angry, because although she knew how to spin a story for the press, there was only one person in D.C. who could reliably keep shit like that out of the papers. And there was no way—*no way*—her mom would've gone to her with this. Once you went there, you *owed* her. Forever.

Taylor had always called her mom *The Fixer*—someone who cleaned up other people's messes before they became scandals.

Everyone else in D.C. avoided calling Jennifer Cane *anything*. At least out loud. People whispered her name behind closed— and locked—doors when they were desperate, and they treated her with a strange combination of awe and fear in person. In fact, Jackie's mom and Aunt Deborah always made sure they fell all over Jennifer and were *thrilled* Jackie and Taylor were such close friends. But Jackie knew it was more of a *keep your friends close, enemies closer* kind of thing.

Jackie didn't know how Jennifer started in her chosen "career." (Seriously, how did someone just get a job fixing political scandals?) But if Jennifer Cane actually fixed even half the scandals people claimed she did, it was impressive. Though she'd never told Laura Beth, Jackie had once overheard her mom and Aunt Deborah discussing how Libby Ballou had turned to Jennifer Cane when her husband, Preston, died while having sex with an eighteen-year-old. Jennifer named her price—six figures—to hush up the scandal. Jackie figured she'd used some of the money to bribe, coerce, blackmail, or who knew what else, to make it go away.

So it was understandable that from Carolyn Shaw's point of view, the most dangerous person in the city wasn't some whack job with a gun. It was Jennifer Cane. Because she knew everyone's dirty little secrets, and wasn't above using them—*even the president's*—if the price was right.

———

Taking a deep breath, Jackie opened the door of her mother's office and stepped in with her head down, hoping to look as contrite as possible.

"Sit down, Jackie." Her mother gave her a wry smile and gestured to an overstuffed chair facing her desk and the windows looking over the South Lawn. "Let's go over it."

Jackie suppressed a sigh as she sat down. "I already told you everything, Mom."

"Well, tell me again," her mother said.

Great, treat me like I'm five years old and I just spilled my juice all over the vice president at the Christmas party again.

But before she could tell the whole story again, her mother said, "I'm sorry—this was a rough way to wake up, wasn't it?" Jackie gripped the edges of the chair. "I wish I could just be your mom and tell you everything will be okay. But I have to be the chief of staff too." She gave Jackie a half smile. "Everything will be okay. But only if there are no surprises later. Tell me everything."

Jackie exhaled loudly and repeated the story she and Laura Beth had confirmed. It wasn't hard. It was the truth. But it didn't matter. The entire time she was talking, her mother shook her head and frowned, like she was just so damn disappointed. It was ridiculous, but Jackie actually felt *guilty*.

And that wasn't fair. She hadn't done anything wrong. "You know this whole thing never would have happened if you hadn't made us invite Whitney. She was the one who brought the guys over to our table and she probably mentioned who I was."

Her mother shook her head. "You need to learn how to

control people like Whitney. And the way to control her is to make her part of your group, whether you like it or not. You know how politics works."

Like I didn't know she was going to say that.

Jackie almost opened her mouth and blurted out how over-blown this whole drama was—they were Just. Talking. But if she did that, she'd lose it and end up crying. Tears at a time like this would just piss off her mom more. After all, tears were a woman's biggest enemy. Even the most organized, put together, intelligent woman would be dismissed as "hysterical" and "hormonal" in a man's world—all it took was just one tear.

So Jackie just waited. And swallowed the words—and the potential emotional breakdown.

"Have you talked to Andrew yet? We're going to need to present a united front and quickly dispel any break-up talk."

"Mom, it's under control!"

What if I want to break up with him? Then what will you do?

Her mom nodded. "As far as the public goes, we'll take the same approach as the Bushes did when the twins got caught: 'No comment.' Any statement to the press will keep the story alive.

"As for Tracey Mills and her Web site, once I let her know her daughter's involved in this too, she'll back off and take the picture down. That'll probably keep it out of the *Washington Tattler* too. Thank God it doesn't come out until Monday—that gives us three days to kill the story.

"Now, you need to be clear on what you're going to say to Deborah. You'll start off with an apology, then give a truncated version of the truth. Don't tell her anything you don't have to."

"Okay."

"If she brings up Andrew," her mother said, studying the

small GPS monitor showing the president and vice president's exact locations at any given moment—they couldn't even pee without her knowing it. "Tell her, again, that it's not what it looks like. Just stay on message. She's in her office. I'll buzz ahead to let her know you're on your way."

And dis-missed.

Jackie stood up to leave, feeling like she was eight years old.

"Oh, and one more thing," her mother said as Jackie reached the door. "You need to call your father and explain all this to him. He'll be wondering what's going on. As soon as you wrap up your apologies to Deborah and Andrew."

Jackie nodded. She could just leave him a voice mail. He'd be too busy with work to take her call.

"And Jackie!" Her mother picked up the phone to let President Price's secretary know Jackie was on the way, then looked back up, meeting Jackie's eyes. "It's still you and me. We'll get through this fine."

Jackie managed a small smile before closing the door and turning right, past the open doors of two of the president's other top advisors and past several Secret Service agents whispering into their sleeves. They nodded at her to keep walking. She could feel their eyes boring into her back.

So awkward.

The Secret Service knew just about everything that went on in the White House. So of course they were aware of the Princeton mess. Sure, they had more important shit to worry about, but hey, they were guys—they had to be wondering if it was true, if she'd cheated on Andrew with some random guy in a bar.

"It's pretty amazing, right?"

"More like freaking awe-inspiring," I whispered as I stood in the center of the room and swallowed the fact that I, Jackie Whitman, was in the Oval Office. Alone. For the first time.

Well, I was with Andrew, but what did that matter?

I took a slow turn, trying to memorize every detail—the twelve-foot windows with their heavy gold drapes; the high-backed leather chair made specially for JFK's injured back; and the presidential seal wherever you looked, encircled by fifty stars on the presidential flag, woven into the rug, on the stationery, even on the ceiling frieze. There were no words to describe this room where the most powerful leaders in the world had started wars and destroyed governments, spread democracy and ended slavery. A-Mazing wasn't even enough.

My eyes fell back on the president's chair, behind the desk. "Oh my God! Can I sit in the chair?"

Andrew laughed. "Whatever you want."

I rushed behind the desk and threw myself into the chair, squirming around to get comfortable. My heart was fluttering, and I was so light-headed I thought I was going to faint. I looked up at Andrew, standing in the middle of the room, just watching me, and I beamed at him. I hadn't really noticed before how his eyes lit up when he smiled.

Andrew walked over to the desk and spun my chair around to face him. He leaned in close and locked on to me with his warm green eyes. My pulse raced. What was I doing? This was Andrew . . . my best friend. Not just some hot guy.

We stayed like this for what seemed like twenty minutes but was probably only twenty seconds. And just when I thought he was going to do something that would change everything, he grinned and pulled me to my feet. "When I'm president, you can help me decorate this room," he teased.

My pulse was still racing, but I quickly shot back, "And when I'm presi-

dent, you chauvinist, you can serve me coffee in here." Not that I had any po-litical aspirations, really.

"We'll take turns, President Whitman," Andrew laughed.

We were standing so close, I felt his body vibrate as he chuckled. But all I saw were his lips. They looked soft and warm. I wanted to kiss Andrew Price.

That's the first time I realized I loved him.

She had loved him. So much.

But things were different now. They'd lost something, and she just wasn't sure they could get it back.

Jackie's iPhone buzzed and she glanced at the text from Lettie. *Do you think Tay's death could have been something other than an accident?* What was she talking about? Jackie wanted to text her back right then, but she was already outside the president's office. Lettie would have to wait. She pushed the bizarre question from her mind and stood hesitantly until Agnes Ford noticed her. "Oh, Jackie!" she said. At least someone was happy to see her here. "The president is expecting you. Go right in."

Performance time.

The president was at her desk, signing a stack of papers.

"Hi, Aunt Deborah," Jackie said brightly, plastering on a cheerful smile as she entered the room, and moved in quickly, ready to give her a quick hug, just as she usually did.

"Jackie," she said coolly, gesturing to a pair of ugly striped chairs usually reserved for visiting heads of state. "I need a moment to finish this up. Have a seat."

Jackie nodded and kept her smile in place despite the fact that she felt like she might dissolve into tears any second. What was it with the suddenly wanting to cry all the time?

Calm down. Even breathing. Focus on something else.

She studied the room while she waited. The Oval Office décor usually changed with every administration, depending on the First Couple's tastes. Aunt Deborah, boasting that she was saving taxpayer money, hadn't altered anything, though she did insist on fresh flowers. Jackie's mom had told her that in truth, Aunt Deborah had kept the Oval Office the same as a reminder that she had a job to do and only a limited time to do it.

Aunt Deborah *had* added framed photos of famous female politicians to the walls. Also a reminder—of the women who had come before her who had also broken through the glass ceiling. Aunt Deborah and Benazir Bhutto—who'd later become Pakistan's first female prime minister—as Harvard undergraduates. Aunt Deborah with Hillary Clinton, campaigning together. Aunt Deborah and New Zealand's former Prime Minister Helen Clark at her election party. Even Aunt Deborah and former conservative British Prime Minister Margaret Thatcher during her last trip to London.

Still waiting, Jackie squirmed lightly. The chair, stuffed with the original horse hair, prickled her ass and she couldn't help but feel this was an intentional punishment.

"All right," the president said, and put down her pen, eyeing Jackie skeptically. "Let's have your side of things. From the beginning, please."

Jackie swallowed. "I'm sorry, Aunt Deborah. I'm so sorry for embarrassing you." She quickly repeated her story, tears of anger and humiliation spilling down her cheeks despite how hard she tried to keep them inside.

And it wasn't an act. She hated disappointing her mother—

who worked so hard, all the time, always for other people. She also hated that she'd created problems for Aunt Deborah, who, aside from being the most powerful leader in the world, was also an amazing woman with a strength Jackie admired. A woman Jackie loved. But even more than that, she hated that she embarrassed herself *and* Andrew for no reason. *Nothing. Happened.*

Aunt Deborah frowned as she walked over to Jackie.

"I want you to understand my position, Jackie."

"I do." Jackie nodded. "I really do."

Aunt Deborah opened her mouth to say something else, but the door opened, interrupting her. Agnes stepped in. "Madam President, the ambassador and her team are waiting for you by Marine One."

"Tell them I'm on my way." She stood up, indicating to Agnes to leave the door open. "I have to go. Come, walk with me to the helicopter."

Aides carrying briefcases and talking into cell phones suddenly flanked them, as Jackie speed-walked down the carpeted hallway to keep up with Aunt Deborah.

"You know, Jackie, when you live in the public eye, you have to be *on* all the time. You can't ever let your guard down."

Jackie nodded, her throat tight and her face flushed.

"It's the publicity drummed up by my political enemies that's the problem, Jackie. They seize on every misstep that I and the people around me make. Sometimes that means I have to be tough on the people I love."

She paused for a second when they reached the doorway to the South Lawn, hidden from the gaggle of reporters standing behind a rope line. The helicopter blades whirled and once they were outside, the noise of the engine would be deafening.

"But I'm not just the president," Aunt Deborah said. "I'm also a mother, and this publicity doesn't just hurt Andrew's image, it hurts his feelings too."

At that, Jackie was filled with resentment. It was true, she was his mother. But it was also easy to forget sometimes. Aunt Deborah was the one who'd thrust Andrew into the spotlight. Sure, it made him look like a pussy if his girlfriend was cheating on him, but wasn't that partly Aunt Deborah's fault for making him wear a promise ring—it had been her idea—and stand around like a prop in the background? It didn't seem fair. Hot anger flared through her and she clenched her hands into fists.

Aunt Deborah put her hand on Jackie's shoulder and spoke into her ear.

"I know this must be hard on you and Andrew. But you have to remember, no matter what the truth is, the *perception* looks like you were cheating on him, going behind his back. In our world, perception is reality."

In my case, it just looks that way. In your case, your husband cheats on you all the time and you let him get away with it.

"Stay out of the public eye for a while, unless, of course, you're with Andrew," Aunt Deborah said. And then Jackie's mother was there, ushering people along. Before moving forward with her chief of staff, Aunt Deborah squeezed Jackie's arm, looked her dead in the eyes, and smiled. "If it was easy to be us, we would want to be someone else."

With that, Jackie's mother waved good-bye as she and Aunt Deborah moved toward the helicopter, conferring in each other's ears about something else—something more important than Ankie's image, and Jackie was glad.

NINE

Escorted by a Secret Service agent, as was customary, Jackie made her way to the family residence on the second floor of the White House. Each step she took brought her closer to facing Andrew. Her emotions roiled as she tried to figure out why the hell he hadn't called her yet.

Her hands actually shook with anger. Was he just too much of a coward to confront her? Or did he just not care what she did because their relationship was already over in his eyes, and he was just stringing her along to keep favor with public opinion? And did he think she would stand for that kind of relationship? That she would be willing to settle for some freaking phony sham of a relationship like the one his parents had? Because if that's what he thought, he had another thing coming. This would never happen with Eric. Eric was decisive; he'd man up and tell her exactly what he was thinking. There wouldn't be this guessing game.

But beneath the anger, her heart pounded, her feet echoing her pulse with each step. Because what if Andrew really did think they were over? What if this whole time the reason he wouldn't sleep with her was because he wasn't in love with her anymore? Or even worse. What if he still was in love with her and this dumb picture that wasn't even *true* was going to break them up? Regardless of her doubts about the relationship, she didn't want something stupid to come between them.

Jackie felt the panic settling in deep in her chest. She opened her mouth trying to take calming breaths, but she felt frozen.

Her heart was racing, and she still hadn't taken a breath.

She needed to calm down. She counted backward, took two deep breaths, and steadied herself. She could do this.

Twice, as they were walking, she could have sworn the agent gave her a dirty look—some kind of cross between condescending and disgusted. Both times she was tempted to justify herself and explain the photo to him—to scream, *"It was just a misunderstanding!"*

The agent left her at the top of the grand staircase. And she paused.

Andrew's room was across the hall from the Lincoln Bedroom. President Clinton had been infamous for using it as a freebie for dozens of wealthy Democratic Party donors. Aunt Deborah put a stop to that and kept the room for the family's visiting friends.

During the beginning of his freshman year, Andrew would invite some of his friends from college. But the novelty of staying in the White House had eventually worn off for most of them when they got their own apartments and realized he was still essentially *living with his parents.*

Andrew's college roommate, Endicott "Cotty" Brewster-King, was really the only guy who still got a kick out of staying over. He'd bring a flask of gin and a copy of French *Playboy* (he claimed to read porn in five languages, as if that was some kind of accomplishment). Then he posted pictures on his MyLife page and used them to pick up girls.

Jackie put her hand on the doorknob to Andrew's room, but hesitated. Because she didn't really want to go inside. She was light-headed, as if she hadn't eaten or had stood up too quickly, and for the millionth time that morning, she looked down at her phone, telling herself she was checking to see if Whitney had called her back—she hadn't. But some part of her was hoping to see a trademark text from Taylor—*At least ur hot, J*—or something equally unrelated to anything going on that would make her feel better.

Thinking of Taylor gave her the strength she needed. *Who the hell is Andrew Price, anyway? You're Jackie Whitman.*

With that, Jackie opened his door, slipped inside, and closed it behind her.

The room was dark—the heavy navy-blue curtains pulled tightly across the windows, blocking the light. And for someone who had a *maid,* it was remarkably messy with clothes, books, video games, and an empty pizza box strewn across the floor. Andrew had chosen the Queen's Bedroom (named after all the royal guests who'd slept there) as his because it was the farthest from his parents' room.

Jackie had helped him decorate it. They'd gotten rid of all the stuffy antiques, including the Victorian four-poster, and gone shopping at Crate & Barrel and Pier 1. Aunt Deborah had even let them paint the walls dark blue, and after they'd spilled paint (accidentally on purpose) on the Persian carpet, they'd gotten a sisal rug to replace it. (Though Taylor and Cotty discovered it was bad for rug burns, not that it was an issue for Jackie.)

Andrew himself was beneath a mass of white sheets and a navy comforter. His face completely buried, his sandy brown hair the only clue he was actually that lump under the covers.

So he doesn't know.

Only instead of relief that she'd be the first one to tell him about everything, relief that he'd hear her side first rather than get a version from the press or his mother, Jackie's fears fell away, replaced by irritation. She'd been stressing all morning over why he hadn't called her, and he'd been sleeping in past noon?

Jackie moved over to the bed, her mood softening when his face peeked out from under the covers and offered her a sleepy smile. With his rumpled hair and bright green eyes, he looked just like he used to when they were little kids, when their parents would let them have sleepovers, and she, Andrew, and Scott would set up tents and sleeping bags on the beach right outside the Prices' house in Martha's Vineyard. They'd stay up all night playing cards and daring one another to go into the ocean or sneak up to the house and spy on their parents. It never failed: the next morning, she'd wake up to find Scott gone (he'd always go back into the house in the middle of the night) and Andrew giving her that same sleepy smile.

She *loved* that smile.

"It feels like I haven't seen you forever," Andrew whispered.

She breathed in his familiar soapy clean scent and the hard place in her chest melted. Moments like this, he was so perfect.

She glanced over at his dresser to see the framed picture of the two of them at the inaugural ball. On the wall behind it were pictures of Andrew on vacation chatting with Daniel Craig on the set of a James Bond movie, Andrew joking with Miley Cyrus backstage at a Bono fund-raiser, Andrew and Jackie at his senior prom, even a framed *Teen People* cover featuring the two of them as the hottest teen couple.

Andrew rolled onto his back and the covers fell away, revealing his toned arms and chest, and she wanted to just slide into bed with him, snuggle underneath the covers, and curl up in his arms and forget the rest of the world.

But she couldn't. Because as soon as he turned on the TV or plugged in his phone (he must have let the battery die *again*), he'd know something was up and wonder why she hadn't told him right away.

"So when we were up at Princeton—"

"Oh yeah, how was that?" Andrew asked. But before she had the chance to answer, he took a deep breath. "Do you smell that?"

She did. She'd smelled warm chocolate the moment she'd entered the private residences. Which only meant one thing.

"My dad must be between girlfriends again," Andrew chuckled. It was a half-hearted attempt at a joke, though. They both knew it was too true to be funny. Bob Price suffered from classic boredom and his coping methods of choice were women and baking. Jackie'd overheard Aunt Deborah complaining that he'd started cheating even before they were married and that she was pretty sure he'd slept with a waitress or two on their honeymoon.

"I hope it's chocolate-chip pancakes and not Nutella crepes," Andrew said, lightly scratching his chest.

Jackie nodded, allowing herself to be distracted by thoughts of Bob Price to avoid mentioning the scandal brewing outside this room.

There was a reason she called Andrew's parents *Aunt Deborah* and *Bob*. And it had more to do with just the fact that Andrew's dad was frequently absent—on the road promoting educational reform, his pet project. He'd never been around when she was a kid, and for some reason, he never seemed to want to be in the same room as her or her mother. As she got older, she also detected some pretty strong animosity between Bob and her father. Not that it mattered, though, since she hardly saw either of them.

But she couldn't say that to Andrew. He still loved his dad and despite the affairs, Andrew seemed to sympathize with him lately. He'd recently stuck up for his father in an argument. After all, as First Husband, Bob Price's days were filled with the same duties assigned to every first lady since Dolley Madison. Mostly he unveiled or toured things. He gave the same uncontroversial speech filled with platitudes and he knew it by heart.

"Thank you, [RANDOM PERSON IMPORTANT TO MY WIFE'S CAREER], and all you wonderful folks for coming out to see me. [RANDOM CITY/TOWN/COUNTRY] has always been a favorite of mine. Seeing [RANDOM NAME/PLACE/OBJECT] reminds me of . . ."

Besides, Andrew reaped the benefits of all the baking his father did.

Andrew's warm fingers on her bare arms, trying to pull her into bed, jolted Jackie out of her reverie. She moved a few inches away from him. "We have to talk."

He groaned and rolled to press his face into a pillow. "Why

does every girl start bad news with that same phrase?" he mumbled.

Jackie bit the inside of her cheek to keep from snapping at him.

"I've got something to tell you and I don't know how to start," Jackie said, waiting for him to roll back over and look her in the eyes. She didn't want to make a confession to the back of his head. "This is important."

He sat up and rubbed a hand over his eyes. "Okay, what's wrong?"

"You obviously haven't seen any newspapers or TV this morning," she began. "Or listened to the messages that are bound to be on your cell. But when you do—"

"Shit, what now?" Andrew sighed.

"When Laura Beth, Lettie, and that new girl, Whitney, and I went to Princeton for the tour and all that, we ended up going to a bar afterward. It was Whitney's idea—"

"Yeah, I bet that took a lot of arm twisting. Please don't tell me you need new fakes. You know how much trouble I could get into for hooking you up with those."

"If I needed new fakes, I could get them myself," Jackie snapped.

Andrew opened his mouth to fire back at her, but she didn't let him.

"Just stop interrupting and let me tell you the problem!" He did. And she blurted everything out before he could interrupt her again.

"Jesus Christ, Jackie, are you bullshitting me? Were you hooking up with this guy?"

"Of course not. Did you *not* just hear anything I said!"

"Why the hell are you yelling at me?" Andrew said, raising his own voice. She hadn't realized she'd been shouting until he'd pointed it out. "And how can you blame me for asking? Every time we're together lately we end up fighting."

"You can't just put all the blame on me. You've started fights, too!"

Andrew opened his mouth—who knew what he was about to say? Whatever it was, he stopped and tilted his head to the side, stretching his neck. Then he nodded. "You're right. We haven't seen much of each other so far this summer. Plus, you're under a lot of pressure with applying to college and we're both stressed and upset about everything else."

About Taylor. He didn't need to say her name for Jackie to know what he meant. But it suddenly occurred to her that he *never* said Taylor's name anymore. She was about to ask why when he started lecturing her about Whitney.

"I think I know how to handle someone like Whitney." Jackie bristled. "Don't treat me like I'm some kind of freaking moron. You don't think I *know* she's only looking out for herself? She's not about to end up as my new best friend or anything."

"I know, but—"

"No, I'm serious. Stop. I hate it when you treat me like this. Just because you're older or a guy doesn't mean I need your freaking advice. I might occasionally just want you to freaking listen. It's shit like this that always leads to a fight."

Andrew reached out and grabbed her hand. "You're right."

"What?"

"You're right. You don't need advice from me," he said with

a shrug, while his thumb traced circles on the back of her hand. "I was just worried about you."

Her anger evaporated as she looked into those green eyes.

"Your mom is super pissed about the photo," she said.

He just rolled his eyes. "What else is new? If she doesn't want the press stressing over our relationship, she shouldn't use every press conference as some kind of photo op."

"She's worried about you," Jackie said, trying to sound like she meant it.

"You mean she's worried about my image and how it reflects on her," Andrew said with a bitter laugh. "Don't try to sugarcoat it."

His smile was a little lopsided, the way it was whenever he was trying to cover up the fact that he hated his relationship with both his parents.

"I've missed you," she whispered. And she meant it.

A smile broke over his face. "I always miss you," he said, pulling her onto the bed and into his arms.

Jackie's lips tasted like vanilla sugar cookie, and when she opened her mouth he tasted the fresh mint of her toothpaste on her tongue. He loved that her tastes were so predictable and so classic *Jackie*. He loved that every time he kissed her it was the same delicious flavors. He wanted to devour every part of her.

He put his hands on her waist, grabbing her and pulling her even closer until she was straddling him. And then he reached up and pulled her hair loose.

God, I want her.

Her hands slid up his chest and pushed him back into the headboard and her kiss intensified as if she wanted to devour him back. And suddenly his stomach twisted, and he felt empty and nauseous inside, and he couldn't stop himself from pushing her away. Even though he *knew* she'd take it the wrong way. She always did.

"What the hell, Andrew?" She sounded pissed. "When are you going to throw that freakin' promise ring away?"

He looked down at the silver ring on his finger and twisted it nervously. It was becoming a habit that he couldn't seem to break. It wasn't the promise ring. But how could he tell her that?

"This is so stupid," she said. She slid off the bed and tied her hair back up. "It's not like I'm Taylor."

It suddenly felt as if the air temperature had plummeted and Andrew shivered. "What the fuck do you mean by that?"

As soon as Jackie visibly recoiled from him he wished he'd said it differently. "What I mean is that it's not like you and I are a one-night stand. This isn't some kind of meaningless game. I know you thought Taylor was a slut, but—"

"What the fuck does she have to do with it?"

"Nothing, that's not the point. I'm just saying we're not like that. I love you and you love me. Sex is a natural expression of how we feel about each other."

"Now who's treating who like a child?" Andrew huffed. He got off the bed and pushed past her. As if he didn't understand sex. As if he didn't fucking think about her all the time, about the way she'd look underneath him, about the way she'd feel or the way her breath hitched when she wanted him. He wanted nothing more than to rip off her clothes and finally get to experience what he'd always imagined.

But he *couldn't*. And he didn't need her to constantly make him feel like shit about it.

He wracked his brain for some kind of excuse to get away from her.

And then he remembered. *Dad and I are supposed to be doing something together today.* "I told my dad I would go with him to some benefit for kids in the Southeast projects, and I'm running late." It wasn't until later that afternoon, but Jackie didn't need to know that.

Despite being the most powerful city in the world and one of the richest, most people who lived in Washington weren't privileged. Most of the struggling families lived on the east side of the city, just blocks from the Capitol. Most of them were also black. The city was one of the most racially segregated in the country, with the nation's highest AIDS and infant mortality rates and some of the worst public schools.

Typically, presidents stayed cloistered behind the White House gates.

But Washington was home to the Price family now. Every couple of weeks they'd eat at some popular local hangout, like Ben's Chili Bowl—a black-owned restaurant that was a Washington landmark—or go to a Nationals baseball game or the movies or volunteer at a soup kitchen. For some of the city's worst-off residents, it was their first glimpse ever of a member of the First Family.

"I'm sorry but I've gotta get ready. Maybe you should go."

He went into the bathroom and shut the door behind him, without looking back, and tried to ignore the fact that he knew her well enough to know she was probably gritting her teeth and looking up at the ceiling to keep from crying.

———

Jackie had already cried once today. She would not do it again. She blinked everything back and took a deep breath before she headed for the door. No reason for the Secret Service agent to think things went badly.

On her way out, she saw Andrew's phone on the nightstand. She'd called him five times and texted him even more. He obviously hadn't seen them yet—she could get rid of some of the more desperate ones.

She dropped her purse on the floor and quickly went over and plugged the phone into the charger. As soon as the screen lit up, she clicked into Andrew's texts. Apparently she wasn't the only one filling up Andrew's inbox.

There were texts, maybe a dozen of them, from a number she didn't recognize, all unanswered.

Lounging in the shade by Laura Beth's pool, Whitney choked back some of the bourbon she'd lifted from Libby Ballou's bar and tried to think about the best way to get information on Jackie and Andrew.

There was definitely trouble in paradise where the two of them were concerned.

Whitney's phone buzzed and she looked at it with a frown. "Jackie again."

"You aren't gonna answer it?" Laura Beth asked.

Whitney shrugged. "She's coming over later, right? We might as well just talk then. I don't know what the fire is about, anyway. She and Andrew are like the perfect teen couple and all that."

Laura Beth was silent and Whitney pulled her Ray-Bans down to stare at her. LB was wearing a brand new Dolce & Gabbana bikini, her skin had finally passed from that pinkish sunburn into a light and even base tan, and her hair was pulled back and pinned underneath a Patricia Underwood hat. With her eyes on her own brightly colored cocktail drink, Laura Beth said, "They used to be, but some things change, I guess."

Whitney stretched out and played disinterested. "Of course, I mean I can't imagine being with the same guy for so long. Talk about bor-ing."

"Oh, but it's Andrew!"

Interesting.

Laura Beth seemed to realize she'd just betrayed her own feelings and tried to backpedal. "He's a really great guy, but I see what you mean. Jackie's never really even dated anyone other than Andrew."

"Never?" Whitney asked. How could Jackie never have dated? What a prude.

"Not really, except for when she had that little fling with Scott."

"Who's Scott?"

"Oh, Scott Price, Andrew's brother," Laura Beth said, wrinkling her nose. "They, you know, *hung out* when we were in like ninth grade, but he's got 'issues.' After the Prices sent him away to reform school, Andrew and Jackie got together. So I guess it was a good thing Scott got sent away."

She must be thinking she could have gotten him if Jackie wasn't in the picture.

Whitney couldn't believe the jackpot she'd just stumbled upon. She didn't know anything about Scott Price's issues, but she could leave that to her mom to find out. In the meantime, she couldn't think of a juicier story. "Washington It Girl Jackie Whitman in Secret Love Pact with Andrew's Brother."

When Jackie left the White House, she'd managed to flatten all the wrinkles out of her dress *and* she'd borrowed a pair of sunglasses to keep the press from recognizing her. One of the Secret Service agents had driven her out and, at her insistence, dropped her near the edge of Georgetown.

Walking down Pennsylvania Avenue, she replayed the scene between herself and Andrew over and over again trying to figure out what his problem was, and every time she came up empty. It was like they had suddenly dissolved into an old married couple without the benefits.

She'd tried to tell herself the good outweighed the bad. He did care about her. He'd been understanding about the whole photo thing and he'd instantly made her feel less guilty about hurting their mom's careers. So what if he wasn't ready to have sex with her? Did that really matter *that* much?

Only it did.

She wanted to feel *wanted,* the way Eric wanted her and couldn't keep his hands off her.

She knew Andrew loved her, but maybe love wasn't enough. The fact that she had to make all the moves and then suffer the humiliation of rejection made her feel like some kind of undesirable slut. And frankly, that overpowered everything else.

Her eyes watered again and she was thankful for the sunglasses.

She should just end it. They could take a break. Maybe if he dated around and realized what he was missing, he would want her the way she wanted him.

Jackie held her breath, trying to steady the avalanche of emotion threatening to spill out. As she crossed the bridge into Georgetown, she focused on Rock Creek Park below her. The national park, twice as big as Central Park in New York, cut a lush, narrow swath running north-south through the middle of the city. People hiked along the creek, spotting woodpeckers and ducks and an occasional fox. It was almost easy to forget the city was just a few yards away.

"Jackie!"

Someone behind her was calling her name.

She turned around. It was Eric. Again.

He looked amazing in a charcoal gray suit, white button-down shirt, and gray tie. The sun gave his dark hair an attractive shine, and she found herself wishing his blue eyes weren't hidden behind black-framed sunglasses.

"Thanks for helping me escape today—you saved my life," she said.

He lifted the sunglasses, as if he knew she'd want to see his eyes. "Running into each other twice in one day. It's fate, obviously." He winked before pushing them back down.

For a second she felt chilled and feverish all at the same time. And then she remembered she was wearing this stupid blue dress. It probably looked like something Senator Hampton Griffin's wife might wear.

"I'm glad I ran into you, but I had something more private in mind for that big *thank-you* you promised me," Eric said. His low, seductive voice was enough to make her forget the dress and go weak in the knees.

He glanced at his watch.

"Look, I've got to meet a lobbyist at the Four Seasons at one, but can we hang out for a few minutes?"

She knew she should make up an excuse. The last thing she needed was someone from the press seeing her with another guy. Especially a Republican senator's aide. And besides that, she'd *just* come from apologizing to her mother, and Andrew, and the president. She couldn't do that again.

"Baked & Wired isn't far. We could go there," Eric suggested.

"Sure," she said. What was she thinking?

When they turned left up Thomas Jefferson Street, the delicious smell of rich espresso and warm cookies wafted past them.

Baked & Wired was more than just the little bakery it looked like on the outside. They roasted their own coffee beans and turned out some of the best cupcakes in the city. Jackie, Taylor, and Laura Beth would bring Lettie there every Thursday after school to celebrate her day off from work—and off from all of her crazy after-school clubs and extracurricular activities. Taylor would order cappuccinos for herself and Lettie, Laura Beth would get a cupcake (coconut was her favorite and it came in a retro parchment muffin cup), and Jackie usually had the chocolate chip cookie that was somehow soft, crisp, and crumbly all at the same time.

She was about to order a huge, extra-sweet vanilla frappé, when Eric ordered macchiatos for both of them. Which was a good thing. A macchiato seemed more *adult*. But she was also starving. She contemplated asking for a chocolate-chip cookie. She could always tell him she hadn't eaten all day (it was the truth), but she bit her tongue. She didn't want him to think she was a kid in a candy store.

They got their drinks to go and walked a few yards to a park bench overlooking the narrow brown waters of the C&O canal.

"Those reporters can't get enough of you, especially after that photo," Eric said, sipping his coffee. "You shouldn't let them intimidate you. My experience is they're really not all that smart—you just have to know how to work them."

"You saw the photo?" She hated that he had seen her looking wasted in a stupid college bar with some loser. "It's not at all how it looked."

"Of course not," Eric laughed. "The press just wants a story. You'll just need to give them a better one."

Jackie let out a breath she hadn't realized she was holding. She was so relieved. Not because she didn't want him to think she'd cheated on Andrew. He already knew *that*. But she didn't want him to think she would cheat on Andrew with just anyone.

"The daughter of that new gossip columnist was with us," she explained. "She was flirting with some guys and it all sort of went downhill from there."

"Oh, so you know Tracey Mills? I've heard rumors about her. I'm surprised she ran that photo if her daughter was there. Some of these reporters will do anything for a story. You should see what they say about Senator Griffin. That he's a Bible-thumping zealot and a hypocrite . . . I spend half my time on the phone yelling at reporters for the crap they write."

"Well, he is pretty conservative," Jackie said, and then instantly wished she hadn't. She didn't want to get into a political argument with him.

But Eric just smirked and leaned closer to her. He looked around, like he was making sure no one was close enough to hear them. "Just between you and me, I'm not really a Republican. I don't really buy his whole conservative schtick," he confided in a low voice.

"Then why are you working for him?" Jackie asked, surprised. He shrugged.

"I met him through my uncle. I was just out of law school and looking for a job that would get me somewhere fast. I didn't want to be some glorified gofer at a law firm waiting for years to make partner."

Normally she would have been disgusted that he was just like so many other guys who lived in Washington, willing to work for—and stoop to—anything in order to get ahead. Jackie came from a long line of loyal Democrats who would no more work for a Republican than reinstate the monarchy. But politics was a game of compromise that everyone, including her own mother, played. Sometimes it meant supporting things you didn't really believe in to get other people to support something you did. It was about choosing your battles. And she was just so damn relieved that he didn't share his boss's right-wing views. Though she hadn't bothered to ask him about politics when he was feeling her up in her mom's office.

She blushed, remembering how amazing his hands felt on her body.

And now he was confiding in her. Being more honest with her than he probably was with anyone else.

"So, what did Andrew say?" Eric asked.

For a minute she thought he meant about the two of them. Then she realized he was still talking about the picture. "Oh, um, I just told him it was nothing. He's fine," she said dismissively, trying not to let him see how flustered she felt.

"You guys have always had such good press until recently. It looks like the press has finally realized you're all grown up."

Jackie couldn't tell where he was looking behind his sunglasses, but she imagined him eyeing her with longing and thought of how Taylor would handle an older guy. And then she did it. She looked Eric up and down and gave him what she hoped was a seductive smile. "It's about time."

Eric's smile widened and he moved even closer. "Maybe you've outgrown Andrew," he whispered. His lips were inches from hers—like he might kiss her *right there*!

"Ohmygosh! Jackie Whitman! How are you? How's your summer been?!"

It was the last person Jackie wanted to see.

"Well, now." Angie Meehan's saccharine voice almost made Jackie cringe. "*Who* is your *friend*?" Her eyes were all for Eric and she looked like she had just won the lottery. Angie's father was a lobbyist and a friend of Senator Griffin's. Another reason to hate her.

Angie's best friend, Charlotte Sallister, stood next to her, weighed down by shopping bags. She smiled and stood expectantly, almost bouncing as she waited to hear Jackie's answer. Jackie immediately leaned slightly away from Eric, composing herself.

"Angie, Charlotte." She nodded. "This is Eric Moran, a Senate aide my mother asked me to show around."

"Ladies." Eric stood. "So good to meet you both."

Angie opened her mouth to say something, but Eric, immediately dismissing her, looked back down at Jackie.

"It was nice to see you," Jackie said, smoothing her hair behind her ear.

"Oh, you too!" Charlotte said. "You'll be at Aamina's party before we go back to school, right?" Jackie nodded. "Fantastic! I can't wait to see you and Laura Beth!"

Jackie nodded again and Charlotte smiled as she turned away. Angie muttered a good-bye and left as well, but looked back long enough to shoot a glare in Jackie's direction.

"I'm gonna have to get going," Eric said, drawing her thoughts away from Angie. "But when can I see you for my thank-you?"

She wasn't about to tell him she was likely grounded. "I'm pretty tied up over the next few days," she said. "My mother's making me go with her to that big awards ceremony at the Kennedy Center over the weekend and . . ."

Eric grinned. "Perfect. I'm going with the senator. We could arrange to run into each other there. How about nine o'clock at the far end of the south terrace? We can find a quiet corner to be alone."

Jackie knew she shouldn't say yes. She didn't want to hurt Andrew and it was obvious this wouldn't be another random encounter over coffee. If she got caught, at the *Kennedy Center* no less, Andrew would be justified in hating her and they'd probably never speak to each other again.

But before she knew it, she heard herself saying, "Sounds like a plan."

"Great. Nine o'clock, then," Eric said just as his phone rang. He stood up. "It's the senator again. I gotta go, sorry."

She wondered if she should kiss him on the cheek, or give him a quick hug, or a little wave—but he'd already turned away from her, talking into the phone.

As she walked toward Laura Beth's, it dawned on her that Andrew would be at the awards ceremony too. So would her mom and Aunt Deborah. Plus, she was under orders to avoid any public appearances with unauthorized male escorts.

Screw it. I have outgrown Andrew. And I've outgrown my mother and Aunt Deborah telling me how to live my life.

TEN

An hour later, all four girls were seated in overstuffed chintz chairs on the Ballous' screened-in porch, the overhead fan on high speed. Mosquitoes buzzed frantically outside, reminding Laura Beth of the swarm of photographers and journalists who had all but attacked Jackie at the White House.

Not that Laura Beth would have complained about all the attention if it was happening to *her*. Of course, she wouldn't have gotten into *any* situation, true or not, that would have the press questioning her loyalty to Andrew.

"It's bad enough having to face your boyfriend after something like this, but I had to deal with his *mother*. I know it's just Aunt Deborah, but when she puts the whole 'I'm the president' act on, it's like she's a different person," Jackie said.

"Well, she has to be, doesn't she? It's just part of the job,"

Lettie said. It was practically the first time Lettie had spoken since she'd arrived at the house. She hadn't touched the food the maid had laid out, either. Laura Beth had asked twice if something was wrong, but Lettie just shook her head. Whatever was bothering her, she wasn't sharing.

"I guess," Jackie said, sinking farther into her chair.

Laura Beth giggled. "Jackie, remember that time, you, Taylor, and I were gonna play Barbies and GI Joes with Scott and Andrew?"

Jackie burst out laughing. "And she gave us a big lecture about Barbie's inaccurate proportions and took away the dolls?"

"How long has Scott been away at school?" Whitney asked.

"It'll be two years in October," Jackie said. "But he comes back for holidays and stuff. He likes being out of the limelight." But now that Whitney had spoken up, Laura Beth watched as Jackie's attention focused on her again. They'd already had the whole *"It wasn't me!"* discussion about the photo, and Laura Beth, for one, thought Jackie had been a little too hard on her. After all, there was no *proof.* And Whitney had practically been in tears about the whole thing.

"Did you talk to your mom yet?" Jackie asked.

"I called her earlier, but she didn't answer," Whitney said. "I'll talk to her tonight, but don't get your hopes up about anything. She's such a bitch. She doesn't care that you guys are my only friends in D.C. All she cares about is her bullshit career."

"You should tell her this isn't L.A.," Jackie said. "She should watch what she says. Embarrassing President Price could turn into an international incident."

Laura Beth smirked at that. While she felt bad for Andrew

and she hoped his feelings weren't too hurt by the scandal, she thought Jackie was overreacting a little.

"We shouldn't have even been at a bar in the first place," Lettie said. "At the very least, we shouldn't have brought those guys over to our table."

"Please, why else go to a bar if not to get wasted and hook up?" Whitney laughed.

"I don't regret that part," Laura Beth agreed.

"Really?" Lettie asked. "Has that guy you were into even called you or anything?"

Laura Beth's heart plummeted. He *hadn't* called, and she'd wanted him to, even though it was ridiculous since he lived two states away and she wasn't even applying to Princeton. "Well, I—"

Jackie's iPhone started buzzing, and she glanced at it, smiling. "I gotta get this." She got up and disappeared inside the house, and for some reason, Laura Beth felt irritated. Since when could Jackie not take a phone call in front of them? What secrets was she keeping?

Jackie walked down the marble hallway, glancing—as she always did—at the Dale Chihuly chandelier resembling a glorious bouquet of poppies floating over the Lalique dining room table whose legs were made of elegantly etched glass leaves. She walked down the wide hallway, past a couple of small Turner seascapes and a John Singer Sargent portrait of Laura Beth's great-great-grandmother, and ran her hand along the smooth, cool bronze surface of the Henry Moore mother-and-child sculpture on a side table.

Once she'd locked herself in the powder room—one of two on the main floor—she hit the call button on her cell and redialed Eric.

"Hey," he answered.

So he's got my name programmed into his phone. Jackie smiled in satisfaction. Keeping her voice low and breathy, she asked, "Did you want me?"

"Do I ever," he laughed. "I can't stop thinking about you. It's becoming a problem since I can't concentrate on work."

Jackie smiled, feeling a surge of heat through her body.

"I'm looking forward to the Kennedy Center," Eric added, his voice low.

"I'm planning to wear something sexy so you won't be able to take your eyes off me," Jackie said.

"It's not my eyes you ought to be worried about."

"Who says I'm worried?" she laughed, remembering the way his hands had felt on her.

Eric groaned into the phone. "You're making it *impossible* for me to work now. If you keep this up, I won't be able to wait."

Jackie laughed. "Nine o'clock. Sunday night. The far side of the south terrace. I'll be expecting you to make it an unforgettable night."

Eric's voice dropped to a whisper. "I've gotta go, but I plan on it, trust me."

He hung up, and Jackie giggled out loud. She caught a glimpse of herself in the mirror. In addition to her giddy smile, her cheeks were flushed, and her lips looked fuller, like they were swollen purely from the memory of being kissed. Her whole body felt overheated as she moved to the sink and splashed a little water on her face.

Then she opened the bathroom door. Whitney was standing right there.

Shit.

Later that night, Lettie slid into the booth at La Caraqueña across from her parents and squeezed next to her sisters. The ten-booth restaurant, tucked inside what locals would call a "no-tell motel" in suburban Virginia, was her family's traditional monthly splurge and as fancy as they got. And Lettie liked that. She looked forward to the authentic South American dishes served by friendly waiters who knew them well by now.

She tried to concentrate on the menu, but her mind kept wandering to her run-in with Daniel and what he'd said about Taylor's car accident. She'd wanted to talk to Jackie and Laura Beth when they were all together at the Ballous' pool, but by the time she got there from work, Whitney was already there too, and she just didn't want to talk about Taylor in front of her. It could wait, couldn't it? Logically it was a car accident, tragic and unfortunate, but just an accident.

She also couldn't stop thinking about her future and Princeton—only that made her excited and then she felt guilty about being excited when she should be thinking about Taylor.

Even worse, Daniel had refused to say anything else about the accident and she wasn't sure what to believe. He'd lost his sister, after all and no matter how hard this had been for her, Jackie, and Laura Beth, Taylor was Daniel's *twin*. The two of them had a connection no one else could understand. Maybe his crazy theory about foul play was some kind of coping mechanism.

It didn't occur to her that he might want to see her again—until he started texting her. They even had a running discussion going about the political cartoons in the most recent *New Yorker*.

Her father's phone rang, and he got up from the table.

"I wish they had hamburgers here," Lettie's sister Christa complained in English.

"Shh, don't say that," Lettie reprimanded. "You'll hurt Mamá and Papá's feelings."

"But I want French fries." Christa pouted. "With ketchup. And they don't know what I'm saying."

Neither of Lettie's parents spoke much English. It wasn't that they didn't want to learn English—but neither one of them had the time. Plus, it was easy to get by without learning, especially as they both worked at the embassy.

"I want pizza," Maribel joined in. "Why can't we ever go to a real restaurant?"

Lettie was about to scold them, when her mother interrupted and asked—in Spanish—"What's wrong with the girls? Don't let them order dessert. Remember we're having rice pudding at home."

"Everything's fine, Mamá," Lettie replied, slipping into Spanish. She glanced over at her father, who was pacing near the door of the restaurant, still talking into his cell phone. His face was flushed and she could see the veins throbbing in his temples, the way they did whenever he was agitated.

It had to be the embassy calling. No one there cared that it was her father's only day off and the only time they had together as a family. The ambassador was always demanding he come in when he wasn't scheduled.

Her mother must have caught her frown. "We are grateful to the embassy, Laetitia. You should know that better than anyone. Just think of my brother and his family, living without running water or indoor plumbing."

Lettie sighed. *Here comes the lecture about Tío José and Tía María.* As if Lettie didn't think about them and their living conditions all the time.

"I know, Mamá," she said, hoping to avoid hearing the same stories for the next twenty minutes.

Luckily she didn't have to worry. Her father returned to the table, bent down to kiss his wife's cheek, and whispered in her ear. A worried frown appeared on her mother's face, but Lettie knew better than to ask what was wrong. The Velasquez family was a traditional Paraguayan family, and children didn't ask questions of their parents, especially not the daughters.

"Girls, why don't you take these quarters and get a gumball each," her father said to Christa and Maribel. He looked at Lettie. "Take your sisters."

Lettie did as she was told, following her sisters, who clutched their quarters excitedly. But, standing at the gumball machine, she kept a close watch on her parents as they whispered to each other, their heads almost touching. They were acting exactly the same way they did when her mother had found drugs hidden underneath the sofa where her brother Paz slept. After he broke down and confessed that he was running with a local gang, they shipped him back home to join the army. No argument. No second chances.

Thinking of Paz, Lettie felt sick to her stomach. *What if something's happened to him?*

Lettie ran a hand through her hair, ignoring her sisters, who

147

were arguing over which gumball machine was the best for their money.

If it wasn't about Paz, what if her father had found out about the bar in Princeton? If they'd seen Jackie's picture in the news, it wasn't a huge leap to assume that she would have been there too. Her parents didn't pay much attention to the American media, but they had friends who did. If they knew she'd been in a bar, drinking and talking to an older guy . . .

She felt sick. If they knew . . . they'd send her home. Just like they did with Paz.

I won't go!

She wouldn't. She would run away. Or go to Laura Beth's. Her house was so big, Libby Ballou wouldn't even know if Lettie moved in. And if she did? She'd probably be happy to advertise the fact that she'd taken in her daughter's token Hispanic charity case.

Her parents got up from the table and walked toward her.

Her mouth was so dry with panic that her Spanish came out jerky, like it wasn't her first language. "Thank you, Papá, for dinner. I think the *sopa de maní* is as good as Grandmother Velasquez used to make." It was a lie. Nothing was as good as her grandmother used to make, but the restaurant's peanut soup, with chunks of beef, rice, and tiny fried potatoes, was still amazing.

And she needed to say something.

Her father gave her a distracted nod and called to her sisters.

As they left the restaurant and walked to the metro station stop, her mother touched her arm. "We know nothing for certain, but there are rumblings of a coup at home," she whispered.

"Paz?" Lettie asked breathlessly.

"As far as we know, your brother is fine," her mother said. "But rumors are flying and no one seems to know what is real or not."

He could be dead already. And we wouldn't know.

"The reason I'm telling you, Laetitia, is that if the government is overthrown, it is unclear what would happen to the embassy here and to us."

Lettie nodded. She hated working in the kitchen at the embassy anyway. She wanted to get another job for her senior year if it was possible.

Only, if something happened to the embassy . . .

She suddenly realized what her mother was trying to say. If the embassy shut down, they would most likely have to go home. Their visas were contingent on the embassy's sponsorship.

ELEVEN

Jackie tugged on the short hem of her little black Versace dress. She still looked like someone had poured her into it, and with her four-inch Louboutins, she was hovering just on the right side of sexy/skanky. Her heart fluttered with excitement, and she felt a breathless anticipation about Eric and their meeting tonight.

She and her mother had both gone to Ilo to get their hair and makeup done. Now they were seated next to each other in the car as the driver made his way the few short blocks to the Kennedy Center. The arts complex, a living memorial to JFK, staged everything from the latest Broadway shows to classical ballets and operas. Republicans always bashed Aunt Deborah for wasting taxpayer dollars on the arts, but tonight's event was something different: She was presenting the presidential Medal of Honor to two soldiers who'd risked their lives saving fellow soldiers in an ambush in Afghanistan. It was the government's highest military decoration, rarely given to living recipients. "Make sure someone from the press gets a good picture of you and Andrew together looking happy," her mom said, breaking the silence.

Jackie nodded, though the mention of Andrew made her feel anxious. She'd tried to think only about Eric the past few days, but underneath that excitement was a sick feeling she couldn't shake about betraying Andrew. She was so worried about what was happening to their relationship, she'd even started waking up each morning with her hands clenched into fists.

She needed to tell him it wasn't working. She needed to end it.

He'll probably be relieved. He doesn't even seem interested in me anymore.

Jackie glanced at her phone. No texts from Andrew all day. Just Eric: *I'm so hot for you.*

"In fact, every moment you're together, you need to be smiling," her mother was saying. "Don't frown or look cross or anything. If anyone gets a picture with either of you looking unhappy, it's just going to fuel the rumors."

One plastic smile coming up.

"I'm sorry, I know you know all this," she continued. "It's just, if they get too many pictures of the two of you with other people and not together, it won't look good. There will be more speculation. And I don't want you to go through that again."

"Don't worry," Jackie said, managing a smile. "Ankie will be in top shape tonight." The irony settled in her stomach like a rock the size of a fist, weighing down on her.

Her mother smiled. "I know I was hard on you about the picture, but I was worried about you. Bad press can follow you forever."

"I know," Jackie said, her smile widening. Classic Carolyn Shaw Apology, right there. She looked over at her mother, wearing a beige Gucci sheath that accentuated her tall, thin frame without standing out and grabbing attention, her long blond hair swept back into a French twist. She looked beautiful.

It made Jackie wonder how in the world her mother was still single.

Not that it hadn't crossed her mind before. Carolyn Shaw had been named one of the 50 Most Beautiful People on the Hill consistently for as long as Jackie could remember, but her mother rarely dated. Jackie couldn't remember a time since her parents got divorced that her mother had been in a real relationship. But she couldn't remember a time when her parents were in a relationship with each other either.

Her mom was married to her job, and essentially to Aunt Deborah. Who of course was also married to her job. And Jackie assumed that was a conscious decision. Her mother had been the one to suggest Aunt Deborah run for Congress back when her mom was working in the attorney general's office.

But right now, Jackie didn't see a smart, powerful woman. She saw a single parent, who, despite how beautiful she looked, was also frustrated, underappreciated, and lonely.

Which spawned two very important questions in Jackie's mind.

1. What can I do to make her happy?

Because Jackie loved her mother more than anything and despite the issues they sometimes had (didn't everyone have issues with their parents?), her mother was a good parent. The best Jackie knew. When her mother had been a lawyer for the

World Wildlife Fund, an environmental group, she always put Jackie first. She'd come to every dance and piano recital when Jackie was little, every parent-teacher conference and back-to-school night as Jackie got older, and she'd *always* come home for dinner so they could eat together, even if she had to go back to work later that night.

And when Aunt Deborah's campaign, and now the presidency, took over their lives, her mother always thought about Jackie and her feelings. When Aunt Deborah offered her the chief-of-staff position, she consulted Jackie before accepting. Not many ambitious and driven parents did that.

The most logical answer to that question, at least in the short term, other than stay in favor with the press, was to *not* break up with Andrew. Which had been Jackie's plan for tonight. She'd even sent him the classic *"we need to talk"* text earlier today. Things hadn't been right between them for months now, and she never wanted to be a *cheater*.

Maybe she needed to talk to her mom first, since Andrew and Aunt Deborah's images were sure to be affected in some way.

But all those thoughts were overshadowed by a more important, yet more amorphous question:

2. *Is this what I have to look forward to?*

Because Jackie wanted a successful career and the independence to be a strong woman too. But what sort of life would that be—single and successful, but lonely like her mom; powerful and driven like Aunt Deborah, but caught in a humiliating marriage to a philanderer; or stuck in the shadow of a more famous dead husband, like Libby Ballou? Were those really her only choices?

Eric Moran stood at the south end of the Kennedy Center terrace, fidgeting and dying for a smoke. But he'd spent every free moment of the past few days planning this moment and he wasn't about to give in to nervous anxiety and ruin it by having cigarette breath when he kissed Jackie Whitman.

"There you are," his boss said, coming up behind him.

"Oh, hello, sir," Eric said, reaching out to shake Senator Hampton Griffin's hand. It was damp and pudgy and Eric dropped it quickly. "I was just looking at all the boats on the Potomac. You can hear all the drunk Democrats partying in Georgetown."

Old Ham—that's what the senator's staff called him behind his back—nodded. "I cornered Carolyn Shaw a moment ago, but she clammed up on the immigration bill."

Eric nodded, feigning the appropriate interest in Senator Griffin's newest mission to stop the Democrats from destroying American culture.

"That bitch just gave me a smug look when I asked her about the bill's chance of passing. She and the President must think it's a shoo-in now that they got those turncoat Republicans by the balls. That's your priority," he said, poking Eric in the chest. "We've got to find out who they are and what Shaw has got on 'em. I don't trust that bitch."

"Of course, sir. I'm on it." Eric nodded. "It's all arranged for me to see Shaw in her office tomorrow at ten thirty."

"Good. I got a nice little reward in mind for you if you deliver," the old man added, giving Eric a slap on the back before walking away.

Eric knew full well that it was going to be tough to find out which Republicans were willing to cross the aisle and vote with the Democrats on such a controversial issue as immigration reform. But he relished the challenge. It was just one more step on his way up the ladder to success.

He'd had his whole future mapped out since high school. His focus hadn't changed when he got to college—not even when his Delta Kappa Epsilon brothers at Yale tried their best to derail him with their hardcore partying.

So far everything had gone to plan. At twenty-seven, he'd landed a job as a top aide to a powerful senator—so what if Old Ham had some of the most ridiculous political ideas Eric had ever encountered. Making English the official language, Eric could understand (he didn't *agree* with it, but he could put himself in the old guy's shoes), but requiring the Ten Commandments to be posted in every airport restroom? (Yeah, that one he hated getting behind.)

But he'd trained himself to suck it up, especially since he'd started double-dipping by finagling a second "job" on the Senate Judiciary Committee, where the old man was chairman. Money and image were important in D.C. when it came to getting ahead.

Which was where Jackie Whitman came in.

Beautiful and well connected, she would get him mentioned in the society pages. She was young—almost *too young*—but he'd figure out a way to spin the press.

And she's fucking hot.

He'd glimpsed her once tonight in that tight black number. She had a body that should be in a museum. It was that perfect.

Eric glanced at his watch. Almost nine. He looked around the terrace.

The balcony, the length of the entire Kennedy Center, was cantilevered over Rock Creek Parkway with a breathtaking view of the river, the glittering lights of Georgetown, and the National Cathedral. The terrace itself was landscaped with weeping willows and a burbling fountain. The perfect romantic setting.

Someone brushed his shoulder with a hand, stirring his blood.

He turned casually to see Jackie, smiling. "Hey." She blushed, looking around to make sure no one was watching them.

He smiled. "You look fantastic," he whispered. "It's nice to accidentally run into you."

A giggle slipped through Jackie's calm exterior.

"I'm planning to take a quick walk if you'd be interested in following." He didn't wait for her to respond, just went back inside, past the famous JFK bust, through the Opera House foyer, and up the staircase to the Golden Circle Lounge, a private room mostly used by rich donors who wanted to escape the crowd during intermission.

And thankfully, Jackie followed him.

The doorway was roped off and the lights were out, but Eric deftly stepped over the rope and unhooked it to allow Jackie into the room. He set the lights to dim and shut the door behind her before pausing to gaze into her eyes and reach for her hands.

Heat flooded her face and rushed through her body, and she struggled to keep her breath even.

"You look *amazing*," Eric said, pulling her over to a red-and-cream-print sofa in the far corner.

He sat down and pulled her in front of him so she stood with her legs in between both of his. He rested his hands on her hips. "I see you're not wearing your chastity bracelet," he laughed.

"I don't have a chastity bracelet." Jackie'd replaced her Capital Girls charm bracelet with a David Yurman woven cable cuff she'd borrowed from her mother.

Eric's hands slid slowly down her dress until they reached the bare skin of her legs. "Glad to hear it," Eric whispered, looking intently into her eyes as his hands began sliding up her thighs, underneath her dress.

Jackie couldn't stop herself from letting out a cross between a moan and a sigh. She leaned forward, putting her hands on the back of the sofa. With a smile that said he knew just how badly she wanted him, Eric tilted his face up to hers and kissed her, lightly at first like he was just teasing. But she leaned into him, and he kissed her harder, his tongue massaging hers.

Eric's fingers grabbed the sides of her thong and tugged. Ever so slowly, as he pulled his hand back down her legs, he brought her underwear down with them.

Jackie had a fleeting moment to wonder how far she was willing to go tonight. She should at least break up with Andrew before *sleeping* with Eric, but as Eric brought one hand behind her to pull the zipper on her dress while the other hand moved up her stomach and cupped one of her breasts, she realized this felt far too good to care about the consequences.

"Come here," Eric whispered, and she straddled him and felt just how much he wanted her too.

She groaned softly against his lips as he slid one strap of her dress over her shoulder, and moved his kisses from her mouth to her jawline, and then down her neck.

And it was like that—her dress unzipped, one strap off, straddling Eric Moran, whose face was buried in her neck, with her thong on the couch beside them—when a flash went off in the room.

Jackie turned toward the doorway in time to see another flash go off. She'd been in the public eye and a target of the media long enough for her body to know instinctively what those flashes meant.

She leaped away from Eric and frantically struggled to get her dress back on as her mind caught up.

The lights flicked on revealing Senator Griffin in the doorway, a glass of champagne in one hand and his cell phone in the other. "Jackie Whitman, good to see you."

If she hadn't spent the day *not* eating in order to make sure she looked amazing in the dress, Jackie would have thrown up right there in front of the senator. She was dead. He would go to the press in a heartbeat and these pictures would ruin *everyone*.

"Eric," the senator laughed. "I'd say I was surprised at you, but then again . . ."

He paused to leer at Jackie, who actually did gag a little that time.

Eric jumped to his feet. "Sir, it isn't want you think."

"Nothing to be sorry about, my boy," Senator Griffin continued. "No one can blame *you*."

Angry, embarrassed, ashamed, and devastated, Jackie shook with emotion, but she refused to stand there and listen to the senator insult her any more. She needed to find her mother and confess everything. She would be furious, but she would know what to do.

Jackie moved toward the door without even a glance back at Eric, but the senator blocked her path.

"Now, now," he said. "I have a solution to this embarrassing chance encounter that will satisfy all of us."

Jackie's heart pounded in her chest as she looked back to Eric, who was sitting on the couch as if nothing was wrong. When he noticed her expression, he just shrugged.

So much for a guy who'd fight for me.

"I don't want to cause a fuss, Miss Whitman," the senator said, stepping closer. "I'd hate to see President Price and that son of hers—not to mention your own dear mama—all upset over your behavior yet again. This can be our secret. As long as you cooperate."

A rock sank in Jackie's stomach. "What do you mean *cooperate?*"

"As it turns out, I've heard your mother is compulsive about keeping paper files and notebooks on everything she does," the senator began. "It's not a very smart thing to do, security-wise, but she sure is organized. And it's going to make your job much easier."

Jackie stared at him for a moment. She couldn't breathe. Could he really be insinuating he wanted her to go through her mother's *files?*

"It just so happens that Eric is going to meet with your dear mama tomorrow at ten thirty," the senator continued. "He's going to suggest they take a stroll around the Rose Garden while they talk, and *you're* going to show up at her office to look for something for me."

"No way," Jackie said, turning to Eric. For a minute she thought he'd set her up for this, but then she saw the look on his face. He seemed completely mortified—and surprised.

"If you can't help me out," Senator Griffin said, "I understand. I just hope the newspapers don't get ahold of any more gossip about you, or, *God forbid,* more photos. Embarrassment like that could ruin your future, not to mention the futures of everyone else affected by your betrayal."

Senator Griffin tucked the phone into his breast pocket. "Think about it—just don't think too long."

And then he left.

Jackie couldn't believe it. He was *blackmailing* her! Sure, she'd heard stories of it happening, but they were *stories.* That couldn't be really happening—and certainly not to *her*!

She felt Eric's hand on her shoulder, but that was no longer any source of comfort or excitement. She shrugged it off.

"Are you all right?"

She whirled around. "Am I *all right*? Do I look fucking *all right*?" she seethed. "How did he know we were here? Did you tell him you were meeting me?"

"No, of course not," Eric said. "He must have followed you."

"Don't even try to say this is my fault! This is your skeezy boss who is now planning to blackmail me into . . ." And then it hit her. Whitney. Standing outside the bathroom when Jackie had been talking to Eric on the phone a few days ago.

That traitorous bitch. She must be responsible for the Princeton photo too.

Jackie turned back to Eric. She'd deal with Whitney later. "How could you even work for such an asshole? You didn't even try to stop him!"

"Come on, Jackie," Eric said. "He's a tough old bastard, sure, but he's no different from the rest of them. This is how the game is played. Look at your mother. She's as tough as anyone." His smile suddenly looked condescending, and she wondered why she hadn't noticed how arrogant he was.

"Yeah." Jackie nodded. "'Look at my mother' is right. You think she'd let someone blackmail her? You can tell your scumbag boss to Fuck. Off. I won't be blackmailed by anyone."

Eric grabbed her arm. "Wait, what are you going to do?"

"Tell my mother everything," Jackie said.

Only when Jackie tried to pull out of Eric's grasp, he held on. "Think this through. President Price can't afford any more bad publicity. The press already thinks Andrew is a spineless puppet of his mother's."

Jackie gasped, tears burning in her eyes. She hadn't heard anyone talk about Andrew like that.

"This will hurt President Price's career and end any career in politics Andrew hopes to have."

"So what, you just want me to let your boss blackmail me?" She shook her head. "You're no better than he is."

For a moment, Eric looked stung. "Wait," he said. "I can get him to erase the pictures. Or I can get his phone and erase them myself."

That *would* be the best possible solution to this mess. Erase the evidence and pretend it never happened.

"The problem is, we're running out of time," Eric said. "He wants those names first thing tomorrow. I can't get to his cell before then. But if you do this one thing for him, I'll make sure he destroys the pictures immediately after."

"You want me to do it?" she asked, her voice trembling.

"It's just a couple of names," Eric said, and his expression turned pleading. "It's nothing that terrible, I swear. I was going to try to get the names anyway."

Jackie thought about how the photos would look spread all over the tabloids. How could she talk her way out of that?

Swallowing the lump in her throat, she nodded. "I'll do it. Just make sure he gets rid of those photos."

Jackie moved to leave and Eric put a hand on her elbow. Not to stop her—he barely had a grip on her. Apparently just to reach out and touch her.

"I still want to see you again," Eric said, and for a moment, Jackie thought he might be as devastated as she was that the night had turned out this way.

But she shook her head. "I can't think about that right now."

Andrew sat in the front row reserved for VIPs, next to Carolyn Shaw and the empty seat where Jackie was supposed to be, and listened to his mother as she began her speech.

"We live in a great country, where we value truth and honesty and openness; where we can trust our government to do what is right for all people," his mother began.

The 2,300-seat theater had deep red walls, rich gold and red curtains, and a spectacular Lobmeyr crystal chandelier that resembled a delicate snowflake. And every seat was filled. But it was a good thing no one in the audience had a bullshit detector.

Andrew knew just as well as anyone else in a political family, everyone was corrupt.

"But no government is perfect," his mother continued. "It's only as good as the people who nurture it. People like these heroes standing behind me tonight." She gestured to the people on the stage. "These brave souls were willing to sacrifice their lives to save others. As a result of their actions, the families of the soldiers they saved were able to welcome their loved ones home. Our country welcomed them home. And we welcome them home, here, tonight."

Andrew spotted Jackie as she slid past a few people in their row and sat down next to him. She looked pale and her eyes were red as if she'd been crying. Not that she looked bad. She always looked beautiful, but whenever she tried not to cry, her skin paled and the skin under her eyes reddened.

His mother presented the Medal of Honor to two of the veteran soldiers, and the audience applauded.

Andrew reached his hand across Jackie's lap and took one of her hands and gave it a squeeze. She turned and smiled at him, but he didn't need to be a mind reader to know that something was really wrong.

And he knew she'd been frustrated and upset with him for the past few months. He just didn't know how he could fix it. Everything he did seemed to just push her further away.

He pulled her hand up to his lips and softly kissed it. "Come home with me tonight?" he whispered.

She shook her head.

Despite everything—how awkward and tense things had been between them and how he could see the gap between them widening into an abyss—he still hadn't expected her to say no. It was such a role reversal that he just looked at her, mouth slightly agape, heart thumping, his eyes welling up. Because this request had been a last-ditch effort to salvage something—to really show her how much he wanted her. But apparently it was too late. That's what her text message earlier had meant.

She really is going to break up with me tonight.

"I'm just really tired and I'm not feeling that well," she said, obviously taking note of the strain on his face.

"I understand," Andrew whispered. Only he didn't.

TWELVE

Call me when you get it.

Jackie looked at Eric's text again and dry heaved into the toilet in the White House bathroom. She'd choked down a few bites of a bran muffin and half a banana that morning, walked to the White House in jeans, a hoodie, and sunglasses, and then promptly thrown up. She pulled herself up and went to the mirror, washing her hands and throwing some cold water onto her face.

She looked like death. She'd barely slept last night, and it showed. The dark circles under her eyes stood out against the sickly pallor of her skin. Looking at her reflection, she couldn't believe she was about to go into her mother's office and betray the two people she loved most in the world.

Only she already *had* betrayed them. That was the problem. Twice last night, she'd gotten out of bed and walked all the way to the door of her mother's room intending to wake her up and tell her everything.

Even worse, she'd called Jennifer Cane and then hung up on the third ring.

She didn't have the kind of money to buy a cover-up. And despite her friendship with Taylor and Daniel, Jackie had always felt a little uncomfortable around their mother. She didn't trust her and she couldn't help but worry Jennifer might use the pictures against her in the future.

Jackie looked at her watch.

10:36

God, what if she couldn't even find the names Senator Griffin wanted?

No, she had to do this. If it got out that she really had cheated on Andrew, with photos to prove it, he would be the laughing-stock of the country. She was well aware that the general public had gender biases and when girls cheated on their boyfriends or husbands, half the country said, *"What a slut!"* and the other half said, *"What a pussy, he couldn't hold on to his girl?"*

If Jackie Kennedy had been caught cheating on JFK, he would have looked like less of a man. It would have hurt his popularity.

Jackie was determined to *at least* make it up to Andrew by making sure those pictures didn't get out. Straightening her back, she swallowed down all of her unease and reminded herself this was a *one-time thing*. She'd go in there, find the names, and get out.

And never see Eric Moran again.

Jackie left the bathroom and met the Secret Service agent outside the door. He didn't mention how long she'd been in there and she wondered if he'd heard her throwing up. At least these agents were discreet. The last thing she needed was "Jackie Whitman Pregnant?" rumors in the tabloids. Especially since she was still a virgin.

When they reached her mother's office, it was empty. (*Shocking!*) Jackie just shrugged at the agent and said she'd wait for her to get back.

Then she was in.

Her mother was immaculately organized; not a single stray paper was out of place, and Jackie had a momentary panic. She was never going to find anything and get it back in the right place in time!

10:39

She moved to her mother's desk anyway, and opened drawer after drawer. Paper files. Her checkbook. Notebooks on campaign ideas. Folders with press clippings of Andrew and Jackie. The police reports from the night of the crash. The medical report on Taylor.

Jackie's entire body went cold. She couldn't think of any good reason why her mother would still have that paperwork. She glanced at the door and then scanned through the pages for the blood alcohol level, wondering if her mother had covered something up.

But no. Taylor hadn't been drinking.

Was there some other reason her mother had these papers here? Maybe there was more to the accident than Jackie—and everyone else—knew. Could Lettie have been on to something?

Her phone vibrated and she dropped the papers and almost screamed. Good thing she held it together, though. She put the papers back and glanced at the phone, hoping it wasn't Eric.

It wasn't.

It was Laura Beth asking about birthday plans—the last thing on her mind right now.

10:41

Sweat trickled down her back and her hands stuck to the papers as she moved them around. Tears burned her eyes and her breath came too fast, like she was hyperventilating.

10:43

Her eyes kept flying back to the door, ears strained to hear any sound in the hallway.

Then she found it. A list of names written down in a spiral notebook filled with graph paper. Next to each name, she recognized her mother's shorthand, and realized instantly why Senator Griffin wanted *Jackie* to do his spying. Her mother had taught herself shorthand when she was in high school and working part time as a legal secretary. Only she hadn't followed the regular conventions. If she didn't know something, she just made it up as she went along. She and Aunt Deborah joked all the time about how even the Navy wouldn't be able to decode Carolyn's shorthand.

But Jackie could.

Armed with the information she needed, Jackie closed the notebook, put everything back in the drawer, and started to leave.

But something was nagging at her.

She looked back at the desk and recognized the lined yellow pad of 4×6 Post-it notes that *had not* been on the desk before.

Shit. She must have pulled them out of a drawer and forgotten to put them away.

10:47

Jackie was running out of time. Her mother would never let

Eric take up more than half an hour of her time. She ran back to the desk and wracked her brain, trying to remember which drawer the pad had come from.

For a second she thought she heard footsteps coming toward the door, but it was just the pounding of her heart.

Okay, think. Which drawers did you open first?

She opened each drawer in the same order she had before. Only they all looked neat and orderly. None looked to be missing a pad of Post-its.

10:50

Jackie opened the middle drawer. Why not? If it was *her* desk that's where she would put them. Only there was no space for them. And they just didn't look right. God, if she didn't figure out where they were supposed to go, her mother would know she'd been here.

Then she remembered.

The Post-its were in the same spot as the file on the accident and Taylor's death. Jackie pulled open that drawer and the Post-its fit right where she remembered them. She had a lingering temptation to open the file again, but squelched it. She needed to get out of here. Now.

"Miss Whitman?" the Secret Service agent asked when she was several steps down the hall.

Heart racing, Jackie turned around. *What if he heard me rifling around in there?*

"Did you want me to tell Miss Shaw you stopped by?"

Jackie nodded. "Of course. But tell her it wasn't anything important. I just wanted to talk to her about our plans tonight."

He nodded, and Jackie let out a breath she hadn't realized she was holding.

171

An hour later, she called Eric from a pay phone (wasn't that what they did in the movies?).

He answered on the second ring. "Eric Moran speaking."

"Eric. It's me," she whispered.

"What? Who?"

"From last night," she seethed. "You wanted me to get something for your boss."

"Right, double-o-seven, what's up with all the secrecy?"

"Don't act like a freaking jerk. Do you want the names?"

"You got them?" He sounded almost as relieved as she felt. "I was worried when you didn't text me back."

Like she cared that *he'd* been worried. "Miller and Frederickson."

"Which Miller? There are two."

"Dammit, Eric, they're not both Republican."

"Oh yeah, of course. You're right."

He didn't say anything else—didn't even thank her.

"What about the other matter?"

He sighed. "I'll take care of it. I told you I would."

"How will I know for sure that they're destroyed?"

"I'll have to convince you in person," he laughed.

Crap. That meant she'd actually have to see him.

"I'm serious about seeing you again. You're all I can think about, Jackie."

"Don't say my name! And God, do you think being black-mailed is a turn-on, because, lesson in girls: it's not."

"Sorry. Look, let's get together in a few days after I get the pictures destroyed," Eric said. "You'll be able to see that I'm sincere, and we'll go from there."

"Whatever. Call me when it's done." Jackie slammed down the receiver.

If her mother ever found out . . . Or worse, if Senator Griffin managed to change Miller's and Frederickson's minds . . . The immigration reform was set to be the most radical change in federal law in years. Millions of aliens, legal and not, were relying on immigration reform to help them stay in the United States. It could mean the difference between Lettie being kicked out of the country or being allowed to stay and graduate from college. Not to mention, President Price had staked her presidency on this platform. If the reforms failed, it could cost her a second term in the White House.

And it would be Jackie's fault.

Tiffany & Co. was abuzz when Laura Beth and Andrew walked inside, flanked by two Secret Service agents. Laura Beth couldn't help basking in all the attention when the manager of the store approached them.

"Hello, Mr. Price. Your package is ready for you," he said. "Is there anything else I can help you with?"

Andrew smiled and turned to Laura Beth, and her heart must have actually skipped a beat, she felt so flustered. "What do you think? Should I get the matching earrings too?"

"Y'all know what I always think," Laura Beth laughed, pulling on her hair. "More is more!"

Andrew laughed, and his grin just about made her melt.

"Yeah, I know you. I don't know why I bothered asking." He turned to the manager. "Can we get matching earrings for the necklace?"

It was so sweet and romantic, Laura Beth almost wanted to throw up.

"Of course, sir. Let me escort you over here, and I'll have one of our sales associates pull the earrings and let you see them."

Laura Beth followed them to the counter. They were picking up Andrew's real present for Jackie's birthday and then she was helping Andrew pick up a fake present to give Jackie as a joke. It was a tradition they'd had since they were kids. They'd always gotten fake horrible presents for each other. One year, Laura Beth got the most hideous-looking cardigan she'd ever seen—seriously, it was white with huge pink and green watermelons all over it *and matching buttons*.

Of course, alone time with Andrew was so rare that Laura Beth had tried on ten different outfits before settling on a bright red Jason Wu dress. She'd even pleaded with Pierre at Aveda to squeeze her in for a blowout.

She was a bit disappointed that Andrew showed up wearing an old pair of khaki shorts and a Georgetown basketball tee, his hair still wet from the shower. He spent the first five minutes in the car teasing her about how many hours she must have spent getting ready. But all her efforts paid off when he told her she looked *beautiful*.

While the salesgirl was wrapping up the earrings, Laura Beth pulled him over to the engagement ring counter. "Mama says when she was a girl you couldn't find colored diamonds if your life depended on it. Look, now they're everywhere."

"Thankfully, I'm not exactly shopping for one of those yet," Andrew laughed.

"But look, they're just gorgeous," Laura Beth said, pointing out an exquisite pink diamond. "What do you think of that one?"

Andrew shrugged.

"It's so beautiful, but do you think I should maybe go with something more traditional? A simple brilliant cut?"

Andrew laughed. "Since when do you do anything simple?"

Laura Beth blushed. "Well, it'd have to be at least five carats of course."

He gave her shoulder a playful squeeze. "That's my favorite thing about you, Laura Beth. You're always so over the top."

She beamed at him.

"So do you think Jackie will like the earrings and the necklace?" he asked.

"Of course," Laura Beth said, even though she had been hoping to avoid the topic of Jackie as much as possible. "You did a great job picking out something so elegant."

He nodded, but didn't look convinced.

"Why wouldn't she like them?" Laura Beth asked before she thought better of it. The last thing she wanted was to encourage him to talk more about Jackie.

Andrew shrugged and looked as if he was about to say something. Only he paused and just stared at her.

Okay, so she didn't want to talk about Jackie, but she *did* want to be there for him. A good girlfriend was loyal. She reached out and touched his arm above the elbow lightly. "What is it?"

Andrew shook his head. "We're just . . . I don't know. We

haven't even spoken since the veterans thing at the Kennedy Center."

This is it! They're really breaking up! Laura Beth tried to calm down her excitement and look concerned, but she couldn't help being surprised. She'd never heard him sound so bitter. She had to change the subject quick.

"How was the awards ceremony?" she asked. "I really wanted to go, but well, you know how Mama is. She didn't want to be seen at a *Democrat* function."

Andrew smiled. "It was a great ceremony, I guess. I asked Jackie to come over, but she wasn't feeling well, so I just went home and watched this cool indie flick Scott recommended. You know how she gets after those big events I'm always dragging her to."

Laura Beth did know. Jackie constantly complained about being in the public eye. Which was ridiculous. "Oh, I just couldn't get enough of those sorts of events. All that attention and political excitement is just so much fun."

Just another on a long list of reasons of why Laura Beth would be better suited to be with Andrew than Jackie. Andrew Price and Laura Beth Ballou together—it could be like the American *Romeo and Juliet,* crossing partisan lines for love.

"How's dance going?" Andrew asked.

Laura Beth beamed. That was so like him to remember the little things she loved. "It's amazing as always. You know, dance is the only time I just really feel free."

Andrew nodded. "Yeah, Jackie always tells me how amazing you are. Have you applied to Juilliard yet?"

But Laura Beth didn't get a chance to respond because a salesgirl came over to them with the two packages, packed into the trademark turquoise-blue boxes, with their crisp white satin ribbons. "Would your girlfriend like to try on an engagement ring?" the girl asked.

Laura Beth felt a thrill shoot through her.

Until Andrew laughed. "Oh, Laura Beth's not my girlfriend. She's like my sister."

He couldn't have insulted her more. Unless he'd compared her to his mother.

"Do you want to go to other stores?" Laura Beth said, abruptly trying to change the subject and salvage the afternoon. After all, this stretch of upper Wisconsin Avenue was the Rodeo Drive of D.C. and her favorite place to shop. And the *only* thing that could make a spur of the moment shopping trip better was Andrew. "We could see what Max Mara has in for the fall, or we could go to Ralph Lauren, and I could help you pick out some corduroys and a blazer for football season. Oh, and then we could grab lunch?"

Andrew shifted on his feet. "I can't, Laura Beth. I'm not going to have time for that. We still need to pick up the other stuff from Rodman's," he said, referring to the family-run discount emporium where he wanted to pick out the stupid joke gift for Jackie. "We can grab a hamburger to go at Five Guys if you're hungry."

Not at all what she wanted to do. "Oh no, it's fine."

He shrugged, and then smiled as they left Tiffany's. "You need to give me a college update and tell me all the latest Libby gossip."

"Oh, Mama! She's even more out of control than usual," Laura Beth said as they walked to the car. "She's been planning her fund-raiser for Afghani schoolchildren for months. At first it was gonna be an Arabian Nights theme until someone thought that wasn't PC. Then when she decided to hold the Afghan thing at the Hay-Adams, she started worrying that one of the guests would get so drunk they'd fall off the rooftop terrace. So she's paying for a special lattice barrier covered with fresh roses."

Andrew laughed. "Seriously? Won't that cost as much as the event raises?"

"Probably. You know Mama."

Andrew smiled and opened the car door for her. The day wasn't a complete wash. Andrew listened to her, and that was important. Sure, he'd said she was like his sister, but guys with girlfriends were obligated to say stuff like that, and sister was better than nothing.

When he and Jackie broke up, Laura Beth would be there to comfort him, and then he'd see her as more than "like his sister."

And they would break up. Laura Beth was counting on it.

THIRTEEN

Despite the way her heart raced at the prospect of seeing Daniel again, Lettie, wearing a cute Marc Jacobs dress (a Laura Beth hand-me-down), stood still while Libby Ballou fussed over her hair. She wanted to ask him more about Taylor's car accident and his theory about it. She needed to understand what he thought happened. But she also just wanted to *see* him.

"Darlin', you could just look so pretty if you put a little more work into it," Mrs. Ballou said, brushing Lettie's hair away from her face. "You should let Laura Beth take you to Pierre for your birthday this year."

Lettie nodded, but knew better than to say anything. Noncommittal responses were always best with Laura Beth's mom.

They were waiting for Jackie and her mother inside Cafe Milano, the Italian restaurant in Georgetown where you went if you wanted to see or be seen. Not surprising, because for someone who complained as much as she did about publicity and her picture in the tabloids, Jackie still really liked to be seen.

Lettie couldn't help feeling excited. The restaurant was famous, the food was amazing, and the servings were big enough that she'd be able to take some home to her sisters. And she had good memories here. She and Taylor had gone to Cafe Milano a few times for lunch last summer.

Then the doors opened and Lettie looked up, expecting to see Jackie or even Andrew.

Instead, she saw Daniel.

Her heart fluttered in her chest as she stared at him. He wore a light blue polo shirt that made the blue of his eyes look even more startling, a plaid sports coat, and khakis with tan flip-flops. It was an eclectic fashion statement (Lettie could only imagine what Laura Beth would have to say about it), but she liked it. After all, he had the tanned, laid-back California look going for him and it was nice to finally hang with someone who didn't look like he'd stepped out of a magazine.

Then he saw her.

A smile lit up his face, and Lettie felt both embarrassed by the attention and thrilled that he looked happy to see her. Daniel brushed a hand through his shaggy, sun-kissed blond hair as he walked straight toward her.

Lettie felt the blood rush to her face and looked down at her feet and when she looked up again, Daniel was there.

"Laetitia," he said, taking her hand and bringing it to his lips, hovering over her skin for a second, his breath tickling her skin, before he kissed the back of her hand softly. She loved the way her full name sounded on his lips, but the whole thing was so suave and obviously staged, she couldn't help but laugh at him.

"I was hoping you'd be here," Daniel added, suddenly more serious.

Her mouth inconveniently decided to dry out right at that moment. So she just stared stupidly at Daniel for a minute trying to think of something clever to say. She didn't have much experience with guys, not that it mattered since she was hardly interested in them—she usually would have said whatever was on her mind. If they liked her, great, if not, whatever. Only the problem was that every seemingly intelligent thought in her mind had just flown out the window, and for some reason, she cared what Daniel thought of her.

But Laura Beth came to her rescue, for once.

"Daniel! Oh my Lord." Laura Beth threw her arms around him and pulled him in for a hug—before pulling back and taking in his clothes. "What are you wearing? Where did you get this thing?" She wrinkled her nose and pointed to the plaid sports coat.

Daniel smiled and shrugged, his gaze momentarily resting on Lettie. "Goodwill. You don't like it?"

"Goodwill?" Laura Beth gasped. "You mean like someone already wore it before you?"

Yeah, Laura Beth, just like the hand-me-down you gave me to wear tonight.

"Lots of people, probably."

But Laura Beth, peering over Daniel's shoulder, was no longer listening. "Look! There's George Clooney. Oh, I wonder how long it'll take Mama to notice."

She frowned. "He looks so old."

As if summoned on cue, Libby Ballou reappeared, bourbon in hand, and announced, "Darlin', when y'all get to be women of a certain age, no gentleman is too old."

"Or too young," Daniel whispered in Lettie's ear.

The door opened again. This time, Andrew and his Secret Service agent, Mark, entered and Lettie immediately waved them over. She hadn't seen much of Andrew so far over the summer, but she'd always really admired him.

As he got closer, though, Lettie felt Daniel stiffen. Tension seemed to radiate in waves off his body. She looked up at him to see his jaw set in a line, his face in a scowl glaring murder at Andrew.

Suddenly she was thinking about the crash, and about what he'd told her.

He can't possibly think it's Andrew's fault.

The warm smile slipped off Andrew's face when he saw Daniel, but he came over to them anyway. "Lettie, it's good to see you," Andrew said, giving her a loose hug. "Laura Beth, you look beautiful as always," he added, hugging her also.

Laura Beth giggled and Lettie tried not to roll her eyes. When did all her friends get so boy crazy?

"Hi, Daniel," Andrew said, offering his hand.

Daniel just stared at it, and for a second Lettie thought he wasn't going to shake hands. But he did, and from the grimace on Andrew's face, it looked like there was some kind of machismo thing going on.

Andrew opened his mouth to say something, but he didn't get the chance.

"You must be Andrew. I've heard *so much* about you," Whitney said, walking over to them. Instead of Whitney's typical skank attire, she was actually wearing an outfit that left almost something to the imagination. She still looked a little slutty in Lettie's opinion—Whitney was tall and miniskirts just ended up looking way too short, but this was definitely an improvement.

Maybe she's not as bad as we thought.

"So you really do wear a purity ring? And it's not a scam?"

Or maybe not. Lettie stifled a sigh. She tried to always think the best of people. But Whitney really made it hard.

"You must be Whitney," Andrew said drily. "I've heard a lot about you too."

"And who are *you*?" she said, noticing Daniel.

A rush of possessiveness went through Lettie as Daniel introduced himself.

"Cane?" Whitney asked. "So you're . . . ?"

"Taylor was my twin sister," Daniel said.

"Oh, I'm so sorry to hear—"

Daniel cut Whitney off with a wave of his hand. "Yeah, we've all had a tough time," he said as he glared at Andrew. "But Andrew most of all, I bet."

Jackie's mother had lifted her house arrest for her birthday. She, Laura Beth, and Lettie had met up earlier for lunch at Pizzeria Paradiso in Georgetown to share a fiery Atomica pizza with salami and hot pepper flakes, and she'd complained about Whitney.

Only neither Lettie nor Laura Beth complained back.

Laura Beth even stuck up for Whitney, claiming she was fun—"like Taylor!"—and Lettie, well, she did what she always did—"We should try to give her a chance. She's new."

And honestly, what could she say? It's not like she could fess up about Eric at the Kennedy Center. After all, it was horrible and embarrassing, and she just wanted it to be over so she could pretend it never happened.

She had planned on telling them about finding Taylor's medical records on her mother's desk. She wanted to tell *someone,* but if Laura Beth and Lettie were going to take Whitney's side all the time, maybe she couldn't trust them anymore. She felt betrayed.

Now she and her mother were pulling up outside Cafe Milano, where all her *friends* were supposed to be, and Jackie couldn't have felt more alone.

Suddenly she felt intensely angry at Taylor for leaving her here to face all this shit by herself. She and Taylor were supposed to be friends forever. They had plans.

"What will I do without you when I'm at Yale?" I said, moaning into one of the dozen silk pillows scattered on Taylor's bed.

She just laughed. "I'll come visit you. How else will I get to sleep with a Yale professor?"

"I'm serious, Tay!" I sat up, throwing a pillow at her.

Standing in front of her mirror, applying her signature red lipstick and heavy DiorShow Mascara, she dodged the pillow and looked at my reflection in the mirror. "Do you really think I'm Yale material? I would die of boredom."

"So what are you going to do after graduation? Just stay here?"

"Travel the world." She rolled her eyes and grabbed a book off her dresser. 1000 Things to Do Before You Die. *She tossed the book to me. "I'm going to do it all and then write an exposé on which country has the best lovers."*

Taylor came over and climbed on the bed, while I leafed through the dog-eared, highlighted pages.

"And of course, you'll come visit me on all your school breaks," she said with a smile. "Maybe we'll even invite Laura Beth and Lettie along, if they promise to be fun."

"Capital Girls take the world?" I asked.

"Why not?"

The Italian owner of Cafe Milano himself greeted Jackie and her mother at the door. "Signora Shaw, Signora Whitman, your party is already seated. I'll show you to the table."

Jackie watched her mother, who looked so happy, it was hard for Jackie to keep from smiling back, forgetting for a second how screwed up her life was and how worried she was about it all.

"After you, birthday girl," her mother laughed. "And here, before I forget." She pulled a thick lavender envelope from her purse. Jackie's name was printed in big, curling letters on the front. "From Aunt Deborah," her mom said as she handed it to her. "She wanted to be here, but the Egyptian president's schedule had to be rearranged, and of course we want to be accommodating."

There were moments every once in a while where it struck Jackie that Aunt Deborah was the *president*. When Jackie turned seven, she'd accidentally dropped the cake her mom had ordered, and Aunt Deborah made her a new one; now, she was turning eighteen, and Aunt Deborah couldn't be there because she was meeting with the president of Egypt. It made her head spin.

"Thanks, Mom," she said, tucking the card into her purse. "And tell Aunt Deborah thank you too."

The restaurant Jackie picked was practically a Washington institution, packed with politicians, high-society philanthropists, and actors in town to testify before some fawning panel of congressmen about their latest pet cause.

Its private rooms were a favorite venue for book launches— and in D.C. there was always some famous journalist or political consultant writing a tell-all about backroom sex and politics. If Taylor had traveled the world and written that exposé, this was where they would have had her book launch party. It was one of the reasons Jackie had chosen Cafe Milano when her mother asked where she wanted to have her birthday dinner.

Jackie took in the restaurant as they moved through it. White linen tablecloths, yellow roses, and brass candlesticks at every table. Their table was along a back wall that gave them some privacy as well as a good view of the room and the other diners. (The party had originally been booked in a private room, but her mother thought it best to prove to the world everything was okay with Ankie.) When her mother told her the new plan, Jackie almost told her she should fly a banner with their names inside a big heart and the words "still celibate" underneath. But after everything that happened with Eric, Jackie was just a little glad there *was* still an Ankie.

Even if they hadn't spoken since the awards ceremony.

She just wanted everything to go back to the way it had been before. Before Senator Griffin and his blackmail, before she kissed Eric Moran, before Taylor died. But she didn't know how to get back to *before*.

At the table, Andrew was seated next to her father in a cashmere Brooks Brothers blazer. On the other side of him was an empty seat—hers—with a huge long white box with a red velvety ribbon.

Her heart lifted and a giddy rush of excitement flooded her. Long-stemmed roses came in boxes like that, and Andrew knew how much she loved everything that said *classically romantic*. He knew her so well.

And yet, thinking of everything he didn't know—about Eric and how she'd betrayed both their mothers—her heart sank. *Don't cry, don't cry, don't cry.* It took everything she had to hold back the tears. What had she ever thought was wrong with safe and comfortable?

She moved toward the table, trying to tell herself she hadn't ruined her relationship with him—at least not yet—and then she saw Laura Beth.

Wearing a mauve print Marc Jacobs dress and with her hair blown out, she would have looked beautiful, only her mascara had run and her eyes were red. It was obvious she'd been crying. A lot. Jackie started to go to her, but her mother stopped her.

"You're supposed to sit between Andrew and Whitney." Of course her mother had a seating chart mapped out and place cards on the table. She could deal with the obvious ploy to put Ankie on display (she wanted to sit next to Andrew anyway and hopefully try to fix things), but she was already pissed off that her mother made her invite Whitney—she certainly didn't want to sit *next* to her.

Jackie's father stood up and pulled her into a tight hug. "You look beautiful. Though it's not surprising, given how amazing your mother is."

Her mother smiled at him, and her face seemed to say, *"See what you're missing,"* something Jackie absolutely loved about her. The divorce had to have been rough on her, yet now, her parents were always able to joke around as if they were just good friends with no baggage between them. And despite all the girlfriends her father had gone through, he hadn't kept any of them around, and Jackie couldn't help feel that was because none of them lived up to her mom.

"Hi, Dad, long time no see," she said pointedly.

He gave her a rueful smile. "Yeah, well, you know how it is, honey. I've been so snowed under at work . . ."

"I know," Jackie said before he made up another excuse. She knew that he meant well, but sometimes it would be nice just to have him around more.

"Can I get you a drink?"

"Don't be ridiculous, Harry," her mother cut in. "She isn't turning twenty-one."

He offered his hands up in mock surrender, but when her mother turned her back he winked at Jackie, as if to say he'd get her something if she wanted it. She just shook her head.

Andrew stood up and gave her a quick hug and kiss on the cheek before pulling out her chair for her and handing her the long box.

Jackie pulled the ribbon off the roses and inhaled the delicate perfume of the pure white buds. "Andrew . . . thank you. You know they're my favorite."

"No, they're from your father. Not me."

For a second, Jackie's throat tightened. Every *right* thing Andrew did filled her with warring bittersweet emotions. The guilty knot in her stomach tightened, because she had ruined them. He was so *right*—the guy girls searched for. Just look at Laura Beth, who would do anything to have him—and Jackie had just thrown it away. And for what? Sex? Not even. Just a quick make-out session with a guy who might have set her up to be blackmailed by his boss.

Wanting to know why Laura Beth was so upset, she leaned into Andrew and started to ask what happened, but he knew what she needed to know.

"Daniel," he said. "He blames me for asking Taylor to drive us on the supply run."

"What?" Jackie hissed. She was reminded of her own guilt for not being in town that night.

"Laura Beth burst into tears and confessed it was *her* fault since she was the one who asked Taylor to go on the supply run."

"That's ridiculous," Jackie whispered. "It was no one's fault. It was an accident." Even if she wasn't one hundred percent sure that was what she believed anymore. There must be something she didn't know if her mother had been looking into it.

Andrew nodded even though he didn't look convinced. Jackie squeezed his hand. Knowing him, he would feel responsible just because he was there.

"I guess Daniel told Lettie he didn't think it was an accident," Andrew said.

"She asked me about it earlier, but I didn't realize Daniel had said something to her."

Andrew shook his head. "He thinks there was some kind of foul play. That Taylor was murdered."

"But—" Jackie was about to say *"who would murder Taylor?"* when it occurred to her that Taylor likely did have enemies, though maybe not enough to actually *kill* her. But her father was kind of sleazy and Jennifer Cane had dirt on everyone—maybe they had a shitload of enemies.

Maybe that was exactly what her mother had been thinking too.

The waitstaff came around with customized menus. Whitney practically threw herself at Daniel, Libby Ballou practically threw herself at Jackie's father, Lettie seemed flustered but flattered by Daniel's attention (when did that happen?), Laura Beth looked miserable, and Jackie's mother tried to make sure everything was perfect and everyone was happy. And Andrew had a hand touching Jackie all through dinner—on her leg, her hand, her shoulder, brushing her hair back from her ear. It was divine.

Or it should have been. It was what she wanted. But instead of feeling amazing, it made her feel even more guilty.

Then the waiters came around with crystal stemmed champagne flutes for everyone at the table—even everyone underage. When a glass was handed to Jackie, she looked over to see her mother standing up and holding her own glass. Her mother winked at her.

So much for worrying about no alcohol.

"I promise not to embarrass you too much," she said, offering another smile. "But I do want to give a quick toast."

"You never did get through a party without giving an impromptu speech," her father chimed in.

Her mother ignored him. "This past year hasn't been easy for any of us. We've all suffered from too much stress and too much heartbreak. Yet we've continued moving forward and we've continued moving up.

"Jackie, one night when you were four, you and I were having dinner, and you told me you needed to learn to tie your shoes. And when I tried to assure you that you would, you corrected me. You said, 'Mom, I need to learn now.' So after we ate, we sat down with your sneakers, but every time I tried to help you, you said, 'I'll do it myself.'"

"That was her favorite phrase back then," her father laughed.

Andrew squeezed Jackie's hand and she smiled. She'd heard plenty of stories about all the times she'd told either or both of her parents she could do something all by herself. But she hadn't heard this one.

"I had to pull out my own sneakers and put them on and lace them up and show you exactly how to tie them. And you didn't want to hear a cutesy rhyme, you just wanted me to stick to the facts.

"We spent a little more than a half hour tying and untying our shoes, practicing so you had it just right, every time, and when we were finished, I told you you'd done a great job and asked why you had to learn to do it tonight. And you told me an older boy at school had made fun of you and you were going to make sure that didn't happen again.

"And I was so unbelievably proud." Her mother's voice wavered slightly and her eyes glistened under the light. "Because even though you were just a little girl, I could see the woman you were going to be. And as I've watched you grow up, you've continued to surprise me. Because not only do I love you, but I admire you and I respect you. And I couldn't be more proud to call you my daughter."

Jackie's own eyes stung with tears, and she smiled back at her mom, who raised her champagne flute. Everyone around the table raised their glass as well.

"To my daughter, a strong, intelligent, determined, independent, and beautiful young woman on her eighteenth birthday," her mother said. "To Jackie."

"To Jackie!" the table echoed. Laura Beth leaned over so her and Jackie's glasses could clink, and Lettie did the same.

Then Jackie lifted the champagne to her lips and took a sip before glancing at Andrew, who leaned in and kissed her cheek. She was about to say something meaningful to him, something so he knew she wasn't mad at him anymore, something to convey that she wanted to go back to *before,* when Whitney cut in and said, "Is there any more champagne? I could really go for another glass."

Jackie turned to glare at her and Whitney just shrugged. "Sorry?"

One advantage to sitting next to Whitney, though, was that Jackie could make sure the bitch didn't take any pictures. She *did not* want Tracey Mills writing about her birthday on some gossip blog.

"Don't worry about her. Do you have any idea how beautiful you look?" Andrew whispered.

Jackie felt her heart beat a little faster. He looked amazing himself. And as he took her hand, she felt even more turned on than she had with Eric. Because he was acting like he still loved her. And maybe that was all that mattered—love. Maybe they really could get back to *before.*

Taylor was always raving about how amazing sex was. How many times had she laughed and said, *"I just can't get enough. I want it. All. The. Time!"* Maybe that was Jackie's problem. Maybe she just needed to get the virgin thing out of the way.

"Are you sure you're not ready?" she whispered back.

"Ready?" he asked, giving her a puzzled look, wrinkling his nose the way he did when he was surprised. Then he cleared his throat. "Oh, that."

"Never mind," she said, feeling miserable all over again. What kind of shitty girlfriend pressured her boyfriend to have sex? "We don't have to go the whole way. Maybe tomorrow night we can go get a coffee somewhere and make out in the backseat of your car. You can just tell Mark to keep his eyes on the road."

Andrew laughed and glanced over at his Secret Service agent and constant shadow. "I doubt Mark could keep his eyes off you. He'd try, but . . ." Andrew's eyes raked over her body, and she felt herself blushing like she was fourteen again.

"Let him look then," she whispered in his ear. "Give him a thrill. Your Secret Service agents are all so discreet. They'd never breathe a word."

Andrew's face turned bright red. "I trust Mark with my life."

His voice seemed to hold a trace of bitterness, and for a second she wondered if he was mad at her for suggesting it. But he was still running his fingers up and down her arm.

"Can you imagine what some of those agents have seen?" Jackie laughed, trying to change the subject. "I bet they know where all the skeletons are. Like, with Clinton and Monica Lewinsky in the Oval Office. I bet they secretly swap stories. One day they'll be talking about us, Andrew, about how you used to sneak me into your room. They won't believe we weren't actually having sex."

Andrew squeezed her hand and leaned into her ear. "I know you get pissed with me sometimes. You know, the whole promise ring thing. But the thing is, Jackie, I get frustrated too."

She nodded, that familiar lump forming in her throat again. She looked up at the ceiling to keep her eyes from welling with tears.

"I don't even know how to begin to tell you—"

She shook her head. She was such a bitch, pressuring him to have sex all the time. "It's okay. We'll know when we're both ready. What's the rush?"

Andrew looked at her like he might say something else, but he didn't.

"Andrew, you have to give Jackie her birthday gift!" Laura Beth said as the waiters cleared the table.

Andrew smiled before reaching under the table and retrieving a bag from Tiffany's.

Oh my God, please tell me it's that Paloma Picasso necklace that was in last month's Vogue, Jackie thought, grabbing at the bag. *Roses and Tiffany's? What was I thinking about him not being romantic?*

"Please tell me it's not a matching promise ring," Whitney said under her breath, just loud enough for Jackie to hear. "I'll shoot myself."

"Don't worry," Andrew laughed. "It's not a ring. But the salesgirl did ask Laura Beth if she wanted to try on an engagement ring."

"That would have been a good picture for those bloodsuckers," Jackie's father laughed.

Even though Jackie wanted to laugh along too, she didn't. Laura Beth probably would have loved to try on engagement rings. Especially with Andrew. She shot her a sympathetic look, but Laura Beth was holding it together, looking unfazed by the laughter.

"Open it. Come on, I helped pick it out."

Excited to see what they'd chosen—if Laura Beth was there, it had to be good—Jackie undid the white bow around the box and opened it up. For a second, she was confused. *What the*— And then she let out a gleeful shout.

Shoving Andrew, she said, "God, you're such a freaking tease," and pulled out a pack of unfiltered Gauloises, French cigarettes with the most disgusting smell ever. Once when their families had been in the south of France, every time she smelled them she thought she'd throw up.

She wanted to freeze this moment. Right now. So she could replay it over and over again. This felt like *before*.

"Anybody got a lighter?" Jackie giggled.

"You can borrow mine," Whitney said as she shoveled pasta into her mouth. She was the only one still eating, and Jackie couldn't help but marvel at how Whitney seemed to fluctuate between starving herself and totally pigging out.

"Oh, darlin', why would you have a lighter?" Libby Ballou asked. "You surely know how bad smoke is for your skin and your health." She lowered her voice like it was a dirty word and added, "Cancer."

"Andrew, you certainly know how to add to my stress level," her mother said, laughing. "Let's not wave those around."

"Yeah, not only might someone think you smoke, but worse they're not even an American brand!" Andrew joked. "My mother would *not* approve!"

"But at least I'm eighteen and I can smoke them legally," Jackie said.

"I'm serious," her mother said. "Let's put them away."

Jackie did as her mother asked.

"Speaking of my mother," Andrew added. "She got you something too." He handed Jackie a voter registration card.

She laughed. "Yeah, my mom already gave me one of those this morning." She looked over at her. "Don't you and Aunt Deborah coordinate?"

Her mother just smiled and shrugged. "Who says we didn't?" For a moment, Jackie imagined Aunt Deborah and her mother standing in the Oval Office and deciding they would both get her a voter registration card to stress the importance of it. And also just in case Jackie lost one. *It never hurts to be over-prepared* was practically her mother's motto.

Talking about the president reminded her all over again of everything that was wrong with her life. An image flashed in her head of Aunt Deborah somehow uncovering Jackie's betrayal, and all the excitement over the silly gift and the teasing fizzled.

"There's something else in that bag," Andrew said to her.

Jackie looked in the bag and pulled out a second Tiffany's box. Undoing the ribbon, she heard her parents and Miss Libby talking about President Nixon. Her mother rolling her eyes, calling him a chauvinist, and her father saying it couldn't hurt to have a strong man in the White House (no doubt to infuriate her mother), and Miss Libby adding her two cents. "He was just so unfortunate looking. And poor Pat was on the homely side too."

And then Jackie gasped.

In the second box was not only the amazing Paloma Picasso necklace, but the matching earrings as well. She threw her arms around Andrew. "You're amazing, thank you so much!"

He gave her a squeeze and she pulled away to look at Laura Beth. "Thank you for going with him! You're the best."

Laura Beth smiled and Jackie turned back to Andrew. "I love you."

He visibly relaxed. "I love you too, Jackie," he whispered. "Don't give up on me."

"Never," she said, squeezing his hand.

And she meant it.

She *would* fix things between them.

When they brought out dessert, Daniel got a phone call and excused himself. Whitney got up a few moments later, intending to follow him into the bathroom and flirt with him, maybe see what information she could get out of him about the "happy couple." Only he just sort of laughed at her and gave her a gentle push before shutting the restroom door in her face.

How am I gonna get anything done in this town if flirting doesn't work? she thought as she walked into the women's restroom.

It was extra disappointing because he'd taken a few pictures on his cell phone at the table and she was hoping to get him to send her the copies to pass along to her mother. Though a lot of them were useless ones of Lame-o Lettie.

Whitney sprayed some breath freshener and walked back into the hall only to see Jackie and Andrew wrapped in each other's arms and whispering together.

She quickly snapped a shot of them with her camera phone (she couldn't go home with nothing) and started to go back to the table when she heard Andrew say, "Jackie, we have to keep the engagement a secret for now. You know everyone will still think we're too young."

"I know," Jackie said. "But I'm just so excited."

Whitney rolled her eyes in disgust. *Who got fucking married at eighteen who didn't live in Hicksville, USA?* But her mother was going to piss her pants with excitement. Ankie secretly engaged? Now, that was news! She'd get enough allowance from her mother to buy a new wardrobe and enough *trees* to last until school started.

FOURTEEN

"So what *guys* will be going?" Whitney asked.

Jackie rolled her eyes and shot a sidelong glance at Laura Beth as if to say, *You insisted on inviting her, you deal with her.* She was so over Whitney. She'd been less stupid lately. The airhead routine was apparently just that—a routine—and thankfully Whitney seemed to realize it wasn't getting her anywhere. But it didn't matter. She still acted like a slut, and her never-ending hunt for a guy was getting old.

Thankfully, Laura Beth took the hint. "It'll be the regular crowd for the most part. At least half the senior class of Excelsior, plus the boys from St. Thomas Episcopal, and Andrew, Cotty, and some of his friends from Georgetown."

"I'm a fan of college guys," Whitney laughed.

The four girls were in the back of a white Chrysler 300 limousine. While Lettie flipped channels on the TV and Laura

Beth dealt with Whitney, Jackie couldn't help but glance up at the sunroof and think of Taylor—who would have been standing in the sunroof, arms spread out wide to catch the wind, and ready to flash any cars full of cute guys who passed by.

They were headed to a party at Aamina Al-Kazaz's house. The daughter of a Saudi diplomat, she lived in a mansion overlooking the Potomac River on Northern Virginia's ritzy Gold Coast. Former House Republican Leader Newt Gingrich and former Vice President Dick Cheney both lived nearby. It was also home to the CIA, not that you'd ever know it, since Langley sat on 258 acres hidden from the road.

"This limo is cool and all, but it'd be way fucking cooler if it came with something to drink," Whitney said as she rifled through the compartments looking for anything alcoholic.

The limo was, of course, courtesy of Aamina. It was totally a bribe to ensure that Jackie and Laura Beth actually *came*. The limo was big enough for Andrew and his friends too, but Andrew had decided to meet the girls at Aamina's after picking up a friend from Union Station.

"And I'm excited to meet some new people."

"Hello, what are we?" Laura Beth said.

Whitney shrugged. "Hey, the more people, the more we can party, right?"

Jackie fought to keep from glaring at Whitney. "Andrew's bringing a friend from New York, Sol, who just broke up with his girlfriend. But he wants him to meet Laura Beth so hands off."

"Hands off?" Whitney asked, raising an eyebrow. "What, are we going to 'throw down' if I talk to the guy?"

Despite her vow to say as little to Whitney as possible, Jackie decided *someone* had to set her straight.

"Look," Jackie said. "Anyone who's anyone at school is going to be there. You need to understand how Excelsior parties work. You can't hit on guys who have girlfriends, and you can't sleep with someone you've just met. Otherwise you'll get frozen out."

"Frozen out?"

"As in bein' your friend'll be social suicide," Laura Beth added quietly, obviously trying to soften the blow.

"Don't sugarcoat it, Laura Beth," Jackie said, her voice edging toward anger. "You'll be an outcast, Whitney, and if you think our mothers will be able to keep coercing us into inviting you places, you're dumber than you look."

"Jackie!" Lettie said, looking up from the TV. "There's no reason to be so mean about it."

Jackie disagreed. It was inevitable Whitney would create a stir. Any new, attractive girl was unwelcome competition to the Excelsior Prep crowd, but Whitney was worse because she was . . . well, Whitney. The way she looked tonight—in a sheer, white, ankle-length gauze tunic, only a turquoise bikini underneath, and a pair of Jack Rogers Navajo thongs in metallic gold—was going to make every girl at the party hate her. And Laura Beth had gone out of her way—Jackie couldn't fathom *why*—to wrangle Whitney an invite.

Jackie wanted to be sure Whitney knew she had no qualms letting her drown. And if that happened, she wouldn't let her take any of them down with her.

"I get it," Whitney said, eyes narrowed.

"Good." Jackie leaned over and cranked the stereo system,

drowning out whatever news broadcast Lettie was watching. She let the music roll over her the rest of the way to cover up their silence. Lettie and Laura Beth both tried to make conversation, but without Jackie, they had a hard time carrying it on, since Laura Beth kept talking fashion and Lettie kept talking politics.

Even if Whitney wasn't in the car, Jackie wouldn't have tried to join in. She was too stressed. For one, the vote on the immigration bill was in less than two weeks, and she wouldn't be able to sleep right until Congress passed it and she knew she hadn't hurt Aunt Deborah's political career. Eric had been texting her at least twice a day since she'd called him last, but she'd been ignoring him. She still didn't have any proof he'd gotten those pictures erased from Senator Griffin's phone and unless he was calling to give it to her, she didn't want to hear from him.

Even worse, pictures of her at her birthday party had shown up in the tabloids, and there wasn't one word about the "secret engagement" she and Andrew had concocted. Which meant Jackie couldn't prove to her mother that Whitney was a gossip spy. And that meant they were still stuck hanging out with her.

At least things between her and Andrew had suddenly gone back to normal after her birthday party. She'd stopped pressuring him about sex, he'd relaxed, and they were having fun again, hanging out, going on dates, making out. She'd even gotten butterflies just seeing him when she showed up unexpectedly at the White House last night. She'd arranged the surprise visit with his Secret Service agent, Mark.

Yet the better things got between her and Andrew, the worse

she felt about betraying him. What had she even seen in Eric anyway? *Ugh!*

She never thought she'd say this about summer, but she couldn't wait to start senior year—anything to take her mind off Senator Griffin and Eric Moran.

"Whitney, look over there, that's the Madeira School," Laura Beth said, breaking their silence and pointing out the lush, sprawling campus.

"So?" Whitney asked with a shrug.

"Their headmistress, Jean Harris, who was just so prim and proper, well, she murdered her secret lover, Herman Tarnower, the famous Scarsdale diet doctor," Laura Beth gushed.

Jackie felt her chest tighten. Taylor had read everything written about it. She had an obsession with morbid gossip like that.

As they pulled into what Taylor had dubbed The Potomac Palace, Whitney took a deep breath, almost a gasp, and Jackie smirked, not surprised. Hopefully the place made her realize how important this first impression would be. The twenty-acre estate came with a tennis court, indoor and outdoor pools, an aviary filled with exotic hand-tamed parrots, a helicopter pad, a stable for the family's Arabian horses, two guest houses, and a six-car garage. It *also* came with a glass elevator with a river view (Taylor and Cotty had sex in it at last year's party and she touted it as the best sex she ever had—not because of Cotty), a bowling alley, and a fifty-seat theater. And of course, the entire estate was ringed by an eight-foot stone wall with guards stationed twenty-four hours a day.

Wait till she meets Aamina.

In public with her family, Aamina looked like a traditional, modestly dressed Saudi. But she was the epitome of a wild American party girl. The summer before their freshman year, Taylor convinced Aamina she had to throw a back-to-school party because the police weren't allowed to come inside a diplomat's house, and the tradition had stuck.

"Be careful of Angie Meehan," Laura Beth warned Whitney as the chauffeur stopped to let a security guard stationed at the massive wrought iron gates check their invitations. "She's the biggest bitch at Excelsior. And watch out for Erin Thomas, she's a suck-up who'd do anything to get into an Ivy. Including sleeping with Mr. Degardio, the Latin teacher."

"That's just a rumor, Laura Beth," Lettie said.

At the mention of Angie, Jackie remembered running into her at Baked & Wired. It suddenly occurred to her that Whitney wasn't the only one who could have tipped off Senator Griffin. Could Angie have done it? Would she really be that desperate to see Jackie fall?

"Oh, and don't talk to Maddy Manahan," Laura Beth added. "She's a compulsive cheater who pays her way out of gettin' in trouble."

"And I doubt Daria Elliason will be here tonight, but definitely stay away from her," Jackie added, because even if she didn't like Whitney, she felt obligated to warn her about Daria.

"What's wrong with her?"

"She's the self-appointed drug Nazi who turns in anyone who smells like weed," Laura Beth explained.

Whitney laughed. "Seriously, what a loser. Daria Elliason? Yeah, I won't be going anywhere near her."

"And then there's Charlotte Sallister," Laura Beth said. "Everyone knows she's a binge-and-purger. It's why the school started lockin' the bathrooms between passing and durin' lunch."

"So why do you go to this school if it's full of such losers?"

"Every school has losers," Jackie snapped. "And if you do sleep with anyone, make sure he wears a condom. Some of the ones you'd least expect have STDs."

Whitney laughed. "So the promise ring thing is just Andrew?"

Jackie almost wished she was driving so she could slam on the brakes and throw Whitney off her seat.

"Whitney, this is serious," Lettie said. "You need to make a good first impression."

"Yeah, whatever. I won't hook up with anyone until I get your seal of approval," Whitney said, and Jackie didn't miss the sarcasm.

The limo pulled up to the house. And just like the best valet service at the Ritz, an attendant helped the girls out. Aamina's house looked more like a castle than a palace, made of stone with two turrets and a huge Palladian window over the carved mahogany double doors.

They could hear music, splashing, and squealing coming from the outdoor pool. A man wearing a traditional floor-length thawb and a white headcloth stood in the doorway and led them through the foyer, past the woven carpets, gilt antique furniture, heavily embroidered wall hangings, and ornate gilded framed paintings.

"Kinda tacky," Whitney said.

Jackie rolled her eyes, but Lettie frowned. "What do you mean? My house looks like this."

Laura Beth and Jackie both giggled, but Whitney turned to stare at Lettie for a moment.

"Whoa, Lets, that was actually funny." She grinned.

So the *Crapital* Girls were kind of lame. Whitney'd already established that. *But* they got her invited to the hottest party around, it seemed. This place had definite potential.

The pool scene looked straight out of central casting for a movie in L.A. Dozens of perfect-looking kids in bathing suits hanging out on the terrace around the Olympic-size pool. Some were passing around hookahs and pot pipes, and bottles of Grey Goose and Johnny Walker Blue Label were everywhere.

So the caterers in their uniforms toting around hors d'oeuvres were weird. But the rest of it seemed pretty damn cool.

Aamina—at least Whitney assumed that's who it was, she looked Arab—climbed out of the pool and ran over to the girls, giving Lets a quick hug before throwing her arms around Jackie. "I'm so glad you came! I've been dying to see you."

"Of course we came," Jackie said, giving Aamina one of her Jackie Whitman Plastic Smiles. "Thanks for sending the limo. The sound system was amazing."

Aamina laughed and waved it off, as if sending limos for the *Crapital* Girls was no big deal. "Dad gives me an allowance. Might as well use it."

Then she looked at LB. "You promised me this year you'd teach me that awesome dance *and* that you'd sing at the party."

LB blushed. "Well, I guess, I mean—"

Aamina squealed and threw her arms around LB too.

"You must be Whitney," Aamina said. They gave each other

the once-over. Aamina's yellow bikini was at least two sizes too small and she was spilling out of it in all the right places. *Oh, to have boobs like that.* "Come on, I'll introduce you to everyone. Oh, and Jackie, I have to introduce you to my cousin who's staying with us."

Aamina hooked her arm through Jackie's and led them into the party. Hopefully Aamina's *cousin* was an older guy she could hook up with.

Actually, the more Whitney looked around, the more she could get used to this place. And to the *Crapital* Girls, who everyone seemed to want a piece of. They only got to one group of kids before they got mobbed and separated. Aamina pouted a little when Jackie briefly got pulled away from her, but she was easily sidetracked by talking to some bitchy girl about her safari and riding yaks or something. In fact, despite the way people were staring at her—and they definitely were—Whitney felt jealous of the way everyone flocked to Jackie and LB.

Whitney looked around to see if Daniel was there yet, and her eyes caught on a guy just her type: Tall, with the Cali-style blond shag and Billabong board shorts she missed from home.

Whitney sauntered over, put her hand on his bicep—which was rock-hard—and whispered in his ear. "So you actually surf, or you just like the brand? I've always had a thing for guys who could ride a wave."

He turned and looked her up and down before a lazy smile spread over his face.

But the guy standing next to him just laughed. "He knows how to surf, sweetheart, but he wouldn't know what to do with you."

Whitney eyed him. "And you would?" He looked like a football jock, bulky enough that he might have been into steroids.

But right when he was about to say something, another girl moved in between them. "Franklin, Phillip, come into the hot tub pool with me and Elise."

Whitney didn't miss the glare the girl gave her as she dragged the two guys away.

Whatever. I made an impression.

She went back to scanning the party for Daniel, or someone else hot, when she saw Andrew steering someone through the throng. Not just a someone. Tall and muscular, this guy had jet-black hair and a fan-fucking-tastic tan.

Screw LB. First come, first serve.

She glanced around quickly, but Jackie and LB were still with Aamina and some other girls. LB was showing them some dance moves, something that normally would have made Whitney totally gag. But damn, LB could seriously move. All the others struggled to copy her as she tried to talk them through it.

Whatever. They were dancing while *Whitney* was getting the guy. Their loss. Whitney made her way over to Andrew and tall, dark, and hot.

"Hi, Andrew, who's your friend?" Whitney asked.

Andrew stiffened as Whitney put her arm around him, but she just ignored it. Might as well make him squirm a little. What a prude.

"Whitney, this is Sol Molla," Andrew said. "Sol, Whitney Remick."

De-fucking-licious. Sol Molla was what Whitney would have

called ruggedly handsome with dark-brown eyes and thick eyelashes that girls like LB paid money for. There was no way Whitney was giving him up without a fight.

"You're not, you know, into the whole purity ring club, are you?" she asked.

Andrew shifted uncomfortably next to her, but Sol smiled. "Not exactly," he admitted, giving Andrew a look.

Andrew rolled his eyes. "Whatever, dude. Come on, let me introduce you to Laura Beth."

"Oh, I can do that!" Whitney said. *Yeah, right.* "Jackie wanted to see you as soon as you got here. She's over by the pool house." She turned to Sol. "Come with me. You'll just love LB. She's a perfect Southern lady."

Before Andrew could protest, Whitney linked her arm with Sol's and was leading him past the pool, *away* from Laura Beth, who was chatting it up with some random girl, and steered him toward one of the guesthouses.

"So I hear they have king-size beds in all the guest houses," Whitney said, her voice as low and sultry as she could make it.

If Sol was embarrassed, it didn't show.

My kind of man.

"Let's find out."

Whitney smiled. "Sounds like a plan."

From the corner of her eye, Lettie saw Whitney leading someone she didn't recognize into one of Aamina's guesthouses. *She isn't wasting any time. So much for Jackie's and Laura Beth's advice.*

Whatever. She wasn't about to police Whitney.

There were more important things she should be worried about.

Lettie sighed and turned back to the Peruvian maid she'd been talking to. "Make sure they're paying you minimum wage, Geannina," she said. "Don't let them take advantage of you. It's not legal."

Geannina nodded as Lettie slipped a napkin into her hand.

"This is the name and number for a free lawyer who can give you legal advice," she continued. "You're entitled to decent hours. Don't let them make you work sixteen-hour shifts anymore."

"But—"

"No, you said you have your resident alien papers, right?"

Geannina nodded.

"Then they can't hurt you or kick you out of the country," Lettie said. "I promise."

"Thank you, Senorita."

When Geannina disappeared back into the house, Lettie turned back to the party, disappointed Daniel hadn't shown up. She wanted to talk to him more about Taylor, especially since Laura Beth had burst into tears at Jackie's party.

Laura Beth was absolutely giddy when she climbed into her mother's car service with Lettie and Whitney. "This was even better than last year's party!" she gushed.

"It was okay, I guess," Whitney said.

"Oh, don't be ridiculous," Laura Beth said, laughing. "I saw y'all smoking hookah and teaching those guys to blow smoke rings. Aamina was impressed."

Whitney shrugged.

"Well, what about you, Lettie?" Laura Beth asked. "Did you have a good time?"

"Of course," Lettie said, but she sounded subdued. "It was fun to see everyone."

"Well, I just had the best time," Laura Beth announced again. "Sol is just gorgeous. Did you see him, Lettie? *And* we have so much in common! We talked about the opera and the ballet. The Lincoln Center versus the Kennedy Center, and he lives on the Upper West Side near Columbia."

"And to think I thought all guys who liked the theater were gay," Whitney said.

"I didn't like him that much," Lettie said with a shrug.

"What? What do you mean?" Laura Beth asked. When she didn't answer, Laura Beth figured she was just being usual Lettie—too good for a boyfriend. She thought Sol had been a perfect gentleman. She could tell by the way he'd looked at her when she was talking that he was interested, but he didn't try anything. "I can't wait to introduce him to Mama. She'll just love him."

Laura Beth's iPhone buzzed, and she let out a squeal when she read the text. "Lettie, check your phone!"

"What?"

"Jackie just texted us. She and Andrew want to set up a date for the six of us at my pool on Saturday."

"The six of us?"

"Jackie, Andrew, you, me, Sol, and Daniel, of course," Laura Beth said before looking quickly at Whitney. "Oh, Whitney, you're welcome to come too."

"Whatevs, LB, didn't I tell you I have a date on Saturday? I met this totally hot guy in the elevator of my building."

Laura Beth nodded and then turned to Lettie. "This is so

excitin'! If this date goes well, I could have a boyfriend for the back-to-school mixer and the fall dance, and then even prom. And Sol is just so *right* for me. He's worldly. He comes from a respectable family. And he's friends with Andrew!"

And what she didn't say was that he seemed like the perfect guy to make Andrew jealous.

FIFTEEN

Walking to the bus stop, Lettie looked up to see a beat-up 4 Runner following her. After her initial reaction—*um, strange*—her heart beat a little faster, and she looked around hoping to see other people on the street. In Paraguay, someone following you in a dark car meant you should say your final prayers. Here in Mount Pleasant, too, for that matter.

Then the car stopped and the driver rolled down his tinted window.

Daniel.

He smiled, and Lettie felt an almost magnetic pull toward the car. "Most girls I've gone on a date with let me come pick them up."

Heat flooded her face, and Lettie smiled back, her heart hammering harder than a few seconds ago when she thought she might be in danger.

"Is this a date?" she asked, unwilling to play any kind of games. She just wanted to know where she stood.

"Do you want it to be?" he asked with a shrug.

She wasn't sure. If her parents found out, they'd send her back to Paraguay in a heartbeat. They didn't approve of her hanging out with boys. Which was why she was taking the bus to meet Daniel and the others at Laura Beth's pool party. Anyway, she wouldn't have time for a boyfriend, what with senior year, college applications, AP classes, and work.

But then again, it was *Daniel*. Who made her heart do flip-flops whenever he smiled at her. "Maybe this can be a test date?" he offered.

"A test date?"

"Like a trial run." His smile widened. "We'll act like it's a date and see how it goes. If it goes well, we can go on another one—a real date. If it doesn't, we can just stay friends."

She couldn't see the harm in that.

She also couldn't find her voice, so she just nodded and walked around the car. Daniel, in turn, leaned across the front seat and opened the passenger door for her.

"Thanks," she said, thinking it was sweet of him to open the door for her even though it wasn't a *real* date.

"What are you doing on this side of town, anyway?" she asked, puzzled.

"I was hoping to catch you before you got on the bus," Daniel said, and grinned.

Lettie moved several magazine articles off the seat so she could sit down. "What are these?"

"Oh, I thought you might like to have those," Daniel said.

He waited for her to put on her seat belt and then started driving toward Laura Beth's.

Lettie looked at the three magazine articles in her hands, surprised.

Daniel glanced over at her. "Taylor said you collected stuff like that and kept a sort of scrapbook."

Her face grew hot again and her hands went clammy. She'd never told anyone except Taylor about her scrapbook. Not even Jackie or Laura Beth.

"Tay thought it was cool, ya know," Daniel said. "And so I thought of you when I was reading these. The first one's from *The New Yorker* and it's all about who's behind the move to topple the government in Paraguay."

She'd been Googling to find anything she could about what was going on down there, but there wasn't a whole lot of news. Her parents didn't seem to know much, either, and they still hadn't heard from Paz. Lettie kept telling herself that no news was good news.

"The other article's about an ownership society and the decay of American culture," he continued. "Then the one about Taiwan's impending free trade deal with China is from *The Economist*."

Lettie was already skimming *The New Yorker* article and couldn't wait to sit down with her scrapbook, paste in the article, and jot down her thoughts. But she couldn't help feeling let down by Taylor. She'd spilled a treasured secret to someone Lettie hadn't known all that well. Why would she have done that?

"I, um, I think it's pretty cool too," Daniel said. "I've sort of started keeping a scrapbook since she died."

Lettie looked up. "You have?"

Daniel nodded. "I've kept all the articles about Tay and the accident."

"If you really think there's more to it, you have to tell me. I want to know." Lettie's eyes burned, and she blinked to keep from getting weepy.

"Taylor wasn't drunk." Daniel's hands were gripping the steering wheel tightly. "And she was a good driver—a careful driver. I know that sounds crazy to most people because she was so wild, but . . ."

Lettie knew. She remembered the time Taylor drove her to southeast D.C. to tutor some local elementary school kids.

"Dude, L, you don't mind if I keep the radio off, do you?"

Lettie shook her head.

"Good, because I'm a little paranoid about getting into an accident." Taylor flashed her a wry smile. "Don't tell anyone."

"So what do you think happened?"

"Maybe somebody tampered with the brakes or something like that. I haven't figured it out yet," Daniel said. "But I will."

"It could have just been that she swerved to avoid another car. Or more likely, a deer. They're everywhere at night."

On the surface, it seemed absurd to think someone meant for Taylor to die. *Who would want to do such a thing?* But it *was* true that some of the details of the crash didn't quite add up: That stretch of road was a straight shot; yes, it had been raining, but it wasn't torrential or anything and it was a pretty well-lit neighborhood.

"Anyway, if there was anything suspicious, Andrew would have told the police." Andrew never talked about the accident, as far as Lettie knew, not even with Jackie. And Lettie wasn't about to quiz him now. Not after what had happened at the restaurant.

"Yeah—unless Andrew is covering something up," Daniel said. Lettie was struck by the look on Daniel's face. The grief, the anger, the heartache—they were all barely restrained. Her eyes followed the bob of his Adam's apple as he swallowed thickly. "And I really think he is."

Jackie had stopped giving her running complimentary commentary five or six bathing suits ago. Laura Beth had finally narrowed it down to two choices: the DVF print bikini or the black Gottex bandeau one-piece that was the latest craze.

"That's the problem with having so many clothes," Jackie teased, lounging on Laura Beth's bed, piled with discarded outfits.

"But I just can't decide," Laura Beth wailed.

"Wear the bikini," Jackie said. "All guys like bikinis."

"But it doesn't match my nail polish. Do I have time to redo my nails?"

Jackie shook her head. "Your nails are silver. They match everything."

Laura Beth picked up the one-piece. *Finally.* Not that she was annoyed with Laura Beth. After all, the fashion dilemma was keeping her mind off the looming immigration reform vote. She massaged the tension knot in her neck. Her eyes were red and burning from lack of sleep. Not even eyedrops were helping.

"Tell me about Sol," Laura Beth said.

Jackie tried to think of something new, grateful to interrupt her train of thought. "I told you everything I know already."

"But that was hardly anything," Laura Beth protested.

Jackie sighed. She'd already told Laura Beth all the great

things Sol had to say about her on the car ride home with Andrew from Aamina's party. She just hoped Laura Beth didn't ruin everything by being too clingy. After all, she and Sol had only spent one evening together.

"You sure you don't know why he and his girlfriend broke up?"

Jackie shook her head. "Nope. You know as much as I do. Andrew says she dumped him, but Sol wouldn't tell him why. Maybe they didn't have much in common." Jackie smiled. "Not like you."

"If I get in to Juilliard, we'll have even more in common!" Laura Beth gushed. "And we'll be living in the same city."

"Have you told your mom about Sewanee?" Jackie asked, even though she knew the answer. And not that she could blame Laura Beth. She'd have a hard time telling her mother she didn't want to go to Yale.

"I've rehearsed exactly what I'm going to say to her, but I'm gonna wait till just before school starts. That way, I won't have to see her moping around the house all day. You know how she's always had her heart set on my going to her alma mater and going into politics just like Daddy."

Laura Beth sighed. "But I've been doing a bunch of research and even if I don't get accepted at Juilliard, there are other schools in New York with great dance and theater programs."

Jackie nodded. "You should do it. You're an amazing dancer, and your mother will get over being disappointed." She'd always been a little jealous of Laura Beth and the way she could dance. They had actually taken a few dance classes together when they were younger, but Jackie and Taylor had both quit after a few years. Taylor always laughed and claimed they'd be just as good as Laura Beth if they'd stuck with it, but even she had to have known that was a lie. Even at seven, it was clear that Laura Beth was light years more talented. "Remember what Taylor always said: shake what you got, LB. They'll all come running."

Laura Beth turned her back for Jackie to hook the bathing suit. "Yeah, I remember. Hope that includes Sol." She studied herself in the mirror.

"So, are you going to head up to New York for tryouts or something?"

"Yeah. I met this guy through my dance studio who can help me put together a DVD of all my performances," Laura Beth said excitedly.

The words were just out of her mouth when her bedroom door opened and Libby Ballou appeared.

"Laura Beth, what are you doin'?" her mother asked. "You're not thinking of doing one of those hip, hop, happy dance videos are you?" She didn't give Laura Beth a chance to answer. "I hope not. Because all of your guests are already here."

"Oh, Mama, you didn't tell me they were here yet!" Laura Beth said, quickly reaching for her lipstick and applying one more coat.

"I'm telling you now!" Miss Libby said.

Jackie jumped up and followed her out of the room, with Laura Beth right on her heels. She wondered if they were too late—if Miss Libby had put poor Sol through one of her Southern Inquisitions.

When they got out to the pool, Lettie, Daniel, Andrew, and Sol were all seated around the patio table, frosty glasses of lemonade in front of them. All three guys stood when they saw the girls.

Sol looked like he'd just stepped off the porch of his family's summer home in East Hampton. He wore flip-flops, a white Paul Smith shirt with the sleeves rolled up, and 501 Levis. He obviously cared about looking nice, something Laura Beth would appreciate.

Andrew, in pressed khakis and a polo shirt, set her heart fluttering. He opened his arms and she practically ran into them. The feel of him holding her—*God, please don't let me lose this.*

As they sat down, the Ballous' maid, Maria, came out with a tray of cheese and crackers from Dean & Deluca and an array of desserts from Georgetown Cupcake.

"*Gracias,*" Sol said as he grabbed a dessert plate. "*Hiciste al horno?*"

Maria blushed and shook her head. "No, they came from a bakery," she said shyly.

Sol looked like he might say something else, but Libby quickly cut in. "That's so sweet of you to have a little chat with Maria." On cue, Maria retreated into the house.

"I just love to hear a Spanish accent. Preston—that was my late husband, God rest his soul—and I traveled extensively in Spain, but naturally everyone at the Ritz spoke English. Just hearing you now though reminds me what a romantic-sounding language it is, especially when the natives speak it. Lettie of course speaks it too, but there's just something about Spanish men."

"Mama!" Laura Beth said, as her mother winked at Sol.

"Have you been to the Andalucía region?" Sol asked. Jackie was impressed by how smooth he was. Most people had a hard time handling themselves around Miss Libby. "We have family there who have olive groves. It's far enough away from the Mediterranean that there aren't so many tourists."

"You must have to just tear yourself away from there. Europe is just such a marvelous country."

Jackie almost spit out her lemonade. She forced herself to choke it down and ended up having a minor coughing fit. Andrew patted her back and just smirked at her.

"One time, Preston—God rest his soul—and I were invited to an equestrian event outside Paris and who do you think was there? Why, the entire Monaco royal family, that's who. You can't even turn around in Europe without bumping into a prince or a duke or grand duchess or something." She barely stopped to take a breath. "Poor Prince Albert though, the young man has hardly any hair left on his head. What is it about royalty? All those bald pates and no chins. Not to mention the *next* Prince of Monaco. And that *sister* of his, Princess Stephanie! Why, she was so mannish. And talk about bad manners. She virtually turned her back on Preston and me, and . . ."

Miss Libby continued to go on and on about Princess Caroline, Princess Grace—"God rest her soul"—and several other members of the royal family. Jackie half tuned her out and studied Lettie and Daniel, who were sitting so close their arms were touching. When Miss Libby started recalling the night she and Preston—"God rest his soul"—had been in Venice, Daniel leaned over and whispered to Lettie, who giggled and turned red.

Just as well Taylor isn't here to see this. She wouldn't approve.

Last summer, Daniel's brother, Sam, had flirted with Lettie—until Taylor put a quick stop to it.

"I love my brothers, what girl wouldn't? But I don't want them doing my best friends," Taylor told me.

221

"But what if Lettie really likes him? This is the first time a guy has come on to her and she's actually shown an interest in him," I argued.

Taylor just shrugged. "Too late. I already told Lettie he's gay."

"He is?"

"Nah. I made it up."

"God, Taylor, that's just plain mean."

Taylor gave me a weird look. "Do me a favor and drop it."

"So how do you and Andrew know each other, Sol?" Miss Libby asked.

"Mutual friends," Andrew said, jumping into the conversation. Jackie smiled to herself. Andrew was always complaining that he could never get a word in when Laura Beth's mom was around.

"We met last year after a Hoya game in New York," Sol added.

"Do you play basketball like Andrew?" Laura Beth asked.

"Nothing more serious than a backyard pickup game," Sol laughed.

"He does, *however,* play a mean game of polo," Andrew said.

"Now that's a *real* man's game," Miss Libby said. "Why did you know that one time, Preston—God rest his soul—took me—"

"Did you know polo was invented by the Persians?" Andrew interrupted, effectively cutting short another Miss Libby anecdote.

Jackie smiled and squeezed his knee.

"Oh, that's nice, dear," she said, looking back at Sol. "Where are you studying . . . ?"

"Columbia," Sol answered. Once again, Jackie was impressed that Sol hadn't shown an ounce of annoyance while being simultaneously grilled and forced to listen to all her stories. *He really must like Laura Beth.* Jackie wished Miss Libby would just relax and show Sol her other side, the good side, the one that was funny and smart and loving.

"I started as an archaeology major, but I'm not sure now what I want to do," Sol continued. "I volunteer with a philanthropic organization my parents run that promotes understanding between our two countries, and I really love that kind of work. I think I might like to get involved in that as a career."

"Oh, I'm interested in philanthropy myself!" Miss Libby interrupted. "If only people realized that we in the right-to-life movement want to foster understanding too. We have nothing but sympathy and compassion for these poor, young, unwed girls who might be tempted to do away with their babies. Why, one time when—"

"Mama," Laura Beth cut in quickly. "It's been lovely sittin' here and talking 'n all, but it's gettin' so hot. We should really take a swim."

"Oh, of course, Laura Beth, you simply must enjoy the pool." She got up and went over to the bar to add a little bourbon to her lemonade. "It was so great to meet you, Sol, and it was so great to see you, Andrew—and Daniel! I wanted to get a chance to talk to you too, but—"

"I'll just have to come back." Daniel smiled.

"Of course, and y'all are welcome to stay for supper. I won't be in because I have a date tonight. But Laura Beth, just let the chef know how many people are stayin'."

Laura Beth nodded and her mother excused herself and went back into the house.

"Gee, thanks for helping me out, guys," Laura Beth said.

Jackie laughed. "We couldn't get a word in."

"Oh, no," Andrew said, shaking his head. "Don't say that. I got at least five words in."

Laura Beth pointed to the pool house. "You guys can change in there."

As soon as they were alone, Laura Beth grabbed Jackie and Lettie by the hands. "He is so perfect. And he gets along so well with Mama. Don't you think it went well?"

Before Jackie or Lettie could answer, they were all sprayed with cold water. The girls shrieked. Daniel was in the pool, wet hair plastered to his skull. "My bad," he shouted. "Did my cannonball get you girls wet? What was I thinking?"

"Quite an entrance!" Lettie laughed. She got up, slipped off her sundress, and dove into the pool.

Andrew, stripped down to boardshorts, walked up to Jackie. He was frowning, his jaw tightly clenched. *Great. He's gonna get into it with Daniel.*

"Try to be nice for Lettie's sake," she said gently, touching his arm.

He shrugged. "Okay, but I don't know what Lettie sees in him."

"Look, I know he's got some stupid theories about the accident. But try to give him a break. He's still freaked about Taylor. It's like he's got to blame someone in order to make sense of it and you happen to be a convenient target."

He dove into the pool without answering.

Laura Beth spent the whole time in the pool in deep conversation with Sol. She invited him to her mother's Afghanistan fund-raiser. To her delight, he accepted right away. Then he told her his plans for the future—how he was thinking about transferring to Georgetown or Yale and changing his major to international affairs so he could become a diplomat.

"You're thinking of moving to D.C.? In the fall?" Laura Beth was ecstatic.

Sol nodded. "Living here, I could get my foot in the door at the State Department. Even though I'm Iranian, I'm a naturalized citizen—so that wouldn't be an issue—and I speak Farsi, Arabic, Spanish, and French. It wouldn't be for another year or so, though."

Laura Beth's excitement instantly evaporated—so bummed that she felt like crying.

"Here you're thinkin' of movin' to D.C., and I want to move to New York," she said, trying to sound like it was no big deal.

To cheer herself up, she told him all about her Broadway dreams and discovered Sol had a cousin at Juilliard, who he offered to introduce to her.

When Sol mentioned he was heading back to New York the next day, Laura Beth's face fell. "But you'll still come back for Mama's fund-raiser?"

"Definitely." He went quiet for a second. "If it's okay with you, I'd like to come back a lot."

Laura Beth could hardly believe her ears. *He likes me, he likes me, he likes me!*

Sol cleared his throat. He looked really serious.

"Laura Beth, I hope you won't take offense, but we have to get something straightened out. I got the impression your mother doesn't realize I'm Iranian. When my last girlfriend's parents discovered I was Muslim, they made her break up with me."

"How awful," Laura Beth said, thrilled that he was *confiding* in her! "Well, you don't have to worry about that with Mama." Though, to be honest, she wasn't so sure.

He smiled and pushed a strand of hair off her face. At his touch, a shiver moved through her body.

"I hope you're right. If not, I hope we can share more than *a swim* before your mother calls Homeland Security."

Laura Beth thought she'd died and gone to heaven. "You are such a flirt," she said, her face turning as red as her hair. "I don't think Mama will be calling the authorities—unless you . . ."

His brow furrowed. "Unless I what?"

"Take advantage of her daughter!"

She giggled and swam away from him, calling out, "Andrew! Will you protect me from Sol?"

Neither he nor Jackie heard her. They were too wrapped up in each other to notice anyone else.

She didn't know why that disappointed her. Sol was amazing, and she was having so much fun. But still—she wished Andrew would act just a little bit jealous.

"Laura Beth, could you come here a moment?" her mother called from the patio.

Oh my Lord, what could she want now?

Laura Beth pulled herself out of the pool and wiggled her hips as she walked toward her mother, hoping Sol—and Andrew— were watching.

"Yes, Mama?"

"I hope y'all are having a marvelous time," her mother said. "I really like Sol. He's just a darlin' young man. And a Spaniard at that. His accent was gorgeous."

Oh, God. Sol was right. She has no idea.

Laura Beth opened her mouth to correct her, but stopped.

"I've heard Spaniards can be so romantic and most attentive. Why, one time—"

"Mama, you haveta get ready for your date."

"Oh, yes, you're right," her mother said, looking at her watch.

As her mother slipped back inside the house, Laura Beth hoped her date went well tonight. If her mother was involved with a new man, she'd pay less attention to her and Sol.

SIXTEEN

Lettie skimmed over an e-mail from Laura Beth. Another one gushing about Sol. According to Laura Beth, she and Sol had been talking every single night since their pool party two weeks ago. Now he was coming down for the weekend to be Laura Beth's date at Libby Ballou's fancy fund-raiser.

Lettie was in turmoil. She was almost positive it was Sol who disappeared into Aamina's guesthouse with Whitney. She desperately wanted Jackie's advice on how to tell Laura Beth—or *if* she should tell her. But Laura Beth seemed so happy, Lettie'd kept putting it off.

And Sol *seemed* like a nice guy. He was certainly very charming, and had been kind to Maria, who reminded Lettie of her own mother, who'd been a maid since she turned fifteen.

Besides, Lettie had been preoccupied with Daniel—enough so that she hadn't thought of Sol as much as she probably should have. When she wasn't working in the embassy kitchen, she was either with Daniel or thinking about him. They'd been hanging out several times a week. He'd taken her to Saxby's in Dupont Circle, where he'd treated her to a coffee and they'd talked for hours. They'd gone to the National Museum of Natural History to see the American Presidency exhibit, which he said was one of his favorites. He called her daily, and twice she'd been up until three in the morning whispering to him on the phone while her sisters were asleep. They'd even talked more about Taylor's accident, but it was like talking in circles. Daniel didn't have any new information, let alone any proof that it wasn't just an accident.

But today, she was going to decide what to do about Sol, and then do it. And maybe there was a way to protect Laura Beth without upsetting her *or* involving Jackie.

Lettie looked at the computer screen. Thank God it still worked. It was an ancient, clunky model—slow as hell—and like most other things in her life, a hand-me-down. This one was from the embassy, which had also donated a small desk. Somehow her father managed to find room for them in the cramped bedroom she shared with her sisters.

Lettie nibbled on her nails. They were already chewed short—"A nasty habit," Laura Beth always made sure to point out—but it helped Lettie relieve her stress.

She set up a fake Gmail account, found Sol's address through MyLife, and created a new e-mail. Staring at the blank message on the screen, she started to get cold feet. She had no idea what to say—or even if she should do it at all.

What if they can somehow trace it back me?

She steeled herself. She had to do this. Laura Beth was her friend. She had to do something to keep her from getting hurt.

I know what you did at Aamina's house, she typed.

No, that sounded ridiculous, like a bad nineties horror movie or something.

If you ever betray Laura Beth again, your life will be over.

No. Erase that. Way too threatening. And besides, Sol wasn't officially Laura Beth's boyfriend. Guys—and girls (just look at Whitney)—had random hookups all the time. She started typing again.

I know you slept with Whitney. If you know what's good for you, you'll treat Laura Beth right.

But she didn't *really* know that. What if they didn't go all the way? She needed to sound like she knew *exactly* what went down. But of course, she didn't.

She settled on vague with an implied threat.

I saw you and Whitney together at the party. If you treat Laura Beth badly, you'll regret it.

Before she could change her mind, she clicked send.

She created another new e-mail. This one was easy. She knew exactly what she wanted to say to Whitney.

I saw you and Sol together at the party. Unless you want me to ruin your social life at Excelsior you'll be careful about who you choose to betray. If you go behind Laura Beth's back again, I'll make sure talking to you is social suicide. You'll never get any guy to hook up with you again.

It was harsh, and not exactly true—Lettie didn't have the clout to turn anyone into a social outcast. But Jackie did.

"You've seen this, right?" Jackie asked, opening Tracey Mills's gossip blog on her phone. They were in the restroom at the Hay-Adams Hotel for the Afghanistan fund-raiser.

Jackie thrust the cell at Laura Beth, who was reapplying some last-minute mascara. Front and center was a photo of Jackie and Andrew kissing in Laura Beth's pool.

"Whitney must have taken this yesterday," Jackie said. Andrew had surprised her, Laura Beth, and Whitney by turning up with Lettie—he'd picked her up after work—and a big tub of Jackie's favorite Chocolate Fudge Brownie ice cream from Ben and Jerry's in Georgetown.

Jackie took the phone back and read the column out loud.

"'First Son Andrew Price seems to have forgiven Jackie Whitman's little Princeton fling by the look of their hot-and-heavy clinch at Laura Beth Ballou's Georgetown estate. Either that or the water was cold.'"

"Maybe someone took it over the fence," Laura Beth suggested.

"It had to be Whitney."

"Well, at least it shows you and Andrew back together," Laura Beth retorted. "It's not worth worrying about."

She wouldn't say that if she knew what Whitney did to me at the Kennedy Center.

"Gee, thanks for your support, Laura Beth."

"She's gettin' on my last nerve too, Jackie, but it'll be better for us in the long run if we make her think we like her, just like our mamas have said." Laura Beth took a sip of her cocktail. "Besides, Whitney can be pretty fun sometimes, and she didn't embarrass us at all at Aamina's party. Or at your birthday."

Jackie sighed and leaned back against the vanity. Until she had proof, it seemed she'd have to drop it.

"How's my hair look?" Laura Beth said after a minute of silence. "Sol hasn't seen it this way. I hope he likes it."

"Of course he will," Jackie said, but she was having a hard

time concentrating on Laura Beth's updo. Senator Hampton Griffin was an old family friend of Miss Libby's and he was bound to be there. Jackie'd felt physically ill all day, thinking about it.

And what if Eric was with him? She could ignore calls and texts, but she couldn't very well avoid him if he came right up to her. She'd have no choice but to talk to him. The last thing she needed was a scene.

Usually, she loved fund-raisers—most of the time they were just an excuse for a party, and Libby Ballou's were always extravagant and memorable. Jackie had countless Miss Libby stories that stemmed from a fund-raiser.

"C'mon," Laura Beth said. "Andrew and Sol are waiting. And we need to get up there and greet people, otherwise Mama will be mad."

Her mother had invited two hundred of her "closest friends." The original guest list had been closer to five hundred, but she'd told the girls she was sacrificing numbers for exclusivity by holding the party on the rooftop of the Hay-Adams, whose spectacular views of the White House and the Washington Monument more than made up for the limited capacity. Most of Washington's Who's Who, clamoring to attend the party, had flown back from vacation for the evening.

A fourth of the guest list were just wealthy people in the area; a fourth were Preston's former colleagues and other politicians; a fourth were the hottest names in Washington (politicians, authors, and TV personalities); and the rest were PDM ("Potential Dating Material," as Miss Libby called them).

When the girls stepped into the elevator, the rooftop button was already lit up and guests were packed inside like overdressed sardines. When the doors opened, their hostess—in a dramatic black, backless Jo Mendel dress with a beaded halter neckline—was mingling with her guests, welcoming each of them with a carefully scripted personalized greeting. She'd kept her jewelry to a minimum since the dress was so ornate on its own—just a half dozen thin diamond bracelets that twinkled as she hugged friends and enemies alike.

"And how are your darlin' daughters?" Miss Libby asked as Jackie watched her flirt with Republican Senator Jeffrey Ives. He looked good for being in his fifties, with salt-and-pepper hair, hazel eyes, and a strong jawline.

"They're well, Libby," Senator Ives said. "Thank you so much for asking. It was a hard year for them."

"Oh, I know, I'm so sorry to hear about your loss," Miss Libby said as she placed her hand on his arm, just above his elbow, and leaned closer to him. "And how does Frances like her job? Isn't she working on the Hill?"

"She is," Senator Ives answered. "She's working as an educational aide and she absolutely loves it. And Dina's in boarding school, although—"

He kept talking, but Jackie turned away. The man had only been widowed a year, but Miss Libby was already moving in on him. At least this one was her age.

Hopefully Andrew—who was there representing his mother—would make the evening tolerable. And maybe if she stuck by his side, Eric wouldn't dare approach her.

She sat down at one of the tables, next to Andrew, Sol, and Laura Beth, who was introducing everyone within earshot to her "boyfriend."

Once all her guests were seated, Miss Libby tapped her glass to get their attention. "I'd like to thank all you wonderful people for bein' here tonight for such a worthy cause. Each five-thousand-dollar donation will enable us to build half a school. So if any of you are feelin' extra generous tonight, just remember you can always donate another five thousand dollars and tell your friends you are building a school in Afghanistan, which, let's face it, sounds *so* much better than saying you're building *half* a school.

"And we're honored tonight to have with us Andrew Price, the son of our wonderful president and my dear friend," Miss Libby continued. "If there has to be a Democrat in the White House, I can't think of anyone else I'd rather it be."

There was polite laughter and then she gestured to Andrew. "C'mon up here, Andrew, and say a word, please."

Andrew went wide-eyed and looked over at Jackie. "She can't be serious. I don't have a speech prepared or anything."

Jackie had been too busy looking over at Senator Griffin and his wife (who'd obviously just had a facelift) seated a few tables away. Flustered, she looked back at Miss Libby, who'd moved to a podium set up with a microphone, and then at Andrew. "Um, I guess—"

"Give a mini version of that speech you gave last year when you had to talk to the international students at American," Laura Beth suggested. "You know, the one about how the world has become such a small place and we have a duty as world citizens to make it better."

"Thanks," Andrew said, flashing Laura Beth a grateful smile before he headed up to the podium.

Jackie felt instantly guilty. It should have been she, not Laura Beth, who suggested he recycle one of his old speeches. For once she was glad about Laura Beth's crush on Andrew, glad she had always hung on to his every word and practically memorized every one of his speeches.

Jackie got up in search of a glass of champagne, which she planned on pretending was ginger ale if anyone asked.

But when she reached the bar, a voice was suddenly close to her ear. "Miss Whitman, don't you look ravishing this evening."

Her skin crawled and she fought off the urge to turn around and throw the champagne in his face. She didn't need *that* picture showing up in the press.

"It is too bad Eric isn't here tonight," Senator Griffin said.

Jackie almost gagged. She turned around, straightened her back, and held his gaze. "I have nothing to say to you."

But as she started to push past him, he reached out and grabbed her arm and murmured in her ear. "Oh, I don't need you to *say* anything. But I do need you to listen. Because I have something else I need you to do for me if you don't want scandalous pictures of you all over the Internet and on the front page of the *Washington Tattler*."

Jackie's heart sank. If he hadn't been holding on to her, her knees would have given way. Even if she'd known what to say, she couldn't have: the lump in her throat felt like it was strangling her.

"I'm afraid I'm just having the darnedest time with the delete button on my phone," the senator continued. "I'm worried I'll accidentally press SEND instead."

"But I did what you said," she whispered. It sounded lame even to her ears.

"My research department tells me I've grossly undervalued that little item of mine," Senator Griffin said with a chuckle. "I'll have Eric get in touch." He released her arm and walked back to his table.

Eric *hadn't* erased the pictures.

And now the senator was trying to blackmail her *again*.

She was screwed.

Andrew didn't know what was bothering Jackie, but he was ninety percent sure it meant she was about to break up with him. She'd barely said five words to him all night, sitting at their table looking miserable while Sol and Laura Beth danced and laughed.

"I think I know something that will cheer you up," he'd said at one point. He'd pressed her free hand to his lips. She always loved romantic gestures.

"What?" she asked.

"Guess who called me tonight before the fund-raiser to tell me her *sources* had heard we're secretly engaged?"

He watched the life flow back into her as she sat up straight. "She didn't!"

"Oh yes. Good old Tracey Mills, our friendly neighborhood gossip reporter, wanted to give me the opportunity to comment on the reports before she ran the story, since I'm such good friends with her daughter and everything." Andrew laughed.

"Oh, that backstabber!" Jackie said. "I knew she was reporting back to her mother. I *knew* it!"

Andrew felt better looking at the smile on her face. She almost looked like herself again.

"Wait, what did you say to her?"

Andrew smirked. "I told her I loved you, but she needed to

check her sources again because the secret engagement was also a secret to me."

Jackie laughed and he paused to admire her mouth. She was so beautiful.

"And then I said, 'Oh, unless Whitney is your source, since Jackie and I mentioned a secret engagement in front of her, just to . . . you know . . . see if we could trust her.'"

"You did not say that!" Jackie screamed, playfully slapping his shoulder. "That's perfect!"

He laughed. "Glad you think so. Tracey Mills, on the other hand, seemed pretty flustered on the phone."

"I bet."

But over the course of the evening, the smile had vanished. Now, seeing her slumped silently next to him in his Prius, she seemed down again. By the time he pulled up outside her townhouse, he'd convinced himself whatever it was, it must be his fault.

Maybe Daniel or Lettie had planted some crazy idea in her head about the accident.

Just the thought of it made him feel sick to his stomach.

Right then, he almost told her everything. Just confessed it all.

But before he could even begin, she started to jump out.

He grabbed her hand and pulled her into him, inhaling her perfume and savoring the warmth of her body, but she quickly broke away and climbed out of the car. "I'm dead tired. I'll talk to you tomorrow, okay?" Then she shut the door, and walked slowly up to the front of her house.

After months of denial, all of Andrew's doubts suddenly vanished. He had to tell her the truth. Even if it broke them up.

SEVENTEEN

Whitney and her mother were at a stalemate. Even if they hadn't been at opposite ends of the country, they'd still be separated by a giant wall of tension.

Whitney had to hand it to Jackie (and Andrew for going along with it). The Secret Engagement Snafu was a stroke of genius, one that Whitney had *not* seen coming. But as a result, she now had to deal with her mom's wrath. She'd never heard her so angry.

As far as Whitney was concerned, her cover was blown: Jackie didn't trust her anymore and her mother would just have to find a new source to bribe. But of course, her mom didn't see it that way. She was insisting Whitney shut up and suck up and do whatever it took to get back into the *Crapital* Girls' circle.

In between lapses of sulky silences, they'd been having the

same argument for the past four days. The phone calls, texts, and e-mails went something like this:

Mom: *Apart from bad tips, you haven't given me much of anything else lately. Even before your latest screw-up, you weren't any closer to becoming a Capital Girl than you were the day you met them.*

Whitney: *That's not true. Besides, I don't want to be part of their Crapital Girls club.*

Mom: *That's my point exactly, Whitney! You don't have the right attitude. If you're too selfish to see how important this is for me and for my career, then at least think of yourself and how miserable you're going to be living in Washington without any friends.*

Whitney: *(Silence)*

Mom: *I mean it, Whitney, if you ever want to get back to California, you'll need to get your priorities straight.*

Whitney was sick of thinking about it. She got up from the sofa and went to her bathroom. At the moment, the *Crapital* Girls and the fight with her mom were not her biggest worries.

She was late.

And Whitney had always been a "like clockwork" kind of girl.

It could be stress. After all, didn't stress make people late sometimes?

She opened up the bathroom cabinet and groped around for

the home pregnancy kit. Her fingers shook as she held the box, and she almost put it back.

But she needed to know.

Lettie was at GW's Gelman Library when her phone vibrated. She was tempted to ignore it. Most of her college apps weren't due until the last two weeks of December, but she wasn't needed at the embassy until that evening and she'd set aside the whole day to polish them.

But there was a chance the call was from Daniel, and even just *talking* to him made her happy. She'd started playing a game with herself. Every time her phone rang, she would close her eyes, not look at the number, and chant to herself, *"It won't be him, it won't be him."* Somehow it lessened the disappointment when it wasn't and heightened the excitement when it was.

She clicked ANSWER. "Hello?"

But it wasn't Daniel. It was Whitney. Sounding desperate.

"You gotta come over. Right now. Please."

As she stuffed everything into her backpack, Lettie thought about the Butterfly Effect. It was one of her favorite theories. She'd written a paper last year in AP Physics on how it related to quantum physics. How one tiny event could have far-reaching effects and actually change the course of history. It was amazing to think that something as small and insignificant as the flap of a butterfly's wings might create enough tiny changes in the atmosphere to alter the path of a tornado, or even prevent one.

Lettie was currently a victim of the Butterfly Effect.

Hers started when she ran into Daniel at Taylor's grave. If he hadn't smiled at her, if his eyes hadn't told her how he understood her, she never would have sat next to him at Jackie's birthday dinner. If she hadn't sat next to him, she wouldn't have given him her number or agreed to go on a fake date at Laura Beth's pool. And, of course, if she hadn't gone on that date, she wouldn't have gone on more dates. And if they hadn't started dating, he wouldn't be calling her every day, and she never would have kept her cell on at the library.

Which led to this moment: answering her cell when Whitney called.

A half hour later, Lettie was ringing Whitney's doorbell. When Whitney pulled open the door, her eyes were red and her hair was wet and flat.

Irritated that her plans for the day were ruined, anxious that Daniel hadn't called yet, and annoyed that Whitney almost definitely gave her mom the photo of Jackie and Andrew kissing in the pool, Lettie was a little more blunt than she intended to be.

"You look like shit."

"And you look like a fucking raccoon," Whitney snapped. "What's with the bags under your eyes?"

Lettie followed her down the hallway to Whitney's bedroom. "I haven't been sleeping much." She had one theory about why Whitney wanted her here, and she thought it'd be best to just tell Whitney flat-out. "You're not getting any gossip out of me."

Whitney scoffed. "Tell that to my mother the next time she calls."

Looking around the room, it struck Lettie as odd that Whitney hadn't bothered to decorate it. The walls were white

242

and bare. She didn't have any pictures, posters, or anything that gave the room character. It looked like she'd just moved in; not like she'd been living here for two months.

They sat on her bed, Lettie perched on one corner, trying not to get too comfortable since she wanted to leave ASAP. She didn't want to blow the whole day. Definitely not on Whitney.

Whitney didn't say anything. For seventy-five seconds. Lettie counted.

Then she finally broke the silence. If Whitney didn't want gossip, then what *did* she want? "Did you want to talk about your mom?" Lettie asked.

Whitney huffed. "Not really. She's such a bitch. She wants me to spy on everyone for her blog. She's always used me as a source, and whenever I don't want to do it, she calls me selfish. Me! Like she's not using *her own daughter* for her career!"

Lettie sort of understood. Her parents put their jobs before everything else too. But it was a necessity, not a choice. After all, if they lost their embassy jobs, for any reason, the whole family would be shipped back to Paraguay.

"I never even wanted to move here," Whitney continued. "And now I have to start a new school. For *senior* year. All my friends are three thousand miles away. My dad is never around. And Excelsior sounds way too intense. What if I can't keep up?"

"Don't worry about school." Lettie felt bad that the girls had never once stopped to consider Whitney's point of view. They'd never given her a chance. Yeah, she was a pain, and yeah, she could be rude and full of herself. But that didn't mean she didn't have feelings. "Your parents can get you a tutor. Even the smart kids use them. The school office has a whole list."

Whitney raised her eyebrows.

"Don't look so skeptical," Lettie laughed. "You'll have a great year."

"Not if I'm pregnant."

Lettie thought she must've heard wrong. "Wait, what?"

Whitney threw herself onto her back and flung an arm over her face. The whole bed shook. "My period is late. I bought a pregnancy test, but I'm too nervous to use it."

"Oh my God, Whitney!"

"Whatever. Just forget I told you."

"Um, no," Lettie said. "You were right to tell me. But you really *have* to take the pregnancy test. It could be a false alarm. And if it's true, it isn't the kind of problem you can just close your eyes and wish away. You need to *know*."

Lettie stood up and grabbed Whitney's arm. "Come on, right now," she said, pulling Whitney off the bed. "Where's the kit?"

In the bathroom, Lettie read out the instructions on the back of the box. It didn't seem too complicated, just pee on the stick, leave it out for a few minutes, and then check to see if it had a (+) or a (−). Pregnant or not pregnant.

"Hey, do you want some of these?" Whitney said, grabbing a couple of pill bottles and offering them to Lettie. "This one is Ambien. They'll help you sleep like a baby, and these"—she pointed to the second bottle—"will help you stay awake when you're working."

"Adderall?" Lettie said, reading the label. "I don't have ADD."

Whitney laughed. "Neither do I."

Lettie set the bottles down on the counter. She had no intention of taking them. "Okay. I'll be in the bedroom. Call me when you're done, and we'll wait together."

"Okay," Whitney said, her voice suddenly sounding younger and more nervous than it had a moment ago.

"Hey," Lettie said. "No matter what happens, we're in this together."

"No offense, Lets, but I just don't really swing that way."

"Yeah, hysterical, Whitney," Lettie said with a roll of her eyes.

Back in Whitney's room, Lettie sat on the bed, feeling shaky. What if Whitney *was* pregnant? And with Sol's baby?

Hiding in the back of Ebeneezers Coffeehouse near Union Station, with her sunglasses on and a baseball cap pulled over her eyes, Jackie sipped her mocha latte and waited for Eric to tell her what the *hell* he wanted.

"Look, I'm really sorry about this," he said, leaning closer.

She wanted to pull away from him, but she moved in so she could whisper, "Just tell me what he wants, and let's get this over with."

"The senator thinks your mother has lots of good polling data on the PAPPies," Eric said. "He needs you to get it for him. He wants it all. He needs to know what kind of threat they pose to the Republicans, especially during the next election."

"You've got to be kidding me! That could be thousands of pages! Tell the Republicans to do their own research."

"Look, it's not that bad, it's just—"

"Don't tell me it's not that bad," Jackie said. "You're not the one betraying your family and being forced into this situation."

"You don't think I'm being forced into this?" Eric threw his hands up. "I like you. I want us to have a relationship. But he's my boss. My job's on the line."

"You don't even like your job."

"Yes, but I have to consider my career. My future," Eric said. "I'm not some kid fooling around before I go to college."

"Right." Jackie rolled her eyes. "Like that's what I'm doing? Meanwhile, you're working for a guy who blackmails girls who are barely legal, and gets behind ridiculous conservative platforms you don't agree with. Don't get all superior with me."

Eric downed the last of his coffee and stood up. "Jackie, please be reasonable. I told you what he wants. He's giving you a week to come up with it. I'm sorry."

As he walked off, a panicky desperation set in.

She had two obvious choices in front of her. Give Senator Griffin what he wanted. Or wind up as front-page news.

But if she gave in to the senator, would it ever end? He'd keep demanding more. And she couldn't keep spying on her mother—it was eating away at her—and she obviously couldn't rely on Eric to make it go away. And besides that, she didn't think she could put up a front for much longer. She felt like crap, she couldn't sleep, she could barely eat, and she was taking it out on Andrew.

But she couldn't let the photos go viral either.

That left choice number three: trading one blackmailer for another.

Taylor's mom.

EIGHTEEN

Jennifer Cane didn't resemble Taylor in either looks or personality. They both had blue eyes, but Taylor's were a piercing ocean blue, while Mrs. Cane's were dark, like lapis lazuli. And unlike Mrs. Cane's compact, athletic build, Taylor was thin with lean curves that even Jackie envied. And while Taylor had white-blond hair, wore heavy eyeliner, mascara, and deep red lipstick (all Dior), and owned every item from Betsey Johnson's line, Mrs. Cane wore her light brown hair in a low ponytail, very little makeup, and always wore the same thing: a black knee-length skirt and suit jacket covering a white shell—the professional attire of a typical Washington female powerbroker. Everything about Taylor had said *fun, wild, party!* And everything about her mother said cold and calculating.

"So you have a problem?" she asked.

She and Jackie were sitting across from each other in

wingback chairs in the Canes' formal library. Nothing warm and fuzzy there that would make you want to open up. Jackie tried to imagine it was Taylor—not her no-nonsense mom—whom she was spilling her guts to.

And she just fell apart.

The floodgates opened, tears streamed down her cheeks, and between sobs (and probably half incoherently) she related everything that had happened with Eric and Senator Griffin.

Taylor's mother didn't interrupt even once, though at one point, she pulled out her iPhone.

Finally done, Jackie felt spent, as if she'd just run a marathon. All she wanted to do now was lie down and fall asleep for a few days before facing the world again.

"You obviously want these pictures deleted," Mrs. Cane said.

Jackie nodded. "It was just a terrible mistake. I don't know what I was *thinking*."

Jennifer Cane cracked a smile, and a little bit of Taylor seemed to peek out. "You weren't, of course." She tapped two of her fingers against the iPhone. "And you want me to take care of it now?"

Jackie felt like her heart had stopped. It sounded like she was about to talk price—money or favors, it didn't matter. Jackie had neither to offer. "What could I ever do for you, though?"

She shrugged. "That remains to be seen."

Jackie ran a hand through her hair. *Please, please help me.* She had nowhere else to turn.

Mrs. Cane frowned. "Don't look so worried. I don't deal in blackmail. I deal in favors. When I take care of this, the pictures will be gone, so I won't be holding them over your head. But at some point in the future, I might ask a favor of you."

Jackie straightened her back, summoned her courage, and looked right into her steely eyes. "And if I *don't* return the favor?"

"Then you don't," she said. "That's a risk you and I both take."

The hidden warning in her words didn't escape Jackie. Failure to return the favor would create a powerful enemy.

"And you're *sure* you can get the pictures deleted?"

She laughed. "From Hampton Griffin? I'll have it done before the end of the day."

Palpable relief washed over Jackie. She stood up. "If you're willing to take the risk that I won't return your favor, I'm willing to risk asking you for one."

Mrs. Cane's face broke into a rare smile. She held out her hand to shake Jackie's. "Then, Jackie Whitman, you have yourself a deal."

Whitney emerged from the bathroom, grinning, and Lettie breathed a sigh of relief.

"It's negative?" Lettie asked, though the answer was pretty clear.

Whitney did a little dance, shaking her rear end as she waved around the pregnancy test.

"Here, let me see it," Lettie said, standing up and grabbing it out of Whitney's hand. She wanted to make sure there was no mistake.

Sure enough, a big blue (−) stared back at her.

"I'm not preggers!"

"Seriously." Lettie laughed in sheer relief. "I was trying not to get ahead of ourselves and think about how much that would suck, but . . . well, it would suck."

"You're telling me!"

Whitney flopped on her bed, burying her face in her pillows. When she looked up, Lettie had never seen her so serious. "Thanks for being here for me, Lets. You're a good person and a good friend."

Lettie nodded, though she didn't feel like she'd been a good friend at all. It had taken a pregnancy scare to get her to see Whitney as a real person. "Do you want to go catch a movie or something?"

"Really?"

Lettie shrugged. "I've been going crazy, waiting for Daniel to call me. A movie would be a fun distraction."

"Shit, just invite him along."

"What? Oh, no, I could never do that."

Whitney shook her head in amazement. "Oh, Lets, you're such a prude sometimes. Just text him and tell him we're going to a movie if he wants to meet us there."

"But—"

"No buts. I mean, it's not a date because he's just tagging along with the two of us, but it'll make him feel like he's starting to win you over. You can't make guys do *all* the work. They've gotta think you're interested too."

Lettie wasn't so sure about that. But she pulled out her phone anyway and texted Daniel.

"You know, if you don't get your period soon, you should go to the doctor," Lettie said. "Even if you're not pregnant, there could be something wrong."

"Whatever," Whitney said with a dismissive wave. "Being on the rag interferes with my sex life anyway."

"Ew, TMI!"

Lettie's phone chimed. As she read the text from Daniel, a slow smile crept over her face.

"What's he say?"

Lettie held up the phone so Whitney could see.

I'm in for a movie. Where and when?

"Sweet!" Whitney said. "And let's stop at CVS. I need to buy a giant box of condoms so I never run out again. After this scare, I might make them wear double."

Lettie rolled her eyes and grabbed her backpack. Whitney would never replace Taylor—no one could. And she'd never be as trustworthy as Jackie or Laura Beth—they'd been through so much together. But it would be nice to hang with someone carefree for a change, someone with the kind of crazy energy Taylor had.

She went into the bathroom to pee. Washing her hands, she stared at the dark circles under her eyes that Whitney had mentioned. She really did need to get more sleep.

On a whim, Lettie grabbed the two pill bottles on the counter and poured out a handful of each. She probably wouldn't take them, but it couldn't hurt to have them just in case.

Overwhelmed with relief, Jackie walked to her car on an adrenaline high. The danger was over and she'd handled it without going to her mother. She'd taken care of it herself.

But now she was dying to tell someone. She turned the key in the ignition and headed for Laura Beth's house.

The maid led Jackie into the family room, where Laura Beth

lay sprawled on a wine-colored Victorian sofa, wearing one of her favorite Juicy Couture exercise suits, watching a *Project Runway* marathon.

"Wow, how bored are you?" Jackie laughed.

Laura Beth moaned. "Sol's back in New York. But at least we've been Skyping every night. I had such a great time with him when he was here."

"Really? I'd never have guessed," Jackie teased as she joined her friend on the sofa. She was glad Andrew's matchmaking was working. Laura Beth didn't have all that much experience with guys.

"Yeah, especially after Mama's party," Laura Beth said. She lowered her voice. "Mama's upstairs. I don't want her to hear. But I get why you've been so mad at Andrew about not having sex. I could tell Sol really wanted to do it the other night. I mean, I could really tell. And I wanted to, too. Not that we *did*. He was a perfect gentleman. It'll happen soon, though. I just know it."

Jackie felt a pang of envy. She'd always thought she'd be the first one after Taylor. But she didn't say it.

"Sol and I are making plans to see each other next weekend," Laura Beth added. "We can do couples stuff now with you and Andrew. Won't that be awesome?"

Yeah, if there still is a me-and-Andrew. On the drive over, Jackie had decided the best way to fend off Jennifer Cane's favor was to come clean with Andrew—and her mother. It would be horrible telling them, but once they knew, Mrs. Cane wouldn't have anything to hold over Jackie's head.

Which meant there was a distinct possibility that Andrew and Jackie wouldn't be together next weekend.

Might as well start coming clean now. "Laura Beth, I've got something to tell you."

Laura Beth sat up.

Jackie repeated the same story she told Jennifer Cane—the Kennedy Center and the blackmail. Except, this time, she managed to hold it together. Instead of sounding like a blubbering idiot, her voice only cracked once or twice and she didn't cry at all. As clichéd as it was, getting it off her chest really *did* help.

"Oh my Lord!" Laura Beth said, looking distraught. "I can't believe Uncle Ham would do that! Tell me you're kidding."

Jackie shook her head. "I wish I was."

"Well, don't do anything else for him!" Laura Beth was practically shouting. "He might be an old friend of our family, but he's evil. And Eric! What a creep. He must have been in on the plan to set you up."

"No, I think it was Whitney."

Laura Beth looked stricken. "Whitney? What's she got to do with it?"

Jackie sighed. "We were all at your house when I was talking on the phone to Eric, arranging to meet him. I went into the bathroom when he called, and when I came out, Whitney was standing right there. She must have heard the whole conversation."

"You really think she'd do that, tell someone what she heard?" Laura Beth asked. She squirmed as if uncomfortable.

"Think about it—it all fits," Jackie said. "She probably told her mother, who called Senator Griffin to ask what he thought about his big-shot aide hooking up with the White House chief of staff's underaged daughter."

Before Laura Beth could answer, Libby Ballou strode into the room.

"What in the hell is goin' on now?" she demanded.

"It's nothing, Mama," Laura Beth said quickly. "It's just boy stuff."

"Nonsense, my girl, I heard every word."

Jackie sucked in her breath. Crap.

Miss Libby walked over to the sofa and squeezed between them. "Jackie Whitman, for someone so astute you've managed to get yourself in a right pickle. And I'm appalled, absolutely appalled, at Ham. Why, Preston—God rest his soul—never would have stooped so low as to blackmail children."

"Mama, this is a disaster," Laura Beth said, her voice shaking. "This could destroy Jackie."

"No, I've got it under control," Jackie said. "I went to Taylor's mom. She's going to take care of it. Get the pictures deleted and everything."

Laura Beth's eyes widened. "Taylor's mom? You went to Jennifer Cane?"

"I had to, I—"

"Oh, baby," Miss Libby said, cupping Jackie's face with her hands. "Please tell me you didn't."

Jackie's heart thumped. Just moments ago, she'd felt so good about her decision. But now, seeing the worry in Miss Libby's eyes, she wondered if she'd made a terrible mistake.

"You don't think she'll take care of it?" Jackie asked.

"Oh no, she'll take care of it all right. This'll be a piece a cake for Jennifer. But you'll have to face the consequences of this decision down the line. Believe me, I know."

Jackie looked at her nervously. Was she worried for Jackie

or for herself? Had Jennifer Cane demanded a favor in return for covering up the fact that Preston Ballou died in a young woman's bed?

"And if—God forbid—anything like this ever happens to any of you girls again, you come to me first," Miss Libby said. "I can take care of things like this, and you won't have to worry about me having some hidden agenda."

She looked so grim, Jackie started to worry all over again. *Maybe telling Andrew and Mom won't stop Jennifer Cane asking for favors, after all.*

"Oh, Mama, what could you have done?"

"Why, Laura Beth, they don't call Libby Ballou the Velvet Steamroller for nothing." She beamed.

"The what? What are you talkin' about?"

"That's what they used to call me behind my back, back when your daddy was alive. They also had a name for your daddy, but it's nothing a lady could repeat. However, suffice it to say that between Preston's politickin' and my flirtin' we knew just about everything that went on in this town. Why, this one time . . ."

As she launched into one of her stories, Jackie replayed the scene in the Canes' library. She wanted to believe Jennifer Cane would help her out because of her friendship with Taylor, not because of any future payback. She was cold and calculating, but she was also a mother—and Jackie had been her daughter's best friend. That had to count for something.

Didn't it?

NINETEEN

Without even knocking, Jennifer Cane walked into Hampton Griffin's office. The senator had his back to her, his chair swiveled around to face the window behind his desk. He was tapping his foot impatiently, talking to someone on speakerphone.

Jennifer swept her eyes around the room. Two things stood out: the huge, antique mahogany desk piled with papers, and the ornately framed photo of him chopping wood with his hero, Ronald Reagan, on the president's Santa Barbara ranch.

Jennifer smiled to herself. A man like Ham had to wonder how he had gone from those glory days to this: pleading with a gossip columnist.

"You can't use the story yet, Ms. Mills," he was saying. "The Bible says those who have patience inherit what has been promised."

Jennifer heard the gossip columnist snort. "Well, it also says the meek shall inherit the Earth and neither you nor I believe that one."

Ham gave a weak laugh and cleared his throat. "Well, you promised *me* you'd get me information. I want to know if this talk about impeachment is getting serious."

"I'll see what I can do. But I don't see why I can't run with this Jackie story now." *So. Tracey Mills knows about Jackie's little tryst too.* Jennifer couldn't believe her luck, stumbling on this little gem. She moved in a bit closer so she didn't miss a word.

"Ma'am, I told you that it does not suit my purposes to give you those photos at this point in time. I don't know how you do things in Hollywood, but around here it works this way: If you make nice with me now, I will be real *nice* to you when the time is right."

"Nice doesn't pay my bills, Senator. I need gossip that I can use. Now. All you've told me so far is that Jackie Whitman was photographed at the Kennedy Center in a compromising position with your aide and that I can't run it."

He gave an exasperated sigh.

"I *promise* you will get those photos once I'm done with them. In the meantime, just to keep you happy—and as a sign of good faith—I will give you another juicy tidbit that you can use in your story when I finally give you the go-ahead."

"Now I'm intrigued."

"You know Laura Beth Ballou, I believe?"

"Yes, she's a close friend of Jackie's."

He chuckled. "Are you quite sure about that? Guess who tipped me off to Jackie's romantic little rendezvous at the Kennedy Center?"

"No! Why would she do that?"

"According to the little lady herself, she overheard Jackie Whitman on her cell phone making her plans for the evening and decided to call me to put a stop to it. She thought I would be outraged that my aide was consortin' with the enemy—especially an underaged one."

"She did that? What a fool."

"I was surprised myself, especially with her being the daughter of the man who wrote the book on dirty politics. She obviously thought she could come to me as an old family friend . . ."

They both laughed.

"But your patience will be rewarded, Ms. Mills. Eventually, you will get the photos and the story."

Satisfied that she'd heard enough, Jennifer walked right up to the desk and pressed the END CALL button on the phone.

Ham whirled around.

"What the hell . . . ?" He stopped cold.

"Hello, Ham."

"Jennifer? I didn't realize you had an appointment to see me today," he said, feigning an air of superiority. "Unfortunately I'm going to have to excuse myself. I have a meeting. Perhaps we could reschedule."

She laughed. "I don't do appointments in this town. You, of all people, know that."

"Yes, well, it's always great to see you," he said. "You are looking lovely as usual, my dear, but—"

She interrupted and cut to the chase.

"I thought you might like to know that I have a friend who recently saw you go into the Willard Hotel with a beautiful dark-haired intern."

He looked at his watch and started to rise out of his chair. "Really, I must excuse myself—"

"My friend, of course, is an excellent photographer."

Ham sat back down.

"Really, Ham, you should be a little more discreet," Jennifer chided. "I have enough pictures of you with interns to make Tiger Woods look like an altar boy. Your constituents will be demanding you go to rehab for a sex addiction. They'll want your head . . . among other things."

She tossed him a USB drive with all of the pictures she had, in the event he didn't want to take her word for it. Though she'd dealt with him enough to know he *would* take her word for it.

He did.

"And you of course have copies of the pictures on this drive . . . elsewhere?"

"Of course," she said with a smile.

"What do you want?"

She held out her hand. "Your cell phone, please."

"How do you know I haven't made copies?" He sounded slightly smug.

Jennifer shrugged. "I doubt you did. You're about as computer savvy as a toad." He was also arrogant, which meant he thought he was so untouchable he didn't need to back up his evidence.

"And if I give you the phone . . . ?"

"I'll delete the pictures, and so long as they don't somehow resurface, on Ms. Mills' blog, for instance, or anywhere else, those pictures of you won't be released to your wife and the public."

"You just want the photos deleted? Nothing else?" he asked.

Jennifer nodded. He pulled the cell out of his breast pocket and handed it over.

"You must be really worried about that immigration bill passing to stoop to blackmailing a young girl. Must have cost you a pretty penny in favors to flip those two votes." She straightened a photo of his wife on his desk. "But I'm sure you covered your tracks. Whatever you promised them must be buried deep in another bill—the appropriations bill, maybe?"

It took him a second to regain his composure. But it was enough time for Jennifer to confirm all she needed to know— he'd done exactly as she'd guessed. Not that it was all that hard to read him. Hampton Griffin was not a particularly tricky man to figure out.

Jennifer opened his cell and quickly found the two pictures of Jackie and Eric. For a moment she contemplated sending copies of the photos to her own phone. But a memory suddenly took over—five-year-old Taylor and Jackie, snuggled up in bed for a sleepover. She hit the delete button before she could change her mind.

Besides, the way to use Jackie was to befriend her. A person's sense of loyalty could be a powerful weapon.

She put the cell on his desk.

He sneered at her. "You know, Jennifer, I know plenty about you too."

"And?"

"Blackmail is the least of your skeletons," he said, puffing his chest out. "I know you and Libby Ballou covered up how Preston died that night—in the arms of a sweet young thing showing him a good time. And I also know it's not the first time you and Libby covered up one of Preston's indiscretions."

If you think you can trump me when it comes to playing this game, you're a bigger fool than I thought.

"I also know the truth about how you and Preston Ballou really earned your fortunes," she said with a smile. She let the veiled threat sit for a moment. "It's been nice catching up, Ham. Please keep in mind that Jackie Whitman was my late daughter's best friend."

"Yes, I've always thought of you as the maternal type." He sneered at her again. "But you and I both know that sometimes we have to do unpleasant things for the sake of our great nation. I will leave Miss Whitman alone for now, but I'm not making any promises for the future."

Jennifer smiled and nodded as she walked out.

Neither am I.

Jackie was standing next to Andrew's red Prius when she got the call from Jennifer Cane.

"It's done."

"Thank you," Jackie said simply, stifling the urge to gush into the phone about how grateful she was and how she didn't know how she'd ever repay her. Better to keep it brief.

She hung up and got in the car.

"I thought we'd get out near the Reflecting Pool," Andrew said. "We can talk there."

Jackie nodded. What an irony, fighting with Andrew and probably breaking up in the same place where all of them had had such fun. This time last year—and the year before—Taylor had stripped down to her underwear and jumped into the shallow water.

Both times, she'd been hauled out by the police.

"But it's a tradition!" she'd protested to the cops.

The memory made Jackie smile.

"It'll be hard to park there," she said.

Andrew shrugged. "Mark'll make sure I don't get a ticket."

Jackie nodded and glanced at the Secret Service tail in the side-view mirror. Just one more perk of being the president's son. You never got ticketed.

They drove in silence past George Washington Hospital and GW's campus, the tension mounting.

This was it. Jackie knew it. She was going to tell him everything—or almost everything—and then they'd break up. End of the fairy tale. She'd been trying to prepare herself for the worst all afternoon. But it didn't help. She still felt nauseous.

All those good times—the family holidays, the campouts at her father's summer house, the joke birthday gifts, hanging at the White House, kissing in the pool—all of it would be over.

Sure, things between them had been up and down for months. At the start of summer, she'd even considered breaking up with him—when she was obsessing over Eric and mad that Andrew wouldn't sleep with her. Every time she'd looked at him, all she could see was this wimpy guy who was always told how to act, what to say, and even how not to do *it* with his girl-friend. But now, they were getting along again—apart from her crappy mood swings, which had more to do with Senator Griffin and Eric Moran than anything Andrew did. She wasn't even in a hurry to have sex anymore. It would happen when it happened. And it would be great—because he was kind, and smart, and adorable. And he loved her. And she loved him. And that's why she *had* to come clean. Even if it meant risking everything.

Reaching the Mall, Andrew turned left on Constitution Avenue, did a quick U-turn, and pulled up to the curb. The still waters of the long, rectangular Reflecting Pool projected a perfect mirror image of the Capitol at one end and the Lincoln Memorial at the other.

Jackie and Andrew walked—side-by-side, but not touching—along one of the paths that crisscrossed West Potomac Park. The Secret Service agent shadowed them from a discreet distance.

Jackie never failed to be awed by the sight of the floodlit Capitol with its massive cast-iron dome. She turned around to look at the lights blinking on the pointed cap of the Washington Monument.

She spotted a circle of grass surrounded by bushes.

"Let's sit over there. It's nice and private," she suggested.

"Perfect, because I need to tell you something," Andrew said.

Jackie took a deep breath.

"Me first," she said. "It's going to make you angry, but I need you to just hear me out."

He looked puzzled.

"I cheated on you," she said before he could interrupt.

And then she told him about her and Eric in her mother's office, running into him again in Georgetown, and arranging to meet him at the Kennedy Center. She spoke quickly, hardly taking a breath, not daring to look at him.

She even told him about Senator Griffin catching them. She stopped before the blackmail. He would have to tell his mother and then the shit would really hit the fan.

When she was finished, she forced herself to look up. His face was impassive. He wasn't even looking at her, just staring out over the Mall. She had no idea what he was thinking.

"If you want to break up with me, I understand. Really," she said in a low voice, her eyes welling. "But please don't. I know

I've given you a hard time about having sex, but I won't anymore. I don't know why I was obsessing, but it doesn't matter. I love you, Andrew. I really do. And I know there's stuff we still need to work on, but we're great together and we *can* fix it. If you still want to."

Finally, Andrew turned his head back to her. "I hate the thing with Eric. He's such a fucking scumbag. But, Jackie, I already knew."

For a moment, she swore her heart stopped. "What? How?"

"Someone saw you two together at the Kennedy Center and told me later."

"Someone other than Senator Griffin? Who?"

Andrew shrugged. "It doesn't matter who. I knew you were angry about the promise ring, and I'd been avoiding you. I figured this guy was coming on to you, and if there was anything going on you'd tell me eventually." He paused. "I also thought that maybe it meant we needed a break from each other."

It was like he'd punched her in the stomach. Even though she'd convinced herself their break-up was inevitable, part of her had still believed he'd forgive her.

"Do you want to break up?" she whispered, her voice quivering.

"No," he said quietly. "But you might."

What's he talking about? She opened her mouth to ask him, but he started talking before she could.

"You were out of town when Taylor died," he said. "You weren't at the party. And you didn't see Tay—she was just flirting like crazy."

Jackie shrugged. "Okay. So?"

Andrew shook his head. "You don't understand. She was

ella monroe

flirting with *me*. I mean, *really* flirting. Telling me all this stuff about what she wanted to do to me." He raced on. "She even followed me upstairs when I went to the bathroom."

Now it was Jackie's turn to shake her head. *Taylor would never flirt with Andrew. He must have misread her. She was probably teasing, trying to make some other guy jealous.*

But she was stunned by what he said next.

"She was all over me, kissing me, grabbing me, telling me how she had always wanted me," Andrew continued.

"What? No, that's not possible, Taylor would never—"

Andrew cut her off. "I pushed her away and told her no. I told her how I was in love with you, how being with you, falling in love but taking it slowly, not wanting to wreck our friendship, had been what I'd wanted forever. And I wouldn't risk losing you.

"She backed off. But then later, Laura Beth said they'd run out of food and alcohol and asked Tay and me to go and pick up more."

"And you couldn't just say no?" Jackie said, her anger rising.

Andrew didn't answer. He just looked at her, and in that look, she knew. The guilt on his face, the anguish in his eyes, the way he braced himself as if he expected her to hit him. It said it all.

"You *slept with her*?" she asked. "You *slept with* Taylor?"

"Yes," Andrew whispered. "We got in her car and she asked me to take her to Battery Kemble. She swore it was because she needed to talk."

Jackie tried to swallow, but there was a giant lump in her throat. Battery Kemble was a secluded park near the party, tucked into a quiet suburban street, packed with kids playing soccer on Saturdays but deserted once the sun went down.

"She just lost it. She started crying, saying something about how nothing would ever be the same and she needed me to help her. I couldn't understand what she was talking about—or if she was even saying *anything*. But she was so unbelievably upset, she was almost hysterical, so I put my arms around her, just to try to calm her down, to comfort her. The next thing I knew, we were kissing. And then it just happened."

Jackie didn't know she was going to slap him until she did it. Hard. The sharp crack of her hand striking his cheek seemed to ricochet off every tree, every blade of grass, and echo a thousand times in her head.

For weeks, she'd been the one who'd betrayed him. And now, suddenly, her betrayal seemed insignificant. Nothing compared to his. Staring at his shocked face, stained red from her slap, she felt she was looking at a stranger.

"In her car?" she asked. "In the backseat or the front? Or did you get out and do it on the grass?"

"Jackie, come on," he said, his voice breaking.

"No. I want to know!"

He shook his head. "No, you don't. And there's more."

"More?" she scoffed. "How could there be more than *that*?"

"On the way back to the party, I was upset. All I could think about was how I'd betrayed you."

This had to be a dream. A bad dream. A nightmare.

"I told Taylor I was going to tell you what happened," Andrew continued. "And she just completely flipped out. We started arguing and she kept saying how you'd never forgive her and you wouldn't understand."

"She was right about that."

"She kept telling me to drive faster, telling me to hurry up and get her back to the party. She was screaming at me and punching me in the shoulder, and saying she only slept with me because she *had* to."

She had *to? What the hell did that mean?*

"I floored it until I couldn't see my Secret Service tail anymore. I just wanted to drop her the fuck off and go call you."

Jackie thought she'd misheard him. She had to have misheard him.

"Wait," Jackie said. "*You* were driving?"

Andrew was wincing, like he was in physical pain. He ran a hand through his hair again. "That's what I've been trying to tell you. She kept hitting me and grabbing at the wheel. I lost control of the car. And we slammed into the tree."

He'd been lying. All this time. To her, to his mom, to the police; he'd lied to everyone.

Andrew stumbled on.

"When Mark pulled up, Taylor had been thrown from the car. She was lying near the tree and she didn't have a pulse, and he said, 'She must have been driving without a seat belt.'"

"He didn't know you were driving? How could he not know?"

Andrew had asked himself that same question thousands of times. Either Mark couldn't tell who was driving because of the rain or he was covering up for Andrew. He didn't want to know the answer. He couldn't do anything more than shrug.

"He radioed for an ambulance and told them the driver was dead. It just snowballed from there. Everyone thought Taylor had been driving, and the story got out like that, and I was too scared to say anything.

"And that's why I couldn't bring myself to make love to you. I just felt so fucking guilty."

He didn't tell her what a relief it had been when his mother came to him soon after and asked him to wear a promise ring to counter a new wave of Republican attack ads accusing her of being a free-love, pro-abortion liberal. He'd readily agreed, thinking a celibacy pledge would take the pressure off him with Jackie.

"Say something," he said, his voice cracking again.

"What could I *possibly* say?" She laughed bitterly. "You lied to me. For months. About everything." Jackie shook her head.

"Andrew, if anyone finds out about this, you could go to jail."

"I know. Fuck, I know. But it's not even that simple. If I turn myself in now, it would kill my mother's re-election chances, and tarnish your mom's image too. The press would assume it was a cover-up."

"That sounds like you're making excuses."

"I know," Andrew said. "I know it does, but it's true."

Jackie shook her head again.

"What?"

"I hadn't thought there was anything, any more, that could make *me* want to break up with you."

"And?"

"I was wrong," she said, and she walked away.

He watched her, waiting for her to glance back or turn around or something. But she just kept going.

He felt totally drained and lost. Because he knew he'd never find another girl like Jackie. He'd never love anybody the way he loved her.

Whitney punched in the number, steeling herself to channel her mother at her bitchiest. Because she *really* didn't want to make this call. All she wanted to do was go back to Cali, surf, and get high. But that wasn't gonna happen till she made her mother happy. And her mom had made it clear that Whitney's budding friendship with Lettie wasn't gonna cut it. Because poor Lets didn't have the power to get Whitney a permanent membership to the *Crapital* Girls club.

"Hey, Whitney, what's up?" Laura Beth answered.

"Where are you?"

"I'm just at home workin' on my college essay."

Whitney rolled her eyes. What a loser. "We have to talk."

She heard Laura Beth sigh. "You're not still mad that I didn't invite you and that guy you met in the elevator to the pool party, are you? I keep telling you I'm sorry. But I think you would have felt out of place, because it was for, like, *real* couples."

Whitney laughed. "*Real* couples? What? You and Sol? Lettie and Daniel?"

Laura Beth didn't answer.

"Whatever," Whitney said. "That's not why I called."

"If it's because you didn't get to go to Mama's party, I explained that too. We—"

"I know you screwed over Jackie," Whitney interrupted bluntly. "You know, your so-called best friend?"

There was dead silence and for a second Whitney thought LB had hung up on her.

"I don't know what you're talking about." Laura Beth's voice was firm and flat.

"I know you told that old senator about Jackie and Eric hooking up at the Kennedy Center," Whitney said in the coldest voice she could muster. "Are you *that* desperate to get Andrew for yourself?"

"What? No!" Laura Beth stammered. "It wasn't like that at all. I was trying to protect—"

"It's sure gonna look bad to Jackie when she finds out, no matter how you try to spin it."

"No, I . . ." Laura Beth paused, then her voice turned steely. "What do you want?"

Whitney almost felt sorry for LB and her lame attempt to sound tough. Almost, but not quite.

"If I have to stay in this crappy town for my senior year, I want into your little Capital Girls club." She had to catch herself from calling it *Crapital* Girls. "Starting now, you're gonna be my new BFF. And you're gonna make sure Jackie wants to be my BFF too."

"I can't force Jackie to be your friend!"

"No? Well, then, how do you think I should tell her about what you did?" Whitney said. "I could send an anonymous letter or I could just be upfront and give her a call. Or I could let my mom run with the story on her blog. Then *everyone* would know how you sold out your best friend."

"No!"

"Then you're officially my new BFF. And if any of those Excelsior bitches diss me, you're gonna call them on it." Whitney paused for dramatic effect, a smile spreading over her face. "Essentially, I own you."

"Maybe if you weren't such a backstabbing bitch, you wouldn't need to be blackmailin' me to make friends," Laura Beth yelled.

"That being nice to me thing? It starts now," Whitney said. "After all, Jackie's just a phone call away."

With that, Whitney hung up. *Let her sit on that for a while.* It wasn't like she had any choice—this was way better for her than the story getting online, or becoming a *Washington Tattler* column.

Her mom would be off her back now, at least. Senior year might be bearable. And—not that the little Southern Belle Bitch would see it this way—but she'd just saved LB's friendship with Jackie, not to mention saved them both from public humiliation.

In a sick kind of way, I just did something nice.

"That blackmailing, conniving Cali slut!" Laura Beth hurled the phone across her bedroom, then collapsed on the bed, burying her face in her hands. She *hadn't* called Uncle Ham to get Jackie in trouble. After overhearing Jackie's cell call with Eric in the powder room, she only wanted to stop her from cheating on Andrew. Eric seemed like such a creep.

Other than Sol, nothing was going the way she'd planned.

After Taylor died, she'd hoped the tragedy would bring the three of them closer, that going through something so horrible together, they'd become even better friends. Instead, Lettie was spending most of her free time with Daniel or Whitney. And not only had Jackie kept a *huge* secret from her, she'd gone to *Jennifer Cane* for help. And now her senior year was going to be spent at Whitney's beck and call.

What was she going to do?

TWENTY

Lettie couldn't believe how much she loved listening to Daniel talk about skateboarding. Who knew she'd ever care about lip tricks and grinds? But Daniel's enthusiasm was contagious. That's how he was about everything he liked—passionate. Totally different from most guys.

"Wait," she laughed into the phone. "What's a bomb drop again?"

"Only one of the oldest tricks in the book!" Daniel teased. "No, it's pretty easy. All you do is get high up on a platform with a good ramp. Then you drop off the platform with the board in your hand and try to land flat on the ramp."

"And how is this different from the acid drop that you showed me the other day?" she asked

"Good catch. It's not. Same trick, different name." She could tell by his voice he was smiling. "Now that you're an expert, do

273

you want to come with me to that skateboard competition I told you about? I mean, I'm leaving in less than two weeks. I want to hang with you as much as I can."

Lettie didn't have to think twice. Just as she was about to say, *"Of course!"* the front door slammed. She looked up, expecting to see her sisters returning from a play date across the hall.

But it wasn't them.

It was her mother, slumped against the door frame, tears streaming down her face. Something was very wrong.

Lettie's mind was racing. A coup back home must have toppled the government. The embassy was closing. The family would be kicked out of the country.

"Daniel," she said quietly. "I gotta go. I'll call you back later."

She hung up without waiting for an answer. "Mamá, what is it? What's wrong?" she asked in Spanish. She rushed over to her mother, her heart thumping so loudly it was drowning out her own thoughts.

"Oh, Laetitia," her mother sobbed, throwing her arms around Lettie, squeezing her tightly as her whole body shook and her hysterical sobs got louder.

"Mamá, what's happened?" Lettie asked again.

"Esta muerto! Esta muerto!" her mother wailed between sobs. *He is dead, he is dead!*

Lettie's heart pounded in her chest. "Who, Mamá, who is dead?"

"Paz!" she cried.

Lettie thought she was going to pass out. The room was spinning and she sucked in air, trying to catch her breath.

She pictured Paz, caught in a civil war. Dying defending a corrupt government.

A world without her brother just didn't seem possible.

Her mother's wailing brought Lettie back to reality. She thought of her sisters—she didn't want them to see their mother sobbing like this. Lettie guided her mother to the couch, and, wiping off her own tears with her bare arm, she ran across the hall to ask the neighbor to keep the girls until she came back for them.

Back in the apartment, her mother looked as if she hadn't moved. "Mamá, tell me what happened," she said, sitting down next to her.

But all her mother could say was *"No se, no se,"* over and over again. *I don't know, I don't know.*

Lettie had never felt so alone. She wished Daniel were here to comfort her.

The front door opened again. *Thank God, it's Papá.* Surely he had the answers.

But when she looked up at him, his eyes were bloodshot and his cheeks were wet. Her father—her strong, proud father—who never cried. Not even when they'd found out Paz was involved with a gang.

Which meant it was true.

Paz was dead.

The two of them would never again stay up all night listening to Guarania. Never would she and Paz cook Sopa Paraguaya on Mother's Day when the whole family got together to watch *Cerro Cora,* their favorite movie.

Just a few minutes ago, talking with Daniel, she was *so* happy. Now she couldn't imagine ever being happy again. Lettie sank to her knees on the threadbare rug, her own sobs echoing her mother's.

Her face blotched and swollen from crying, Jackie opened her front door, slipping upstairs without her mother knowing. All she wanted to do was crawl into bed, pull the covers over her head, and sleep until this nightmare was over.

Taylor and Andrew. Taylor sleeping with Andrew. Taylor betraying her.

She still couldn't believe it. How could Andrew have done this to her? How could *Taylor*? You just don't do that to your best friend. Maybe Taylor's friendship was an act. If that was true, what else had been a lie?

Jackie looked down at her charm bracelet, which was usually so comforting. She tore it off her wrist and stuffed it in the drawer of her bedside table. She couldn't even look at it without feeling like someone was twisting a knife into her chest.

How many times had she wished Taylor back to life? Missing her laugh, and her advice, and how she always knew exactly what to do and say. Now she just wished she were alive so she could take her by the shoulders, shake her, and scream, *"How could you?"*

But *Andrew* let it happen. He was a cheater and a liar too.

Jackie needed to clear the slate before she could move on.

She needed to tell her mother *everything*. After all, if Taylor had betrayed her, Jennifer Cane wouldn't hesitate for a second.

Jackie forced herself to get out of bed. She could hear her mom talking loudly in her office down the hall.

By the time she got to the office door, her mom was bellowing.

"How the fuck did that happen?" her mother was shouting. Jackie paused, listening on the other side of the door. "Dammit!

You've *got* to be kidding me. How could we have lost those two votes?"

Jackie leaned against the wall for support. She was almost hyperventilating. *Please, please let her not be talking about the immigration bill.*

As if on cue, her mom confirmed her worst fears.

"I want to know how the hell Griffin managed to flip them. Goddammit!"

Her mother went quiet, obviously listening to the person on the other end of the line.

This is all my fault.

"Without their support, we're sunk. The bill doesn't have a leg to stand on. Our two best chances at getting this bill passed just switched sides."

She couldn't bear to listen anymore. Her stomach muscles clenched. She lifted a hand to her mouth and ran for the bathroom, locking the door behind her.

Jackie sank down onto the cool tile floor.

She tried to think. There wasn't any point confessing to her mother now. It was too late. The damage was done. If she knew now, her mother would never forgive Jackie's betrayal.

Just like Taylor had betrayed Jackie.

TWENTY-ONE

Jackie stood over Taylor's grave, wearing her Chanel sunglasses to hide her tears. Last time, she'd wept over the loss of her best friend, wondering how she could live the rest of her life without her. This time, she felt like she'd lost her best friend all over again—someone she thought she knew and could trust who'd plotted against her and seduced her boyfriend.

Because she had *to.* Whatever that meant.

She thought back to last night and her meeting with Laura Beth and Lettie on the marble steps at the feet of Abraham Lincoln. The twenty-foot statue of the sixteenth president seated inside a faux Greek Doric temple looked down the grassy stretch of the Mall.

History had been made over and over in that spot.

A crowd of at least 75,000 fans heard Marian Anderson sing after the Daughters of the American Revolution barred the black contralto from their concert hall, and Martin Luther King had given his famous "I Have a Dream" speech before 250,000 civil rights protestors. Right there.

The Capital Girls made their own history in this spot. It was Taylor's idea to start an end-of-summer tradition freshman year. They'd sit by the Lincoln Memorial until midnight, doing vodka shots and swapping secrets.

Last night was the first time without Taylor.

"You should thank me for this," Jackie said to Taylor's gravestone. "I didn't tell them about you and Andrew. I don't want them to feel betrayed by you the way I do. I don't want to make them any more miserable than they already are."

Jackie didn't know what was up with Laura Beth, who seemed to be moody *all* the time lately—maybe she was having problems with Sol, just like her and Andrew. Lettie seemed permanently stuck in a pit of depression. Paz was officially MIA and presumed dead. She told them she wanted to find some way to honor her brother, and they'd all agreed to start volunteering with wounded vets in the fall. Then Jackie and Laura Beth toasted him with vodka shots, while Lettie held on to hers, not lifting it to her lips.

They talked about senior year. Laura Beth decided she was going to go back to her singing lessons. She seemed more determined than ever to get into Juilliard or some other fine arts school.

And, of course, they dissected Whitney. "Screw her," Jackie had said. "Let her figure Excelsior out herself." She was done with backstabbers. Like Taylor. And Eric. And Andrew.

But Lettie wanted to give Whitney another chance. She insisted Whitney was basically a good person, just insecure.

To Jackie's shock, Laura Beth sided with Lettie. "Even if we can't stand her, it's like Mama says, keep your friends close and your enemies closer. She's gonna be way more trouble outside our group than inside."

Jackie was outvoted, although she grudgingly had to admit that anyone raised by Tracey Mills would be screwed up and deserving of some sympathy. Besides, she just didn't feel like arguing anymore.

Kicking Taylor's headstone lightly, Jackie spat out the words: "So I guess we've replaced you. And you better believe I'm watching Daniel. Who's to say *your twin* is not as conniving as you."

Jackie roughly wiped away the tears with the back of her hand. She was angry with herself for crying over Taylor now. Backstabbers didn't deserve to be cried over.

"What I just don't get is . . . why?" She dug the toe of her shoe into the grass. "Why would you do this? What the hell did you mean by you *had* to do it? What could be more important to you than our friendship? Unless our friendship was just a setup, just some kind of elaborate game?"

Jackie shook her head, then leaned down and whispered to the gravestone, "I'm going to find out all your secrets. You're going to be glad you're dead."

And then, straightening her back—because no one was going to screw with Jackie Whitman, D.C.'s It Girl, and get away with it—she ground her heel into the daisies, and walked away.

Without looking back.

ACKNOWLEDGMENTS

Thanks to our great husbands for their unwavering support, encouragement, and cooking. We couldn't have done it without you. And our heartfelt appreciation to Sara Goodman, Nancy Coffey, and Joanna Volpe, for their belief in this project.

Turn the page for
a sneak peek of

SECRETS AND LIES
A CAPITAL GIRLS NOVEL

Coming in Fall 2012
from St. Martin's Griffin

ONE

The start of school was Laura Beth's favorite time of year. Even better than Christmas. It was when Excelsior Prep buzzed with voices and anticipation, all the girls swapping summer gossip, finding out who was dating whom and who had been where. It was exciting every year, but this was the one Laura Beth had been dreaming of since she was a freshman.

This was her senior year.

And really, her summer news should be the talk of the school. After all, who else had a gorgeous *college* guy as a boyfriend? Unless, of course, you counted Jackie and her boyfriend, Andrew Price, who also just happened to be the president's son.

Laura Beth's stomach knotted at the thought of them. Jackie and Andrew. Andrew and Jackie. *Ankie.* Even though their romance was old news at this point, they still managed to get all the attention—both from the press and in the halls of their school.

287

And who knew if they were even a couple anymore? Jackie certainly wasn't acting like it. Not with the way she had thrown herself at that slimy congressional aide.

But even if they broke up, the press would never let it go. It'd run rampant through the newspapers and classrooms for months. Laura Beth felt a twinge of guilt—it's not that she wanted Jackie to be unhappy. She just wanted her own turn at center stage.

As Laura Beth strolled down the hallway, students parted to make way. Like royalty. *Well, that's one thing that's good about today,* she thought. Her eyes flicked over the groups of girls pressed against the walls and she took mental note of who looked thinner and who had indulged in too many umbrella drinks over the summer.

Halfway down the hall, she stopped next to Lettie's locker and stuck her hand in her brand-new steel gray Kooba satchel—*the* must-have color of the season. Even though she wore Excelsior's mandatory plaid skirt and collared shirt, Laura Beth knew how to stand out. Her auburn curls had been flattened to a sleek sheen and a one-carat diamond stud dotted each ear, completing her refined, polished look.

With a tap, the paper she retrieved from her bag disappeared between the vents of the locker. *I'm just going to buy Lettie a new cell phone and prepay a year's worth of service. She shouldn't be stuck in the Stone Age.*

"What's up, LB?" Laura Beth's heart sank at the sound of Whitney's voice. She turned slowly to face her.

"Planning a party without me?" Whitney smiled maliciously.

And that was the other problem with this year: She was chained to Whitney.

Laura Beth fought the foul words bubbling inside her and put on a pleasant smile. "Hey, Whitney. Are you finding everything okay?"

Always kill your enemies with kindness. Especially if those enemies know your secrets.

Whitney Remick, the new girl at Excelsior and the constant thorn in Laura Beth and her friends' sides, leaned against the wall of lockers. A lacy hot-pink bra peeked out from beneath her white button-up. Laura Beth frowned at the way it flattered her caramel-colored skin. Her own skin was already so pale—especially with everything she'd done trying to get rid of her freckles—that the white uniform shirt always washed her out. Even Whitney's yellow feather earrings seemed to dull the sparkle in Laura Beth's studs.

Honestly, how has she not been sent home dressed like that?

"Things are good—if you like sterile, boring, and prison-like." Whitney's smile grew. "But I have a solution. I'm going to ditch and you're going to come with me."

Stalling for time, Laura Beth dug around in her purse and flipped open a compact mirror to check her reflection. At least she didn't look as stressed as she felt.

Over the summer, when she and her friends first met Whitney, Laura Beth loved her carefree attitude and knack for fun. It filled the void left by Taylor's death.

But that was before Laura Beth discovered Whitney's true motives: spying on them and reporting back to her mother, gossip column queen Tracey Mills. And before Whitney blackmailed Laura Beth into being friends.

"I can't." Laura Beth snapped the compact shut and began

walking down the hallway. Like a yappy dog, Whitney trailed at her heels. "I promised Jackie and Lettie I'd meet them. Right now. Before class."

It was a lie. Kind of. She and Jackie had made plans after first period to meet before third. They wanted to surprise Lettie with a fun lunch off campus—something to cheer her up— and were going to plan it during passing. But Jackie hadn't shown. And that's what had Laura Beth so stressed. Jackie would never forget to meet her. She just seemed to have vanished into thin air.

"Maybe I'll come along." Whitney didn't even bother to hide the threat in her voice. "It'll be a little Capital Girls party."

For a moment, Laura Beth wavered. Whitney could crush her world. Keeping Whitney far away from Jackie was her number-one priority. She'd have to do one or the other—let Whitney come with them, or ditch with her. "If you wait until after lunch, I'll come."

Whitney narrowed her eyes. "Fine. But if you back out, I may have to invite Jackie instead. And who knows what might come up then."

Laura Beth curled her fingers tighter around the handle of her bag and prayed they didn't shake too badly as she watched Whitney disappear into the crowded hallway.

There's more than one way to kill a snake, she reminded herself. *But sometimes the best way is to just take off its head.*

Laura Beth wanted, more than anything, to just freeze Whitney out completely. But if Jackie ever learned Laura Beth was the reason Senator Hampton Griffin—a longtime family friend— had caught her in a compromising position with a staffer, their friendship would be over. And as much as Laura Beth sometimes wished Jackie's life were her own, she would never intentionally hurt Jackie.

She glanced back at Lettie's locker and swallowed the lump in her throat. Whitney may own her, but Laura Beth would never be her friend.

Lettie Velasquez wasn't a crier. She was a rock. Her parents and little sisters relied on her. For the past two weeks, while Mamá wept, Lettie answered the door, accepted condolences and gifts of food from neighbors, and kept the family running.

But as she studied the AP Literature reading list, the sobs she kept hidden threatened to escape.

Her brother Paz was dead. Dead. First Taylor and now Paz. Two of the people she most loved in the world. She knew it was illogical and futile, but she kept asking herself the same question over and over—what had she done to deserve this?

Tears sat hot in the corners of her eyes. *Not here, Lettie. Wait till you're alone. Focus.*

With a long sniff, she turned the combination on her locker and flung the door open. A piece of paper covered in hand-drawn hearts fell to the ground.

Lettie recognized it immediately as Laura Beth's handiwork and scooped up the paper. Unlike her two best friends—Laura Beth Ballou and Jackie Whitman—Lettie didn't have a cell phone. At least not anymore. She'd taken her anger over Paz's death out on it and couldn't afford a new one. Not that she really needed one or its accompanying bill. Well, not all the time, anyway—it would be nice to not always be the last one to hear about things.

Leaning into her locker to hide her watery eyes, Lettie unfolded the note.

Lets! I haven't seen Jackie since first period and she's not answering her phone. I'm worried. Have you seen her?

xoxo ~ Laura Beth

Lettie drew her brows together. Jackie hadn't been in calculus last period either, but Lettie thought maybe she had a meeting with her advisor. Of course, without a cell phone, Lettie had no way of checking. And Jackie would have at least texted Laura Beth if she had to leave, if only to ask them to pick up her homework.

Something wasn't right. A few weeks ago, Jackie casually mentioned the threats the White House had been receiving. About her. Jackie and Laura Beth had laughed it off. But President Deborah Price, and Jackie's mother, the chief of staff, hadn't found it too funny. They insisted Jackie tell them every place she went—ahead of time.

"I love my mom and Aunt Deborah," Jackie said, picking at her sandwich. "I know they want to keep me safe, but these kinds of things are part of being in the public eye."

Laura Beth gave one of her typical dramatic sighs. "It won't be any fun this year if you have to clear everything first."

I pressed my tongue against my teeth. Jackie was right. Public figures received threats all the time. But this was different. She wasn't a politician. "I think it's a good idea. Why take the risk? If the White House is worried, you should take it seriously."

Jackie rolled her eyes and laughed. *"You'd probably be in favor of me wearing a GPS device."*

"If it kept you safe," I told her.

Laura Beth snorted. *"That would be fantastic. We really wouldn't have any fun then."*

Jackie pushed her sandwich aside. *"Don't worry about it, Lettie. It's just a precaution."*

Lettie's eyes scanned the now nearly empty hallway. The bell was going to ring any minute and if she didn't hurry, she'd be late.

With a slam of her locker door, Lettie sprinted toward the stairs at the far end of the hall. She climbed them two at a time and reached the classroom door on the second floor just as the bell trilled.

Hidden just under her desk, Laura Beth's thumbs flew over her iPhone. Technically, she shouldn't have her phone in class, but if the teacher couldn't see it, then what's the harm, right?

J—pls, pls, pls text me. I'm worried about u.

She hit SEND and double-checked the screen to make sure it went through.

Mrs. Stepaniak, the government teacher, shuffled a few papers on her desk as students filed in the door.

Where is she? Laura Beth's stomach rolled. *Oh Lord, what if Whitney already told her the truth and Jackie's avoiding me?*

Laura Beth stared at the door, willing Jackie to suddenly appear. Despite everything, Jackie was her best friend. And no matter what Whitney thought, Laura Beth had only wanted to protect Jackie.

Stop lying to yourself. You hoped she and Andrew would break up.

Lettie skidded into the room just as the bell rang. Her eyes, filled with concern, met Laura Beth's. She hurried to the empty desk next to Laura Beth.

"Have you seen Jackie?" Laura Beth asked even though she knew the answer.

Lettie shook her head. "No."

Mrs. Stepaniak cleared her throat and began calling roll. The desk in front of Laura Beth, the one she had saved for Jackie, sat empty.

"She wasn't in calculus either," Lettie said softly.

As Laura Beth opened her mouth, to ask if maybe they should tell someone, the classroom door burst open.

Startled, she dropped her phone onto the floor.

No one noticed. All eyes were on the man dressed head to toe in black, standing in the doorway. His hands clenched a rifle. A rifle!

"Is Jackie Whitman here?" the SWAT man asked.

"Jackie?" Mrs. Stepaniak called. Every set of eyes turned toward where Lettie and Laura Beth sat. Without Jackie.

Laura Beth's heart pounded. "I haven't seen her since this morning. What's going on? Why do you want Jackie?"

The man stomped down the aisle until he stood directly before Laura Beth's desk. He kept his rifle trained at the ground, but still, being near it made her skin crawl.

"Are you her friend?" the man demanded.

"We're her best friends," Lettie said quietly.

The man pivoted toward Lettie. "Is there anywhere she goes to be alone? Anywhere she may be hiding?"

Bile rose in Laura Beth's throat. Suddenly, the stalkerish calls they'd laughed about didn't seem so funny.

"There's a spot—in the school garden. Sometimes Jackie goes there to clear her mind," Lettie said.

The SWAT member stormed back up the aisle toward the door. "The school is in lockdown. Everyone must remain in this room until further instructed."

The door slammed behind him and the room broke into chaos. Students leaped from their seats and ran to the windows to see the action unfolding out on the grounds. Laura Beth ran in the opposite direction: to Lettie. She folded herself into Lettie's arms and squeezed tightly.

Whitney. The blackmail. Andrew. None of it was important.

Please, Laura Beth prayed. *Please don't let me lose another friend.*